Reader's Choice Award Finalist *Sweet Surrender*
"Julie Tetel charms her readers...a must-read for all historical romance fans!"

—*The Literary Times*

"...Tetel hits the jackpot with this romantic tale."
—*Affaire de Coeur*

Simon's Lady
"...a veritable witches' brew with a bit of whimsy folklore, and an engaging hero and heroine..."
—*Romantic Times*

1994 RITA Finalist *Sweet Sensations*
"I couldn't put it down.... Tetel has a fresh and provocative voice."
—Award-winning author Patricia Potter

"...a totally enthralling tale packed with nonstop action.... Another Tetel winner!"
—*Affaire de Coeur*

Sweet Suspicions
"...a man, a woman, murder and mayhem..."
—*Romantic Times*

"Am I disturbing you?"

When Wesley didn't answer that, Sarah continued guilelessly, "But you're finished, aren't you? I mean, you're dressed—" She ran her eyes over the muscled planes of his torso turned toward her. "That is, you're more dressed than you usually are, and you've finished shaving. So I didn't think I was disturbing you by wanting my turn to lie down." Her smile was especially warm, even melting. "Did your rest restore you?"

The look he gave her suggested that he had been restored to health but not to serenity.

"Hungry?" she asked next. She relished this teasing, testing, pushing, prodding.

He opened his mouth, glanced beyond her to the flaps at the front of the wagon, then thought better of what he was going to say. His eyes narrowed, and she had the most scandalous sensation that he had just stripped her naked....

JULIE TETEL

Sweet SARAH ROSS

Harlequin Books

TORONTO • NEW YORK • LONDON
AMSTERDAM • PARIS • SYDNEY • HAMBURG
STOCKHOLM • ATHENS • TOKYO • MILAN
MADRID • WARSAW • BUDAPEST • AUCKLAND

ISBN 0-373-28965-0

SWEET SARAH ROSS

Books by Julie Tetel

Harlequin Historicals

Sweet Suspicions #128
*Sweet Seduction #167
*Sweet Sensations #182
Simon's Lady #229
*Sweet Surrender #255
MacLaurin's Lady #287
*Sweet Sarah Ross #365

Harlequin Books

Promised Brides Anthology
"The Handfast"

Harlequin Regency

The Temporary Bride
*The North Point Series

JULIE TETEL

has always loved both history and romance, making it easy for her to love reading and writing historical romances. She is from a suburb of Chicago and currently lives in Durham, North Carolina. She has two sons, two careers, at least two points of view and one husband.

Chapter One

May 1836
On the Oregon Trail

Sarah knelt at a shady spot on the bank of the river and wondered what all the fuss was supposed to be about. In the two weeks since she'd left Independence, Missouri, the trip west had certainly not lived up to its arduous reputation. Instead it had been rather more like a pleasant outing. The only disagreeable aspect of the journey—besides the presence of her bratty little sisters, of course—was that horrible Mrs. Fletcher who had joined their wagon train at the last minute. Sarah was determined to put the old gossip in her place before they arrived in Oregon at the end of the summer.

Dipping her hands into the shallow water, she admitted to herself that difficulties might lie ahead. Nevertheless, nothing she had experienced thus far compared to the dire stories she had heard back in Independence. She was inclined to think that the tellers of those tales either intended to scare off the faint of heart or were faint-hearts themselves.

She splashed her face and allowed her sense of self-satisfaction to expand. She hadn't wanted to come on this trip, but she was pleased to judge herself an excellent traveler even when the conditions were far beneath her. No, she hadn't wanted to come, but when she had refused William's insipid offer of marriage, her usually loving mother had been unaccountably angry with her and demanded that she accompany the family on the journey to join her brother and his wife, who had settled years ago in the Oregon Territory.

Even her normally reasonable father had refused to understand the logic of her arguments in favor of staying behind in Maryland, and had cut her off by saying, ''This time, Sarah Ross, you'll not wrap me around your little finger.'' It had been too absurd of him to fail to see that at the mature age of almost twenty-two she was perfectly capable of taking care of herself. Not to mention that she had money of her own—never minding the fact that she wouldn't have access to it for a few more years yet. And to have accused her of wheedling had been unjust!

Drinking from cupped hands, Sarah tasted the purity of the river, felt the chill against her teeth. She was caught short by the stray thought that here one could never feel tired or old. She rose to her feet and critically surveyed her surroundings. The broad green river braided before her and away on either side. Grassland sloped up behind her. An improbable indigo sky bowled above. A dry breeze rustled around her, mixing the scent of grass and sandy loam. The calm pulse of the prairie hummed in her ears.

When confronted with odd experiences, she often imagined how her father—her *real* father, the General—might have reacted, and she paused to consider what he would have thought of the rustic charms of this wilderness adventure. With a sniff she concluded that he would have agreed that she deserved the elegancies of life, not the rigors, and with some distaste she found a secluded clump of trees where she relieved herself. Afterward she adjusted her skirts and twitched her shawl into place. Then she secured the ties of the reticule hanging from her waist and fiddled coquettishly with the brim of her bonnet as if she were stepping out into a fashionable shopping street in Baltimore.

She was about to return to the wagon train circled beyond the slope behind her just out of sight, when the afternoon calm was shattered by piercing cries. Suddenly, she was distracted by glinting flashes of splashing water at the edge of the riverbed about twenty feet away from her. She had taken a half step out from the shelter of trees but quickly drew back in and behind the nearest tree trunk. A large, strange beast was lumbering in the water, balanced only on its hind legs, moving in her direction. Her heart jumped to her throat when the beast turned the bend in the river and began to head straight for the trees.

She would have made a run for it up the grassy slope, back to the safety of the wagon train, had it not been for the effect of a renewed volley of raucous whoops that assailed her ears. The terrifying sounds seemed to be coming precisely from the direction of the wagon train. The thought *Wild Indians!* stabbed through her brain and halted its normal functioning. The vision of the wild beast coming toward her paralyzed her legs. She stood frozen, staring wide-eyed at the beast, who was still upright, hardly swaying at all. Its hair was dark and curled chaotically around its head. Its eyes were a ferocious blue. It looked strong and remarkably surefooted for a—a—

For a human beast. Terror turned to shock, then dissolved into confusion, which meant at least her brain was working again, even if her feet weren't. She blinked. Yes, it—no, he—was a human beast—a human being. It—he, it was definitely a he—was tall. The skin on his face and arms and broad shoulders was brown, as if accustomed to the sun. His skin was a bright burnt pink across his belly and down his—

At that moment she fully registered the fact that the man-beast was stark naked.

She shut her eyes and ducked her head behind the tree trunk. She strained to hear the sounds of the man-beast's approach. Through the clamor filling the air behind her, she detected the splish-splash of feet leaving water. The soft clunk of rock tapping rock. A stick breaking hardly two feet away. Then...

The man-beast stopped running. He was so close to her that she could hear him panting and feel the radiating heat of his exertion. She caught the scent of a body pushed hard, but still strong and healthy. He splayed a palm against the tree next to the one behind which she was hidden, at such an angle that a sinewy forearm muscle appeared in high relief at her eye level. He leaned against the tree and hung his head so that the sunburned nape of his neck was visible to her.

She shrank back, wishing she was invisible. She could tell that the man-beast was winded. If she was going to get away, now was the time.

Her feet wouldn't move.

Then she became aware of a sudden silence more frightening than the savage cries that had rent the air moments before. In retrospect she perceived that the war whoops had been answered with gunfire, but now the guns had nothing left to say. She felt more than saw that the man-beast cocked his head slightly and pricked his ears, as if he, too, perceived the meaning of the deafening silence. She held her breath and hoped she wouldn't faint from the pounding in her chest and thunderous drumming in her ears. She clutched at the crossed ends of her shawl and hung on to them for dear life.

Her poor, overworked heart was subjected to yet another assault when the man-beast suddenly whirled. Before she could even squeak in fright, one of his hands came down to clamp her mouth while the other grasped her shoulder and wrenched her against his sweat-soaked body. She writhed but did not effect her release from his grip. Nose to nose with him, she was eyeing two blue pools swimming with madness or exhaustion.

His gaze came into focus. It roamed her face, circled her bonnet, returned to the hand held over her mouth. He bent toward her ear and croaked softly, "Don't speak. Too dangerous."

She could only stare at him.

To emphasize his point, he pressed the hand at her mouth. On the barest of breaths he demanded, "Promise."

She nodded vigorously. He slowly withdrew his hand from her mouth but didn't release the grip on her shoulder. He moved a half pace away and surveyed her top to toe. Fear and a proper upbringing prevented her from doing the same to him. His hand at her shoulder was squeezing hard enough to hurt her, but some ancient instinct warned her not to reveal any weakness.

The hand at her shoulder began to fall, dragging her shawl with it. He managed to say, "Let go."

It dawned on her that the man-beast spoke a version of civilized English, and a ripple of relief coursed through her. This was followed by a veritable wave of relief when the significance of his request sank in. *He wants my shawl to cover himself!* It took a moment, however, for the command from her sluggish brain to reach the fingers wrapped so tightly around the shawl ends. Eventually her fingers uncramped, one by one, and she handed the large square cloth over to him. She felt better at the mere thought of the man-beast wearing some sort of clothing.

Upon accepting the cloth, the man-beast sat down on the ground, and the next thing she knew, he was tearing the delicate material in two. Her slight surge in good feeling turned swiftly to puzzlement, then yielded to indignation. Instead of covering that which no lady should see, he proceeded to bind his feet!

She didn't know what to make of it. Nor could she observe him at length without causing herself great embarrassment. So she turned her back to him and considered what to do next, now that he—the man-beast, her captor, whatever he might be—was preoccupied. She saw her opportunity to scramble up the slope and see what she could of the wagon train.

From behind her came quiet words that seemed to have rattled up and out a rusted pipe. "Don't go...there...yet."

She never took kindly to orders, and knew of no reason why she should obey one from a naked man-beast, but the tone of that statement was ominous enough to give her pause. She whispered back, "My father and mother are there."

"Not time. Not yet."

"My sisters, too."

To that he said nothing, and his lack of response brought horrific visions to her mind's eye. She stood immobile once again, this time from fear for her loved ones. Perhaps she still had reason to fear for herself, but her best assessment of her immediate circumstances said she didn't. The man-beast hadn't attempted to kill her for the shawl, and he obviously had no weapons concealed on his person. She knew that he was strong, but judging from the muffled grunts and groans coming from him as he worked on his feet, she guessed that his body was in great pain and that his strength was nearly spent.

At thoughts of the fate of her family, her vision blurred and her stomach churned. Go over the slope? Or stay here?

More words broke into her indecision. "If your family is...still there, you can do nothing...for them now," he said. "If your family has...escaped, you are only... exposing yourself...to capture...by the Sioux. Might still be around. Probably are."

The Sioux. She had a hazy recollection of hearing something about them in Independence. "The Sioux are hostile?"

His grunt confirmed the worst. He had apparently finished with his feet, but didn't rise. Instead she heard him settle against the trunk of the tree behind her. She cast a curious, cautious glance over her shoulder and saw that he had positioned himself out of her line of sight. She could see only one corner of his shoulder and an arm bent at the elbow. The hand had disappeared and was no doubt resting against his invisible hip. She supposed she should be thankful for his delicacy, whether or not it had been intended.

He added with great weariness, as if to himself, "No sense killing yourself...unless you've a mind to die."

She slid down the trunk and sat at the base of her tree. So. Here she was in a clump of trees in the middle of nowhere, not more than a foot away from a naked man-beast, and possibly surrounded by Sioux. Anger and outrage and helplessness overcame her. Seizing on the most immediate injustice, she began on a harsh whisper, "Why, sir, did you—"

The absurdity of calling him "sir" stopped her midsentence. She began again, this time very deliberately. "Why, sir, did you rip my shawl and bind your feet when the material could have been put to much better use?"

"My bloody feet," he replied with labored breath, "are blazing...a trail."

"For the Sioux to follow, you mean?"

"For prairie wolves, too. Can smell blood...and a festering wound...a mile away."

Prairie wolves sounded worrisome, but she decided to take her worries one at a time. "If the Sioux are following you, why did they fall upon our peaceful wagon train?"

His reply came after a lengthy pause. "I'm guessing...they think...I found refuge...in your party."

"It's because of you, then, that our wagon train was attacked?"

"Pioneers travel...at their own risk."

The callousness of that remark caused her to raise her voice above a whisper. "So if my family lies dead yonder, I'm not to blame you?" she snapped back.

"Some of your wagons...must have gotten away. The Sioux have not...been able to count me...among the dead."

"What do you mean?"

"They're not looking...for me...here. Not yet. Which means...they might be trailing...wagons that got away."

It was a glimmer of hope for her family but not much more. "Why do they want you dead?"

"I was on their land. Took me prisoner. Got away. Were going to kill me anyway...but now their desire... has doubled. Honor at stake."

"How did you get away?"

"Old tribal dispute. Sioux warriors took off...like somebody set...breechclouts afire. Left me with the squaws."

"That was lucky."

The frail sound that came from his throat was a brittle ghost of a laugh. "Sioux squaws no bargain. Take to torturing with pleasure. Warriors rode off...with all the ponies in camp. I cut loose...started to run."

"You ran? Just like that?"

He drew a deep breath, seemed to strangle on a dry cough. "The squaws came close to catching me...with my hands tied and all. My legs are longer. Knew what would happen...if they caught me."

As intrigued as she was by the notion of Sioux squaw bloodlust, she didn't think the sound of the war whoops she had heard had come from women, and she said as much.

"When warriors returned...they took after me, too. By that time...I had gotten my hands free...and was far enough off...to keep ahead of them."

"You've been running all day?"

He didn't answer for a long time. Then, as if from far off, came the answer, "All day...and day before. All night, too. I've covered...maybe fifty miles...barefoot."

She reassessed the gravity of his physical condition and wondered if he'd survive the night.

"I'm mortal thirsty. The river tempts me...but I'll not risk an arrow through my heart...after all I've done...to stay alive."

"You didn't drink when you were running through the river?"

"Didn't want to waste time.... Stuck my tongue out and caught what drops I could...splashing along."

"But that's nonsensical to run through water and come out of it dying of thirst!"

"I chose the water route...to lose my scent. Not to drink."

"I suppose you've learned your lesson now," she said primly, trying not to feel sorry for him, since he was the immediate cause of her misfortune.

"You could...fetch me water. It might be...worth the risk...to be rid...of your fool conversation...for a few minutes...or forever."

She gasped at the insult and thought it mighty cheeky of a man-beast on his last legs who, now that she came to think of it, might just have to depend on her for survival—that is, *if* she was of a mind to help him survive, which, at the moment, she was not.

"And if you're thinking...of leaving me...to my own devices...I'll ask you...two questions."

Since she was thinking just that, she swerved her head and found herself looking into a pair of blue eyes no longer glazed, but still rimed with red and shot with blood.

"Can you...kill and skin...a rabbit?"

"No, but—"

"And do you know...how to start a fire...with two sticks?"

"Well, I've never had occasion to try, but how hard could—"

"Then the scissors...in the bag...you're wearing...just might save...the both of us."

Surprised, she stared openmouthed at him until she recalled that when he had pressed her to him, he must have felt against his bare thigh the small metal shape in the reticule hanging from her waist. She flushed with embarrassment at the thought of that intimate contact, then turned back around. There was absolutely nothing to say to that, so she resolutely closed her mouth, until it occurred to her that his objective had been to shut her up. But when she opened her mouth again, no words came. So she sat there, speechless, her thoughts colliding so violently and her emotions roiling so precipitously that she was beginning to feel seasick.

The sun shifted. The shadows lengthened in the minuscule glade. The man-beast didn't move from his seated position at the base of the tree. He might have dozed off. He might have died. Her first thought was that it would serve him right. Her second thought was that she would be without someone who knew how to make a fire and find food. She scooted over to him on all fours to see whether or not he was still breathing.

She peered into his face, which was streaked with dirt and sweat. His eyes were closed and lined with fatigue. His jaw was slack and stubbled with several days' dark growth, as was his chin. His lips were so parched they were cracked and white in places. She couldn't risk a glance down the length of his body to check out the feet wrapped in pieces of her shawl, but he was breathing. Definitely breathing.

He was also alert. She had hardly completed her inspection of his face when his hand shot out and grasped her forearm so hard that she yelped involuntarily.

"Don't," he said softly, without opening his eyes, "do that again."

She wriggled her arm, and he let it go. She withdrew to her tree. "Don't make sure you're breathing?" she whispered in return. "Or don't cry out?"

"Both."

"I'm going to get you some water," she said. Sioux or no Sioux, she was pretty sure that his body needed water desperately, and she saw the wisdom of keeping alive the means of her possible salvation. She began to rise.

"Not yet," he said.

Thinking she had not heard him aright, she glanced over her shoulder and craned her neck to see that his eyes were open. He looked up at the sky, around their hiding place, over at the river. "Still too early," he pronounced.

"But you're dying of thirst," she protested.

"I wasn't kidding…about Sioux arrows." He lolled his head on his shoulder and looked at her. His expression bordered on the grimly humorous. "I might need you…as much as you…need me."

"It's something that you admit it," she replied, sitting back down.

He grunted. "Just…my luck."

She was about to respond in kind when she recalled the fifty miles he had covered barefoot. With great restraint, she said, "I'm willing to allow that it is extreme dehydration that makes you disagreeable, so I'll overlook that remark. About the Sioux, though, I judge it to be a few hours ago already that they came through here. They haven't been down to the river, at least, not to this part of it, so it seems safe enough to venture out to get you some water and see the damage that has been done at the wagon train."

"Might have gone…to higher ground…about a half mile away. They have eagle eyes."

She wasn't a complete dolt. "They certainly couldn't shoot me at a range of a half mile."

He regarded her balefully. "Don't want them to discover…our hiding place."

"Oh, I see," she said. "I didn't know you meant that the arrow through the heart would come sometime *after* the trip to the river." At her most proper, she intoned, "You will let me know, sir, when it is time."

"Until then, quiet. Just be…quiet."

She was thirsty and irritable herself and mighty anxious about what lay beyond the grassy slope. But she held her tongue, although the effort nearly killed her. In truth, she didn't want to give him the satisfaction of speaking. He wouldn't have to tell her twice to shut up, but then she remembered that he had, in so many words, told her twice to shut up.

Thereafter her brain was so busy picking the sore of her lacerated dignity—which another part of her brain knew full well was happily keeping her from contemplating worse thoughts—that she didn't hear him the first time he said softly, "It's time." When he repeated it loud enough for her to register it, she looked around her to see that evening was stealing through their hiding place and veiling their surroundings in moving shadows.

It wasn't until she was at the river's edge that she wondered how she would transport water back to him. She looked around for some kind of hollowed-out vessel but no appropriate object caught her eye. She considered filling her bonnet but figured the water would drain out before she could make it back to him. So she settled on her ankle boots, figuring he was too thirsty to be picky. Sure enough, when she handed him two shoefuls of water, he accepted them gratefully and even seemed to acknowledge her resourcefulness with an approving nod.

It was less embarrassing being next to him in the gathering darkness, so she knelt beside him and noted that he didn't gulp the water down. Rather he restrained himself to take it in measured sips. When he paused at some length, she asked, "Can I go over the slope now?"

He took another spare sip, shuddered with relief. He cleared his throat, then uttered his first full sentence. "It's best to go before the moon and stars come out." His voice was deeper and more resonant than she had expected. She moved away from him, and he said, "Crawl, don't walk." When she was at the edge of their hiding place, he added, "Watch out for rattlesnakes."

She squeaked in horror and got down on her hands and knees to crawl through the cover of the grasses and the shifting twilight. The afternoon's wait had been unbearable, but this last crawl up and over the slope was excruciating. She was hoping against hope that when she judged herself close enough to the scene and lifted her head above the grasses, she would find that—

All was well.

Her heart leapt with joy. The spot where her family's wagon had been was empty. Meaning that they, and most of the others, had had time to flee. Her joy turned to sorrow as she recognized the one who had not been so lucky.

She had been traveling with her family in a train of ten wagons. Only one was left at the site, broken beyond repair, and the Widower Reynolds lay facedown on the ground next to the wagon, an arrow in his back. She went over to the dead man, bit her lip to stifle her sob, then did what she had to do.

She crawled back down the slope to the shelter of the trees. She made her way over to the man-beast, who had not moved from his seated position, and announced, "I've brought you some trousers."

Chapter Two

Powell woke from fitful dreams of being chased by white-skinned women and red-skinned women around drawing rooms in Washington, D.C., and over the open prairie.

He cracked his eyes, his chest heaving from dream effort. His bone-dry eyes were soothed to perceive cool, blue moonlight after days of red-seared sunlight. He swallowed once over a painful knot in his throat, but he knew he had had water in the past few hours, and the pain in his throat this night was not as bad as it had been the night before. He figured he was ready for more water now without putting his battered body into shock. He needed a prolonged watering. Mmm. A thorough soaking would be nice.

In a hazy sort of way, he was sorry he wasn't some kind of plant. He might choose to be a vine, and he imagined his legs, stretched out before him, turning into long tendrils. Then he would have only to wait for it to rain, and the backs of his legs could take root in the earth, and he could drink and drink and drink his fill without having to move an inch.

He breathed in. He breathed out. He came to the conclusion that he wasn't a plant but an animal, and animals had to move around in order to find food and water. It was a pity. Especially since he had a fuzzy recollection that a source of water ran behind him quite a few yards away, and his feet were burning as if on fire and swollen to the size of huge squash. He couldn't use his feet to get there, not a chance, but maybe he could slither over to the water. On that thought, he entertained feelings of deep envy for snakes who had no feet to plague them. Fish, too, who moved suspended in gallons and gallons of lovely water. And birds, who could get off their ridiculous unfleshly feet anytime they wanted—

Birds, fish, snakes, vines. He must be thirst-crazed to be having such thoughts, and the only way to restore his sanity was to get himself over to the water. He shifted from his seated position so that he could slide on his belly, and when he moved, he became aware of the lump of coarse material in his lap.

He fingered the lump and determined that it was some sort of clothing. Shirt. No. Trousers, maybe. Yes, trousers. He was reminded of something, and in order to discover what, he had a notion to look around the dark glade where he had taken refuge.

Moonlight dappled the dark and dotted a human form lying a few feet away from him. It was a woman, a white woman, to judge from the outlines of the clothing draped around her reclining body. Her head was pillowed on another piece of cloth—must be her bonnet—and long strands of golden hair turned silver in the moonlight had escaped whatever pins might have been holding them. As pretty as her hair was to contemplate, he was more interested in her skirts and underskirts. Not carnally but practically. He mentally cut up the superfluous yards of cotton she must be wearing and made snares and slingshots and bags and bandages.

He was so cheered by thoughts of all that good material that he began his slithery sliding toward the river. He thought of the woman and couldn't for the life of him figure out what she was doing in the glade with him.

Then he remembered. She was the woman who had been wearing a shawl. Two things about her stood out in his mind. She was an idiot, and she was beautiful. A beautiful idiot. When he had first seen her, she had been bobbing around a tree, and if he hadn't known better, he would have thought that she was trying to attract his attention rather than conceal herself. The tree she had chosen couldn't have been much more than a foot wide, and with her skirts sprouting out on either side of the base, he wasn't likely to miss her once he had come ashore. That is, if he hadn't already spotted her when he had rounded the bend in the river.

The river. It was all coming back to him. He winced at the flood of memories of capture and escape, of the brutal bruising his body had endured during his two days of flight. He had come to the riverbank, fearing at first it was a mirage. He had been heading for the Platte River, knowing it was ahead of him as he ran, thinking it would save him if he could just get there before the Sioux got their hands on him again.

He held a pretty good map of the territory in his head, but his hobbling had prevented him from making an accurate estimate of the ground he had paced out on foot. He had had an even better map of the territory on paper, but that map was in the ashes of a sacrificial fire, and he didn't want to think yet about what had happened to all his surveying equipment. Probably offered to the Teton Sioux god of Wandering Souls, for all he knew. Why hadn't he had the good fortune to run across the Mandans or the Pawnees, instead of the Tetons? He wasn't a fur trader or a bison hunter or even a settler. It was just his luck to have run into the Tetons on a bad day in a bad mood.

And it was just his luck to have run into a beautiful idiot who didn't understand the first thing about life on the frontier. He might even have said as much to her. But she had a pair of scissors in her bag and was wearing yards and yards of useful cloth, and now he had dragged himself over the twigs and the rocks and the sand and was at river's edge and didn't have a thing to worry about anymore.

He put his face in the water and drank. It was cold and bracing and provided as exquisite a pleasure-pain as he had ever experienced. He drank some more and then some more. The more he drank the thirstier he became, and he doubted that he could ever drink enough to have enough excess to piss ever again.

When he needed air more than he needed water, he lifted his head, turned his entire body. He picked the absurd flower-printed bandages off his feet, rinsed them out. Then he flopped over so that he could immerse his blazing members in the cold. The sizzling sting of the water on the open sores of his soles nearly killed him, but almost as quickly numbed his wretched feet, so that the overall effect was mercifully, outrageously sensual. He lay on his back in the sand, his feet in the water, his eyes on the clouds drifting across the diamond dust in the night sky, and thought, *It's good to be alive.*

With his return to life came the return of his ability to plan for the future. He knew where he was. He knew who he was with. He knew his resources. He knew what he would be up against come morning. His chances didn't look good.

Still, it was good to be alive.

He yielded to the pleasure of bathing his feet in ice-cold water and of witnessing the magnificent spill of stars high above. His well-trained eyes picked out the constellations, and he reckoned the lateness of the hour by the hunter Orion walking stiff-legged across the sky. He tried to find the Little Dipper by climbing up its tail from the polestar but lost it in a sky too milky with moonlight.

He could think of ways to improve his lot in life, and the first would be to spirit away the woman with the shawl to the drawing rooms of Washington, D.C. He could picture her perfectly there, chattering all day long with every other woman he had ever known who was exactly like her. He had, alas, no magical powers to transport her from here to there, and the more he accepted her presence in his immediate circumstances, the happier he was that he had a pair of trousers to wear.

Lying naked on the riverbed, he made a mental note to put those trousers on before the first rays of dawn would illuminate him, once again, in all his masculine glory.

Sarah snuffled half-awake to a rumbling in her stomach and a crick in her neck. She squeezed her eyes shut tighter, but her room was flooded with disturbing daylight, suggesting that someone had forgotten to draw the curtains. And her bed was as hard as the earth. She groggily rehearsed the prettily worded complaint she would offer the hostess of the house party she must be attending.

Then she remembered that she was lying on the board she had for a bed in the wagon and regretted having turned down William's offer of marriage. She sat bolt upright, put a hand to her neck and shook her head to alter the unpleasant illusion that she was seated directly on the ground in a clump of trees in the middle of nowhere and in the company of—

A man-beast who was sitting cross-legged with his back to her. He seemed to be tending something in front of him, but at the groan she emitted upon coming fully awake, he turned and looked at her. She was pleased that he was wearing the trousers she had retrieved for him, but the expression on his face did not encourage her to think that she would find him any more agreeable today than she had the day before.

Nevertheless, she greeted him properly. "Good morning, sir. I trust you are feeling better today than yesterday. May I ask if your feet are improved?"

A look of faint disbelief—or was it amusement?—crossed his features. "I'll put it this way," he answered her. "I'm no longer running the risk of fatal infection, but I'm not walking anywhere today. We'll be staying put."

The vision of a tedious day stretched before her. She sighed and felt the wreck of her coiffure, then patted the ground for precious pins that might have fallen while she slept. She picked up her bonnet, brushed it off, took out the stockings she had stuffed inside it. She folded these into the waistband of her skirts and rose to her feet, holding the bonnet by its ties so that it dangled from her hand.

"We've plenty to do," he added, turning back around, "so don't worry about remaining idle."

This was not the first time he had accurately guessed her thoughts. "Do you fancy yourself something of a mind reader, sir?" she demanded, palming several hairpins.

He shook his head and occupied himself with whatever was in front of him. "No, but it's plain you haven't traveled much."

She was sorry that he had turned his back to her, for he missed her rather superior smile. "I'll have you know that I've been to England and back."

To that he made no response.

"Two years ago it was, and my chaperon was an elderly lady who needed more care than she gave. So I assure you that I have dealt with many demanding situations as a traveler abroad and proved myself equal to all occasions."

"Ah. Now tell me. What language do they speak in England?"

Poor, ignorant man-beast! "They speak English, sir, and it is a version very similar to that which you and I speak."

"The dwellings the English inhabit, what manner would they be? And what manner of conveyance do the English commonly use?"

"They live in houses, some of which are like palaces, and they often ride in carriages."

"I see. Tell me something else. What language do the Sioux speak?"

"Indian, I suppose."

"What manner of dwelling do they inhabit?"

"I have heard they live in rough tents called tepees."

"And have you encountered any roads or carriageways in the past few days?"

She caught the man's drift and was annoyed. "I gather it is your objective to emphasize the dissimilarities in my two traveling experiences," she said evenly, "but I can tell you that crossing a vast ocean is a very demanding experience."

"We're not on the ocean now, we don't enjoy the protection of a ship with a well-stocked hold, and we aren't bound for familiar or friendly shores."

Her response was frosty. "You have made your point, sir."

This was hardly the ideal beginning to the day, which, she noted, had hardly dawned. She yawned, then stretched out the kinks in her back and neck. At that moment she caught a whiff of something malodorous. "What's that I smell?"

"Breakfast."

Approaching him, she looked over his shoulder and puzzled over the sight of a jumble of smoking rocks criss-crossed by sticks. "And what is for breakfast?"

"Tree frogs."

She thought she detected a slightly gleeful note in his deep voice, like the kind a little boy might use when dangling a slimy worm before a little girl. Although her empty stomach recoiled when she perceived the outlines of the small, shriveled creatures skewered on sticks, she suppressed her revulsion in order to reply knowledgeably, "The French eat frogs. They are considered quite a delicacy."

He took a stick and held up a wizened carcass. "Want one?"

She declined the French delicacy, citing customary lack of appetite first thing in the morning. She saw him take the frog off the stick and begin to eat it. Feeling nauseous, she looked away and announced her intention to go to the river. She added—with as much dignity as rumpled clothing and a ruined coiffure would allow—that she hoped she could be assured of her privacy.

To her back he said, "It's all we have until lunch."

She heard these words as a taunt and decided to defer the problem of finding suitable food in order to satisfy the most immediate of her bodily needs. She continued in the direction of the river. At the edge of the trees, a thought

struck her. She paused and said, "You haven't warned
me about arrows in the heart and such, but I note that
you've kept the fire low, which I suppose is to avoid giving the Sioux a sign that we're here."

"I've kept the fire low so as not to burn the frogs to a
crisp, and I'm thinking the Sioux have no further interest
in this area. But now that you mention possible dangers,
keep your eye out for the prairie wolf stalking our campsite."

Indians, rattlesnakes, prairie wolves. What next? "How
kind of you to mention it," she said with exaggerated
civility, "for I had completely forgotten about the prairie
wolves following your trail."

"Wolf," he corrected. "Just one. You'll recognize him
by his cropped ear. I think I saw him a couple of hours
ago, but I can't be sure. Not to worry, though. I'd say he
weighs less than a hundred pounds, and wolves have always feared humans, so I'm guessing this one will keep
his distance."

"How reassuring," she said, and resolutely left the
shelter of the trees. As she made her way toward the river,
she dared to wonder whether the man-beast had mentioned the wolf so that she wouldn't run away from him
and leave him to fend for himself. However, just in case
he wasn't the kind to stoop to scare tactics, she kept a
nervous eye out for the wolf.

She saw nothing to disturb her at the river and performed her morning ablutions to the extent that the prim-
itive conditions would allow. She dearly wished for a
comb and a brush and a mirror, but made do with her
fingers. She spent the whole of the time dressing her hair
mentally arguing with that vexatious man-beast, who always seemed to be putting her in the wrong. She donned
her bonnet, then knelt down by the river, cupped her

hands and dipped them in the water. When she tasted the freshness on her tongue and the chill against her teeth, she was arrested by memories of the thoughts she had entertained the day before when drinking from the river at this very same spot.

She had judged the trip to be more like a pleasant outing? She had reckoned that difficulties might lie ahead?

Hah! She hadn't guessed the half of it!

Then, an uneasy thought occurred to her. Was this the "Someday" that her mother had predicted for her? Had she, in some mysterious fashion, brought this present calamity upon herself?

Sarah recalled her mother's reaction upon being informed that her daughter had turned down William's offer of marriage. Her mother began gently enough. "Sarah, love, you've had everything your own way for too long, I'm afraid, and I don't know what to tell you anymore except that you will simply have to stop leading these poor men on."

"Now, Mother, I didn't lead William on."

Her mother's normally serene expression had set into lines of disapproval. "You toyed with Mr. James's affections as if he were a parlor poodle, and if you haven't determined your effect on men by now—especially after all the ruckus you raised in England—"

"Gossip! Malicious gossip, all of it!"

"Then you are a far more insensitive young woman than I had ever imagined! And I don't want to hear another word about 'malicious gossip.' A woman who looks like you and behaves like you can expect tongues to wag on occasion, and given your reputation, I can only wonder how poor Mr. James allowed himself to fall prey to your toils!"

Sarah had been unwise enough at this point to observe, somewhat flippantly, "William isn't poor."

"Indeed not!" her mother had instantly agreed. "Everyone knows he comes from one of the richest families in Baltimore, and he's a fine-looking man, I might add. As much as I love you, I'm beginning to think that my love has been blind and that the gossips have been right. Could it be, young lady, that the only reason why you would crush such an eligible man beneath your heel is that you think far too highly of yourself?"

"But William *dotes* on me, Mother! I couldn't bear a man who dotes on me all day long!"

"Since you don't seem to be able to inspire in a man any other desire but to dote on you, you will be pleased to accompany us on the journey we must make to join Laurence and Cathy."

Sarah had been aghast. "To the Oregon Territory? Me? You must be joking!"

But her mother hadn't been joking, and nothing Sarah had said afterward had persuaded either her mother or her father from their unreasonable position. She had left that particular discussion angered by her mother's gross misrepresentation of her character.

And now, here she was, standing at the edge of a river in the middle of nowhere, recalling her mother's final words. "Someday, Sarah Ross Harris," her mother had said on a note of threat. "Someday, you will get what's coming to you."

For one hideous moment, Sarah was seized by the idea that she had been deliberately abandoned by her mother and father to the Sioux, the rattlesnakes, the prairie wolves and the man-beast. But then her reason reasserted itself. She hadn't imagined the war whoops or the Widower Reynolds's dead body, and her parents had had other opportunities before now to abandon her along the way. Besides which, they wouldn't be capable of doing anything so despicably underhanded to her, would they. *Would they?*

She returned to the clump of trees, repeating to herself that she hadn't wanted to come on this journey, no she hadn't, which was proof enough in her mind that she wasn't responsible for having brought any of her present misfortune upon herself. And the General? What would he have said about the events of the past day? Why, to be sure, he would have agreed that none of this was of her making, and he would have reminded her to be on her mettle.

Once within the shelter she noted that the man-beast had finished his breakfast, for the fire was banked, and he was sitting under his tree, his back against the trunk. The pieces of her shawl were wrapped around his feet, but they were no longer bloody. He looked as if he was about to say something to her, but since she was feeling hungry and out of sorts and unable to take one of his disagreeable comments just then, she said, "I'm going to return to the Widower Reynolds's wagon and see what provisions may be there."

"The Sioux would have already taken all of use and value."

"They didn't take his trousers."

"They don't tend to touch dead white men, and they've no need for white man's clothing."

"I've a mind to go to the wagon anyway."

"Before you go, I want to—"

She held up a hand. "To warn me. I know. Rattlesnakes."

He made no further comment. She left the glade, scrambled up the slope, where she discovered that the broken-down wagon had been picked clean, and returned to the shelter of the trees empty-handed. At least the man-beast didn't annoy her with obvious remarks about having been right.

Instead, he asked, "How many petticoats are you wearing?"

She was so surprised by the question that she answered it. "Two."

"Give me one."

The ensuing discussion roused her indignation, which brought her out of her dejection and partially restored her spirits. It ended with the surrender of one of her petticoats, but she decided to make a virtue of necessity and offered up the white cotton as if it were a magnificent sacrifice. She soon discovered that its fate was even more ignominious than that of her shawl, for the half of it was reduced to long strips that she was told would serve as jackrabbit traps. The other half would be saved for the future.

She was put to work and obliged to carry out the man-beast's instructions while he lounged against the tree trunk. She set up the rather ingenious traps, as directed, which were composed of sticks and strips of cloth and clover. She fetched the man-beast water in her shoes. She gathered the plants that he told her to gather. She flipped back the cuffs of her long-sleeved blouse and used the hem of her skirts to wipe the sweat from her brow. She found two stones he told her to find and kept them with her in case she might encounter the prairie wolf. She was not to use the stones as lancing objects. Rather, she was to chip away at one rock with the other. She was told that that was how Indians made arrowheads. She wasn't expected to actually make an arrowhead, but the chipping sound made animals, like prairie wolves, wary, as wild animals are of anything strange.

The morning ran quickly into afternoon. The afternoon brought the capture of two jackrabbits. After that, the man-beast was busy with her scissors, skinning the rabbits and cooking them over a fire that gave almost no smoke. Then he set about fashioning the hide.

At one moment while the man-beast was involved in scraping out the rabbit skin, she was troubled enough to say, "I can't understand why my family hasn't returned to look for me. That is, if they escaped, which it seems they did. They should be worried about me, no?"

"They're probably thankful you weren't on hand during the attack yesterday afternoon. If they haven't come back for you, it's because they're not able to come back for you."

"Which makes me worried about them, then."

"Of course."

His response to her concern had been reasonable. No gushing sympathy. No unrealistic assurances of her family's well-being, either. But he had offered her a kind of fellow understanding nonetheless, and she was inclined to judge the man-beast the better for it. She had too much to do, however, to dwell on her slightly improved opinion of her partner in misfortune.

In the course of her afternoon's work, she didn't encounter any wild animals, so she didn't have occasion to chip away at her stones, although she was aware at odd times during the day of being watched. However, whenever she looked about her, she saw nothing. No Indians. No prairie wolves. She kept the rocks with her, and when she smoothed them in her palms, her jumping nerves steadied.

The afternoon was spent, and so were her energies. She went one last time to the river, removed her bonnet and splashed water on her face. Heedless of the fact that her hair was tumbling around her shoulders, hairpins askew, she returned to the glade and plopped down on the ground at the base of her tree. She was happy to empty her mind and stare into the lengthening evening shadows.

When the faintest twinklings could be seen in the sky through the leafy arches in the trees, the rude, inconsiderate man-beast tossed two rabbit skins into her lap and said, "It's time to move on."

Chapter Three

Powell rose to his full height, tested his weight first on one sole, then the other. His feet were still torn and sore, but the covering of wet rabbit hide made it easier to stand on them. He flexed his knees and felt the ache of muscles in his calves from the awkward way he had walked trying to spare his feet over the last few days. Still, his condition was no longer bad enough to warrant the risk of playing the role of sitting duck another day.

The trousers were a definite inconvenience. The Widower Reynolds had evidently been a much shorter man than he, for the pant legs reached only to his midcalf. The suspenders did not adjust and were, therefore, unusable. The trousers were too short in the crotch, too, but the waist was snug enough so that he didn't have to waste one of the precious strips of petticoat cloth as a belt. If the beautiful idiot hadn't been with him, he would have preferred to go naked. However, since she was with him, something about keeping to the conventions of dress seemed like a good idea.

He had already packed up the sack he had made from one half of her petticoat. It now held the suspenders, the torn shawl, the strips of cloth retrieved from the traps, and the beautiful idiot's shoes. Her scissors he carried in one of his back pockets. He had already dismantled the rocks he had used for the two fires he had made, the one for the tree frogs, the other for the jackrabbits, which he had built a few feet away from the first. He had scattered twigs and leaves over the warm ground where the fires had been and had disposed of the jackrabbit remains. All day long he had been rescaling the map of the territory in his head to fit the proportions of crossing it on foot. He had charted their course.

He figured they were ready to go.

When he took his first tentative steps toward the riverside edge of the trees, he became aware that the beautiful idiot had not moved. He looked over his shoulder and repeated, "It's time to move on."

She remained seated and motionless at the base of the tree. The twilight silvered the golden hair that was swirling about her heart-shaped face and shoulders like a fallen halo. The soft half-light paled her rosy skin, giving it the texture of flower petals. Her big brown eyes were luminous with a feisty mix of emotions, and her pretty lips were set in a line oddly expressive of seduction and obstinance at once. She had crossed her arms under full breasts and crossed her legs at their shapely ankles. Her feet peeped out from under the flounces of her petticoat and overskirt. The moccasins lay untouched in her lap where he had tossed them.

"You cannot be serious," she stated in that falsely pleasant voice that grated on his nerves.

It took him a moment to absorb the impact of that statement, then another moment to suppress the desire to strangle her. He shifted the sack on his back and demanded, "Are you always like this, or only when survival is at stake?"

"Always like what, sir?"

Why mince words? "Always idiotic." He saw the flash in her eyes shift from seductive obstinance to outright anger. "We've done fine for the day here, but I've no desire to linger longer and make myself easy prey for either man or animal. And I'm assuming you see the advantage of traveling at night, so that I don't have to spell it out for you."

"No, you don't have to spell it out for me, but I'd like to point out that *I'm* the one who's been working all day while you've been sitting around."

He gave her a very deliberate once-over. "You look like a healthy woman, and the amount of 'work' you did is nothing compared to the physical demands that will be put on both of us tonight—which is why I gave you half an hour to rest. We need to move, and the time is now."

She didn't budge.

It would take only one more idiotic word from her for him to leave her here to her own devices. Let her die, for all he cared. But then he thought of her scissors in his pocket, the valuable cloth in his hands and the fact that she had fetched him water more than once today, and he realized that it wouldn't be fair to leave her. But when was life ever fair? Besides which, it was her choice, after all, to stay or come. You could lead a horse to water...and all that.

He turned to go.

"I need my shoes," she said. "I don't see them lying about, so I'm guessing that you have them in the half of my petticoat that you have slung over your shoulder."

"Wear the moccasins I made you."

"I want my shoes."

"Moccasins don't leave the same footprints as white man's shoes, and I had to cut up the laces of your ankle boots to make four ties for our two pairs.'' He saw her lift the rabbit skins and examine the ties. He saw her jaw drop. He cut off whatever idiotic thing was going to come out of her pretty mouth by saying swiftly, ''They'll fit you perfectly. I measured them against your shoes. Now, *let's go!*''

He slipped through the trees and stepped out onto the riverbank, half hoping she wouldn't follow him.

No such luck, but, then again, that was just his luck. He hadn't gone ten paces before she was behind him, asking, ''Where are we going?''

''To deliver you to your family.'' He added, with feeling, ''And without delay.''

''Oh! Why didn't you say so in the first place?'' When she caught up with him, she said, ''You know, we might get along much better if you would explain yourself to me instead of making me out to be an…an idiot! And I could think of you less as a man-beast and in a more kindly manner if I had a name to call you.''

At that he stopped in his tracks and looked down at her. She was looking up at him, her beautiful eyes wide and almost beseeching, but not quite. Her practiced social smile held a hint of something else that he wasn't willing to examine just yet. Instead, he pinned his thoughts on the incredible idea that she had called him a man-beast, and he almost laughed. Good God, she was an irritating woman, but she had a way of diverting his attention from the pain in his feet. He'd grant her that much.

''I asked you your name, sir,'' she repeated.

''Powell.''

''Just Powell? Only that?''

''Wesley.''

''Well, which is the first name and which the last, sir? I'm afraid I cannot distinguish.''

"Wesley Powell," he said slowly. "My name is Wesley Powell."

"Very well, then, Mr. Powell." She nodded her head graciously. "I am Miss Harris."

He regarded her a moment longer, then grunted and began walking again. Really, she had expected no better from the man-beast, but she found that it humanized him to have a name, and such a perfectly ordinary one, although he had pronounced it with a kind of reluctance. Or did his tone hint of challenge?

No matter. Since their immediate goal was to find her family, she was content—if *content* was an appropriate word to describe her emotional state in a situation where her survival was not assured from one hour to the next— to walk along beside him. She hardly needed to be told that he didn't like her any more than she liked him, and she didn't need to be told twice, no, three times, that he preferred her silence to her conversation. However, since she saw no reason why she should behave according to his preferences rather than hers, she continued chattily, "So, Mr. Powell, can you tell me how we are going to achieve the very worthy goal of finding my family?"

"First, tell me whether, before embarking on this journey, you and your family established a meeting place in the event you should become separated."

She had to consider that question at length. She did recall her father and mother discussing such a situation, but she hadn't paid attention to what the outcome of the discussion had been. At the time, she had been thinking it would be a mercy to be separated from her bratty little sisters, but now, imagining that they had met some unspeakable fate—but, no, she turned her thoughts from dwelling on horrors and bent them toward remembering the names of the various stages of the journey that Morgan

Harris had recited on more than one occasion. It seemed logical that her father would have decided that, if separated, the family would meet up at the next landmark.

She said, "Chimney Rock," since that was the only landmark she could recall, and if she didn't say something soon, Mr. Powell would think her an even bigger idiot than he already did—not that she cared.

"Chimney Rock?" he repeated under his breath.

Hoping that the landmark was ahead of them rather than one they had already passed, she repeated with confidence, "Yes, Chimney Rock. Is there something that troubles you in that, sir?"

"Nothing beyond the fact that it lies some two hundred miles and more to the west of here. Did you not identify more proximate meeting points? Windlass Hill, perhaps? Ash Hollow?"

"Ah, yes, Windlass Hill," she said, picking the landmark that sounded the closest. "I had forgotten."

"You don't have the faintest idea of a meeting point, do you?" he snapped. "No, don't answer that question! Tell me instead whether, in one of your two trips to the Widower Reynolds's wagon, you bothered to notice the direction of the tracks of the wagons that had fled the scene?"

She interpreted this question as just another one of his gratuitous attempts to expose her ignorance. She composed herself before answering, "The character of the know-it-all is one of society's least attractive types, in case you didn't know it, Mr. Powell. Now, you might have asked me to notice the direction of the wagon tracks earlier in the day, if you had wanted the information, and you will not waste your breath asking me any more questions of this type if you know—and I make no secret of it—that I didn't want to make this trip in the first place and would far, far rather be in Baltimore!''

He grumbled inarticulately, but she caught several syllables. Although her lady's ears were offended, she guessed that he was cursing himself for having failed to ask her to investigate what seemed, to his mind at any rate, important clues left at the previous day's wagon site. After a few more paces he turned away from the riverbank and made his way up the slope. She supposed she was to follow him, but his long legs scissored through the tall grasses at a faster clip than she could sustain, so she stopped not far from the top of the slope and hung back while he tramped around the wagon site, his head bent toward the earth. After a while, he stopped that activity and stood looking into the distance. He was facing toward the sun, which had set beyond the horizon but which was still streaking the open sky with broad strokes of pink and orange, while the earth below was bedding down in layers of gray shadows.

She refrained from calling out and asking him if she should come over to him or if he was going to return to her or what she should do. She was rewarded for her forbearance when, about ten minutes later, he returned to her side and said, rather grimly, that they would follow the river only for another mile or so. She also forbore to ask what they would do after that, thinking she'd find out soon enough, which she did. A mile, she had already learned, was not a considerable distance in this part of the world, even when one was on foot.

They traipsed along at the water's edge, hidden from sight by the slight slope that rose on either side of the broad river. The air was getting chillier by the minute. She knew that although the temperature had dipped into the cool range the night before, it had not become uncomfortably cold. She was hungry, having only nibbled at a little jackrabbit all day, but she refrained from asking about food on the perfectly good grounds that if she brought up the subject, the perverse Mr. Powell was sure to concoct something disgusting to eat. She would wait until *he* got hungry, then eat what he ate.

At length he stopped abruptly. Looked down at her. In the light of the rising moon the planes of his face were sharp-etched, his expression somber. He nodded to the slope of the bank, which was steeper at this point than at their hiding place downriver. He climbed up high enough to be able to toss the sack over the edge, then moved back down and offered her a hand. She accepted his strong clasp gratefully, didn't protest at the harsh squeeze he gave her or the rough tug that got her up and over the top of the slope.

Once again on her feet, she brushed her skirts off at her knees. He picked up the sack, shouldered it. They were looking out over the valley of the Platte, an enormous table of land that rolled away and merged with the whole of the darkened horizon. By day she knew the land was tufted with green and yellow grass. At night it looked to her more like the surface of the moon, cratered with every shade of gray, or a paradoxically dry ocean, whose dips and rises had been made solid.

When she noticed the direction of his gaze and followed it with her eyes, she saw two patches of white, not far off, crowded up against a slight rise in the landscape. The patches looked like the broken sails of two ship-wrecked vessels. Her heart caught at the implications of that pathetic scene.

He didn't say anything. He didn't look at her. Nor did he immediately move. It was as if he was allowing her to come to terms with the possibilities of the scene that lay ahead before actually confronting the reality of it.

After several long moments passed, he said quietly, "It's as I thought. Back at the wagon site, I saw the two white dots in the distance and suspected something like this. Tell me when you're ready to go over there."

She summoned strength from the General, the father she had never known. She straightened her backbone, squared her shoulders. "I'm ready now."

Together they crossed the open expanse. She feared. She hoped. As they approached the pitiful remains of two covered wagons, she experienced a kind of death herself. Resisted it with every particle of her being. But she didn't resist looking upon the brute scene of the bodies of her former traveling companions, which littered the ground around the two disabled wagons. There were five, stretched this way and that. Some facedown, some faceup, caught in their scattered, equally ineffective paths of flight. Without blinking, she looked at each body in turn. Every moment that passed brought her new life and new hope.

She made the gruesome rounds twice, just to assure herself that hope and the moonlight weren't playing tricks with her eyes.

She pronounced, "So far, so good." Then she laughed at what she had said. "Of course, nothing good has happened to these poor folks, but at least none of them are from my family! It's awful to say such a thing aloud, but I'm happy that if misfortune was to visit our wagon train, it has fallen on others."

Powell didn't reply. He had put his sack on the ground and climbed into one wagon wreck, then the other.

On a hope and a prayer she repeated, "So far, so good. At least as far as I know for now."

He climbed back out of the wagon nearest her, jumped down on the ground. "Nothing," he reported. "Not a pot or pan or sack of flour to be found." He walked over to her. "Don't feel bad about being happy your family isn't among the slain, although it may feel odd to be so happy in the midst of this misery."

She nodded and voiced her puzzlement about another matter. "Two others from this wagon are missing. You see, here are the Kelly brothers." She gestured toward a trio of bodies. "They were traveling together and had left their aging parents behind in Ohio. Now, beyond the second wagon lie Mr. Clark and his grown son Jack, but Mrs. Clark and her daughter aren't there. I'm wondering whether they might have escaped."

"Possibly."

"Which means they might be roaming the hills," she said. "Perhaps we should look for them."

"They might have been captured," Powell replied. "Or they might be lying dead yonder, out of our sight."

"Still, I'm wondering why it is only the men who have been killed outright, and none of the women."

Powell walked around the large dispersed triangle that was formed by the Kelly brothers, studied the sprawled attitudes of the dead bodies. "Do you know whether all three were carrying firearms?"

"I would suppose they did. Every man on the wagon train had a rifle, sometimes two. Why, even Morgan—my father—had a rifle for shooting game."

"Judging from the way these bodies lie, and adding the Widower Reynolds into the equation, I would say that those who were killed outright were the ones doing the shooting. From the placement of their arms and hands, it looks as if each one was holding a rifle that was subsequently taken."

"You must have had a rifle when you were captured, no? Why didn't they kill you outright?"

"My rifle was on my back," he said, "and I wasn't shooting at them. At the time I was sorry to be so defenseless, but perhaps not anymore."

"They were going to kill you anyway," she observed, "and I don't like to think of Mrs. Clark and her daughter facing unspeakable torture. I doubt the two of them would be able to escape the way you did."

"How old is the daughter?"

"About ten."

He considered the matter. "The Teton Sioux might currently have a shortage of women. A ten-year-old girl who could be taught their ways and a woman perhaps still of child-bearing age might be prized rather than killed."

At that Sarah's mind boggled. The phrase "Fate worse than death" drifted into consciousness but just as quickly drifted out. Her thoughts easily embraced the idea of her sisters, if captured, remaining alive, and her mother, too, but stumbled against the notion that they would be condemned to live an Indian life. Condemned? Her thoughts bumped uncomfortably into the image of her father, Morgan, and her brother, Laurence—that is, her stepfather, Morgan, and her stepbrother, Laurence, child of Morgan's first marriage to an Iroquois woman.

Laurence had lived with them since Sarah was a baby, but he had left the Maryland farm already thirteen years ago. Sarah had always been in awe of the remarkable Laurence Harris, who was fifteen years her senior, and she had always been angry at anyone who might have called him half-breed behind his back.

At the same time, she had always been...well, not ashamed of his Indian heritage and the life that Morgan had lived before he had married her mother, but maybe rather confused by it. Or alienated by their background, which had so little in common with hers, and conflicted with hers. Their background was a complication in her life, another strike against her, although few people had ever dared refer to her own background or the disadvantages it had brought her. She had sometimes felt like a stranger in her own country, in her own family. And she had been there first—before Morgan or Laurence or her bratty half sisters!

"You said that even your father had a rifle. What did you mean by that?"

Sarah's tangled musings were cut short. "Only that he's a peaceable man and wouldn't shoot at another person."

She waited for the retort, "Not even at an Indian?" But it didn't come. Instead Powell said, "All right, then. One wagon remains back at the original site and one body. Two more are here, five bodies, minus two women. The other six wagons—"

"Seven," she corrected. "We were ten in all."

Powell paused, then said, "I must have miscounted the tracks. In any case, the other wagons dispersed more to the north than the west. What I don't know is how many warriors descended on your wagon train and how many were spread out looking for me in other parts of the territory. Covered wagons move a lot slower than horses, so in order to get away, the men in those wagons must have killed some of their attackers. I can't be sure of the number, of course, because those bodies would have been long since returned to their villages by their tribesmen to be given a proper burial."

"We don't know that all of the seven other wagons escaped in the end, do we?"

"No, but they made it at least two or three miles, which

is a rough estimate of the distance I could reckon from the wagon site.''

"So which way do we go now?"

He pointed in the northwesterly direction they would travel for the night. "It will be slow going to put the complete puzzle together, but with luck we'll have it solved in the next day or two."

"Speaking of proper burials, do you think we should do something about—" She broke off and gestured vaguely about her.

He shook his head. "No good reason to advertise that anyone has been through this territory, which is what we'd be doing if we buried the bodies but didn't dispose of the wagon wrecks."

She saw the wisdom in that.

"And we don't have any shovels."

"True enough," she agreed. "Then you might wish to choose a pair of trousers that fits you better."

Powell nodded. When he began to walk around the bodies, sizing them up for the best fit, she looked away from the scene and out over the darkened infinity stretching before her, trying to keep fearsome thoughts at bay. She asked quietly, "Do you think we should take another pair of trousers, just in case?"

He didn't immediately respond to that, which made her think he hadn't heard her, but when he came up behind her several minutes later, he said, "I'd like to, but I don't want to have to dispose of another body."

She turned and saw that he was fully dressed. White shirt, torn and bloodied over the left breast. Trousers that fit. Leather suspenders. A pair of boots laced together and slung over his shoulder. She glanced around and saw the body that had been stripped down to long johns, the arrow still sticking straight up from the heart.

"I see what you mean," she said. "We can hardly leave him out in the open, can we?"

"I'm thinking of dragging him into the wagon. If any Sioux pass by here and bother to inspect the wagon, they might think he got caught sleeping. We'll leave the other bodies the way they are. As much as their boot laces would be useful to us, I won't risk taking them."

Together they dragged the stripped-down body into the nearest wagon and dressed it in the ill-fitting trousers Powell had cast off along with the Widower Reynolds's suspenders. When she was climbing out again, her eye was attracted by a flash of moonlight caught in some small object that was lodged under the wheel of the other wagon. When she bent down to inspect it, she was delighted to discover a new-fangled tilt-edged razor.

She held up the miraculous object. "Look, Mr. Powell. I have found a tool perhaps even more useful than my scissors. Why, I'm sure you could put this to use as a fine weapon."

Powell approached her and ran his hand over his chin and neck. "I think it'll make a better razor than weapon, and I can certainly use that."

Annoyed, once again, by the way he seemed to have put her in the wrong, she handed him the precious object, saying pleasantly, "How sorry I am, Mr. Powell, that I didn't discover a comb and a brush beneath the wheel, since we are apparently not in dire need of weapons. It seems that I am not to be credited with any good ideas— not that I am expecting a thank-you!"

He had the grace to smile, and the harsh lines of his face were transformed into a surprisingly attractive arrangement. She dismissed this unexpected effect as a trick of the moonlight.

"Your excellent find of the razor, Miss Harris, will be

useful in a variety of ways, and allow me to compliment you on your suggestion that I choose a better-fitting pair of trousers. It was, perhaps, your first good and useful idea," he said with a slight bow, "but I am confident that it will not be your last."

"It was my second," she corrected. "Remember that I had the idea to bring you the first pair of trousers last night, although I suppose you'll only say now that in taking the Widower Reynolds's clothing, I have left evidence that white folk have come through the area."

"I wasn't going to say anything of the kind, Miss Harris," he said. He picked up the petticoat sack, tied it around the boots hanging over his shoulder so that the ends of the cloth were balanced front and back, and struck out in the direction that he had earlier indicated they would take for the night.

Sarah had no choice but to follow him.

After what seemed to be several miles of walking, they came upon what Powell identified as the tracks from several of the fleeing wagons of the day before. They strained to find signs of wreckage or dead bodies but saw nothing. They were inclined to take it as a good sign.

They followed the tracks, although they had no assurance that the ruts had been made by her family's wagon. The moon rose. They walked. The moon traversed the sky. They walked. And walked until she could feel every step through her soles to the muscles of her calves and thighs and back. To take her mind off her aches and hunger and thirst, she fixed her thoughts on an image of Morgan Harris confronting his Sioux attackers without raising his rifle to them. In her vision the Widower Reynolds fell to the ground. So did the Kelly brothers. Mr. Clark and Jack, too. But Morgan remained standing.

Chapter Four

When the night gave a hint of surrendering to a new day, Powell stopped at a small tree-filled hollow he had found tucked in the shadows of the barren plains. Sarah's leaden spirits lightened at the sight of a spring lazing in the middle of the hollow and ringed by rocks glowing white in the moonlight. Her thirst was stronger than her exhaustion, so she slipped down the rocky slope to splash her face and drink her fill. When she returned to what would be their campsite, Powell had heaped several armfuls of leaves beneath a tree, spread the half petticoat out upon them and offered her a bed. Without waiting for her thanks, he began to fashion his own bed of leaves about ten feet away from her.

She lay down on her back, sure she would never move again. It was a merciful torture to be lying there with every muscle in her body throbbing and quivering. She was only vaguely aware when Powell left the campsite, but she was acutely aware when he returned, for he seemed to be moving about far too busily for a man who had just trudged God knew how many miles on wounded feet.

"What are you doing?" she asked.

"Gathering wood to build a fire."

She felt a faint stirring of hope. "You have meat to cook?"

"I wish," he said. "No, it's rather that we have company."

She groaned when she rose up on an elbow. "Company?" she echoed weakly.

"The prairie wolf. The one with the cropped ear."

She groaned again when she sank back down onto her bed of leaves. "Let's kill it and eat it."

"That might not be so easy. Nor so wise."

"I know it might not be easy, but why might it not be wise?"

He began to stack the wood to build his fire about five feet away from her. He paused at length before answering, "I don't know. Just a feeling."

Her only feeling at the moment was of bare-boned existence. Breathing in. Breathing out. Body stinging with pain top to toe. Stinging, too, with the will to live. She worked sluggishly through the implications of his statement. "So, if it wouldn't be wise to kill it, you must think it's useful to us somehow."

"Wolves have been known to stalk a man or an animal for miles, so I'm not saying he's not out for our blood. It's just that..." He trailed off.

"Did you know it was following us all night?"

"No. I sensed at different times that we weren't alone, but he's a clever one and didn't show himself. He could have easily made a move on us at almost any point, but he's kept his distance. Even now it was only by chance that I happened to catch a glimpse of the silhouette of his ear in the fading moonlight before he ducked into the bushes on the ridge opposite the hollow."

"What's the fire for, then?"

"To keep him at bay."

"Just in case he was thinking of us as dinner, as I was happy to consider him?"

"Let's just say that he might be waiting until we're in a worse way than we are now before going in for the kill. After all, he has to rustle his grub as easily as he can with the least risk to himself."

"If he has to wait until we're in worse shape than we are now," she said wearily, "then he must be in a pretty bad way himself."

Powell brought the fire to life. "Exactly what I was thinking, Miss Harris."

That revived her a bit. She raised herself back up on one elbow and saw that he sat squatted, balanced on his heels, and was tending the fire with a stick. She said, "That's my fourth good idea. The first and second were for the trousers, the third for the razor."

He looked up and met her glance. "Keeping score?"

"With a hungry prairie wolf stalking us, Mr. Powell, I'd like you to think that I'm more useful alive than as wolf bait." She smiled faintly. "Not that I want to give you any bad ideas."

The flickering light from the flames licked the sharp-edged planes of his face and blued the unkempt black curls that spun around his head. Something about the way his eyes narrowed as they rested on her suggested that he was enjoying a private joke. His expression riled her enough to shake off her tiredness.

"Although," she said, rising laboriously to her feet, "it seems you already arrived at that idea on your own."

She moved toward the fire, plopped down across from him so that she was looking at him through the flames. Her bonnet was still tied around her neck, but hanging down her back. She picked apart the knot in the ties and pulled the bonnet off. After folding it in her lap, she attempted to finger-groom the tangles of her hair, which felt as wild and untended to her as the surrounding landscape. Her scalp was beginning to itch. She had a vision of paradise, and it was a hot, scented bath and a luxurious shampoo.

"So how do you do it?" she asked, nodding toward the flames. "Make a fire, that is."

His lips curved up in the barest suggestion of a smile. "So that you'll know how to make one after you've thrown me to the wolf?"

The suggestion took her aback. "You think I'm capable of that?"

Noting her surprise, he replied, "Well now, it seems I've given you a bad idea. But it might have been one that would have come to you eventually, given the right set of circumstances."

She wasn't a bit tired now. She didn't know which danger had alerted her senses more, the one stalking them outside the campsite or the one she felt hovering above the circle of the fire.

"You have experience with Sioux women," she said, hugging her knees to her chin and arranging her skirts around her feet, "which gives you an idea how a white woman might behave outside the conventions." She rested one cheek on a knee. "Does that mean you won't tell me how to make a fire, so that I have to depend on you for food and warmth?"

He shook his head slightly as if to dismiss this absurd, yet not so absurd, discussion. Then he slipped his hand inside his trouser pocket and tossed something over to her. The sparkle of the small objects in the firelight brought her head up. She sat back reflexively so that she was cross-legged Indian-style, and two stones fell in the trough created by her skirts spread across her knees. She picked up the chunks and looked at him in question.

"Iron pyrites," he explained. He withdrew several more pieces from his pocket and showed her how to strike them to achieve the desired result. "Starting fires from sticks is a tedious business, so I was happy to have found these rocks as we walked along the riverbed this past evening. Keep them. You never know when you'll need them."

While she untied the strings of the reticule at her waist in order to slip the rocks inside, she considered the unpleasant possibility that they might be separated. She was about to ask which one of them should carry her valuable scissors, but before she had a chance to pose the question, he tossed another object over to her. The next thing to land in her lap was one of the strips from her petticoat, bundled into a ball, which, she discovered upon opening it, contained a bunch of berries.

"Dinner," he said.

She was catching on to his ways. "So *that's* what you were doing all the time we were walking next to those bushes. I thought you had chosen the route to offer us protection from attack."

"That was part of it."

"You were harvesting the berries as we walked," she said, recalling that she had glimpsed in his hand an occasional flash of metal in the moonlight. The razor's tilted blade would not have been exposed enough for the task, so he must have used the scissors. "I hardly noticed what you were doing, just as I hardly noticed you gathering the bits of iron pyrite as we walked along the riverbed. You were able to bend down and pick them up without breaking stride."

"Which is why I'm still alive."

She decided that he had more useful ideas for her scissors than she did. Instead of asking for them back, she inquired, "What kind of berries are these?"

"The bitter kind," he warned her. Then he opened the bundle he had prepared for **him**self and began eating.

She did the same. Having been forewarned of the taste helped cut the effect of the bitterness. "Not so bad," she said, munching slowly, fighting the ravenous impulse to gobble, savoring every sour flavor.

"Tell me," he said, "what else you have in your bag."

She sighed. "Pins and needles and thread. A few coins. How I regret not having equipped myself more completely! When I think of all that I left behind in the wagon—"

"Better not to think of it."

"Yes, well, the needle and thread can still be useful. I was thinking that I should repair the rent in your shirt so that it doesn't look as if it was robbed from a dead man— in the event anyone should notice the tear and care about it. I could embroider something over it, you see, to disguise it."

"You like to embroider?"

"Not at all! It drives me to distraction, but I can do a respectable bird or two, and I even have the right colors for an oriole."

"An oriole?"

She shrugged. "A Baltimore oriole. It's the first embroidery pattern little girls learn where I'm from. After the alphabet, of course, and the usual flowers."

"That's right," he said, his voice low and lazy, "you'd rather be in Baltimore. Do I assume that's where you're from?"

She heard his questions as conversational, a way to fill the spaces of time that were as empty as their stomachs.

She hesitated over her usual impulse to pretty up her background, but the coziness of the campfire, which contrasted with the vast ocean of emptiness around them, prompted an honest response.

"From a farm just east of Baltimore," she said. "It's at North Point on the Chesapeake. I have many friends in Baltimore, though, and often go into town for one reason or another."

"And now you're on the road to Oregon," he observed. "What did your family grow on the farm?"

"Years ago—well before I was born, that is—it was tobacco. When the Maryland farmers were undersold in that market by the Virginians and Carolinians, the profit seemed to be in the staples, corn and kale and the like. More recently…"

He finished her statement. "More recently there was no profit to be had in anything."

She stared into the flames and watched a succession of miniature jewel gardens grow and die. It was pointless to deny the obvious. No one left a home when it was comfortable or a business when it was profitable. The original colonists hadn't been landed gentry or moneyed merchants when they had left England, and their descendants weren't fat cats leaving the East, either. The word *depression* had been circulating in *The Baltimore Register* with ever more frequency, along with installments from Samuel Parker's guidebook to the Oregon Territory.

It had taken only a recent letter from Laurence's wife, Cathy, reporting on the success of their apple tree farm out west, for Morgan and Barbara to decide that they had worked too hard for too long to have so little. Before Sarah knew it, the Harris family was packed up and ready to go. They were the first in their neighborhood to leave the old soil for greener pastures, but every farmer and shopkeeper in and around Baltimore had heard the enticing reports of the Oregon climate and the timber.

Sarah was of a mind to tell Mr. Powell that *she* had not been obliged to undertake this journey because she was poor. Oh, no! Mr. Powell should know that she had a very fine trust fund on which she could live in the style she deserved and which had been provided her by the widow of her father, the illustrious General Robert Ross of the British army.

Now, Mr. Powell didn't need to know that she wouldn't come into the money before she was twenty-five. Neither did he need to know that Mrs. Ross had threatened to close the account after those catty British "ladies" had tried to ruin Sarah's reputation when she had visited Mrs. Ross two years before. And he certainly didn't need to know that Morgan and Barbara had refused to borrow a penny against the future of that money and that their refusal hurt her in a peculiar sort of way. She knew, however, that to say any of this would leave her open to embarrassing questions.

She looked up and repeated, "No, there was no profit to be had in anything."

If she thought she was going to avoid embarrassing questions, she was mistaken. Powell, who was thoughtfully chewing his berries, asked next, "You're traveling with your sisters, no?"

"That's right. I have two."

"Older? Younger?"

"Both younger. Helen is sixteen and Martha is fourteen."

"Which makes you—"

"One and twenty, Mr. Powell."

"Hmm. I see."

There was something in the way he said, "I see," that

made her think he saw nothing at all. She knew what he was thinking, and it was exactly what that hateful Mrs. Fletcher had said when she had met Sarah. Upon inquiring about Sarah's age, Mrs. Fletcher had smiled sweetly and said, "Oh, I see, my dear. You must have suffered a disappointment in love. No? Well, why else would a woman of your age be accompanying her parents to begin a new life on the other side of the continent?"

Sarah could restrain her vanity no longer. "I'll have you know, Mr. Powell," she said, "that I turned down a very good—no, an *excellent* offer of marriage hardly more than a month ago, and so you needn't think that I came on this trip because…because I was unable to *situate* myself or anything of that sort!"

Her vanity was hardly appeased when Powell asked, "Why didn't you find a way to stay with one of the many friends you have in Baltimore, if you didn't choose to be traveling now?"

Because none of her friends had turned out to be true friends. After Sarah had turned silly William down, she found that the doors to the houses of Olivia and Isabelle and Claire didn't open so readily or so widely for her anymore. Never mind that they were as stuck-up as they were rich. And they had been jealous of her from the start. Oh, yes, jealous.

She said primly, "I don't like to impose," and had to swallow her pride to see the smirk of understanding cross her companion's stubble-darkened face. It was difficult to determine which was the more unpleasant circumstance to bear at the moment: her exhaustion, her hunger, the memory of being so thoroughly snubbed, or the company of this impossible man.

"And you, Mr. Powell?" she asked, gathering together

the tired remains of her dignity. "What brings you to these inhospitable parts?"

"The U.S. government. I'm a surveyor."

The vision of a precise surveyor jarred against her continuing image of him as a man-beast. She was surprised into asking, "Your studies in surveying informed you of how to trap and skin a rabbit and how to build a fire from sticks and iron pyrite?"

He shook his head. "A year of being in the field has done that for me."

"Nevertheless, I don't suppose when you chose such a...a *respectable* profession that you ever imagined finding yourself captive to bloodthirsty Sioux squaws."

"I'll admit," he said, "that I never imagined the surveyor would be regarded as the Indians' worst enemy."

"How so?"

"The hunters they dislike. The pioneers, too. But the man with the magical instruments who looks at their land—just looks!—and works for the Great White Father back in Washington...this man they hate. And, perhaps, rightly so."

"Speaking of the Indians," she said, looking nervously over her shoulder into the blackness, "I'm wondering whether this fire, as useful as it is for scaring away the hungry animals, might not alert any unfriendly humans to our presence."

"Right again, Miss Harris, and I'm none too pleased about still finding myself in Sioux country. So before I set about making the fire, I gave a couple of owl hoots, since to the Sioux, the hoot of an owl is the sign of death."

"That was you?" she replied, amazed. She had heard an owl a while back and, unlike a Sioux, had been comforted by the familiar sound of it. "You seem to have learned a lot of skills in a relatively short time."

"Since boyhood I've been able to hoot well enough to get answers from owls."

"Where are you from, Mr. Powell?"

"Everywhere, Miss Harris, and nowhere."

Thereafter the conversation didn't flourish, and she was inclined to think that they were protected as well as could be expected from their predators, whoever and whatever they might be.

After a while, Powell got up and left the campsite. Sarah felt a leap of panic at his departure and had to suppress a desire to ask him if she could accompany him. After all, he hadn't followed her when she had had occasion to disappear once or twice behind a bush during the course of their long walk, nor had he said a word about it. Still, it was dead of night, the prairie wolf was stalking them, and this was Sioux country. She glanced at his bed of leaves and thought it was distressingly far away from her own bed. However, to suggest making his any closer to hers was unthinkable.

So she drew herself away from the fire and fairly crawled back to her bed. She lay down on her back, intending to turn on her side, but once down, she couldn't move another muscle to turn over. She was captive to the leaves, imprisoned in a body that was not dead but not fully alive, either. With every sense stretched well beyond tiredness, she lay there with her eyes open, her gaze lost in the snarls of the wood and leaves above her head.

The shadows hidden in the branches mingled with the sneaking glow of the dying fire to create weird mind pictures of prairie wolves, of Sioux warriors with feathered arrows cocked in drawn bows. Of William down on one knee, taking her hand in his, begging her to be his wife.

Of the flick of her wrist, that one, brief gesture containing both her surge of triumph and her loss of desire to ever see him again. Of English aristocrats paying her extravagant compliments in darkened corners and then pawing her breasts. Of hoot owls.

The next thing she saw were the sun's rays breaking through the branches above where she lay. She sat straight up, draining the blood from her head. She was woozy from bad dreams and the realization that the sun was already well up in the sky. She ached everywhere in her body, but mostly in her heart, and when she looked around and saw that Mr. Powell's bed of leaves was empty, her aching heart nearly failed her.

She wanted to call out for him, but didn't dare. A moment later she was glad she had kept quiet, for she saw fresh sticks neatly laid for a new fire a few feet away from the previous night's fire. At the base of Mr. Powell's tree she spied a folded white shirt, a pair of moccasins, her laceless ankle boots, a laced pair of men's boots, a few rolled-up strips of white cotton and the torn shawl, atop which glinted a small object she recognized as her scissors. Relief sloshed through her, and she was able to conclude that Mr. Powell was at the spring, most likely bathing.

Given that, she decided to wait for his return to the campsite before going to the spring herself in order to wash. The evidence of the newly laid kindling suggested that he might have found some meat to cook. She was so cheered by the possibility that she decided to make herself useful. She got to her feet and hobbled across the campsite to retrieve Mr. Powell's shirt and her scissors. Then she hobbled back to her bed, sat back down, opened her reticule and began to mend the tear in the upper left front panel of Mr. Powell's shirt.

She engrossed herself in her task and was, perhaps for the first time in her life, soothed by the activity of threading her needle, of setting tiny stitches, of snipping finished ends, of making invisible knots. She saw the head of a delicate golden orange bird come to life beneath her fingers, sprout a wing, perch on the beginnings of a leafy branch. She let her thoughts roam where they willed. They fixed, pleasantly, on the happy reunion she would soon have with her mother and father and Martha and Helen.

Mr. Powell returned to the campsite. She didn't look up at him, absorbed as she was in her handiwork. She heard the small sounds of him lighting the fire and the subsequent snaps and crackles of the flames. Presently the aroma of jackrabbit drifted over to her and brought a watering in her mouth.

"I've roasted meat on a stick for you," Mr. Powell said to her at one point, "and placed it away from the fire on these rocks. You can have it when you're hungry."

"I'm hungry now," she said, still not looking up.

"I don't doubt it," he said, "but you're right not to hurry, since we can't move out of here for quite a few hours yet."

She was in her black threads now and began to place the beak. "Just like yesterday, then?"

He grunted his assent. "The terrain in these parts doesn't provide enough cover for us to travel during the day. I'll do what I can to sniff out the trail of the wagons over the next few hours, but I'm limited in my movements because of that prairie wolf and my lack of a knife. Not to mention the Sioux."

"I've got a bit of work left to do on your shirt," she said, "and could probably spend the day embroidering, if

I had enough thread.'' She held his shirt away from her and regarded it critically. She turned the shirt toward him, then finally looked up. ''You see—'' she began, and got no further.

He was squatting down before the fire and balanced on his heels just as he had when she had last seen him, but there the resemblance between the Mr. Powell of last night and the Mr. Powell of this morning ended, and she wouldn't have known him for the same man if she had not already heard his voice. When she looked up, he met her regard, and her overall impression of him now was that he was much younger than she had guessed, although she had not previously considered him old. She was frankly astounded to discover how thoroughly a shave could transform a man. His face wasn't handsome—she wouldn't go so far as to say *that*—but it was...*compelling*, in a masculine sort of way, all flat planes and clean angles.

His eyes were blue. She had noticed that right away, along with the fact that he was unusually sharp-sighted. But now that his blue, sharp-sighted eyes were focused on her in inquiry and no longer bloodshot, they had a quite distinctive effect. His hair was different, too. She wouldn't call it precisely tamed, but he had evidently washed it, and it was still slicked back from his face and only just beginning to curl as it dried. Then there were his broad shoulders and his muscular chest, which tapered down to a washboard stomach. She had already discovered how strong he was, but she couldn't quite understand why she hadn't made a connection between that strength and the physique that matched it. This lack of connection was all the more curious given the fact that when she had first laid eyes on him he had been naked.

At that she blushed and had the presence of mind to hold the shirt in her hands up in front of her face. She cleared her throat. "You see what I've been doing," she tried again. "What do you think so far?"

He did not immediately respond. In fact, the silence was prolonged enough to give her time to recover her complexion and to peek around the side of the shirt.

He was staring openmouthed in amazement, but his expression was not that of pleasant surprise, nor did he seem particularly impressed with her unexpected skill with a needle.

"I asked you what you think, Mr. Powell."

He closed his mouth, then opened it to say, "It's a bird."

"An oriole, yes. I told you so last night."

"I didn't think you were serious about putting it on the shirt."

Any trace of embarrassment vanished. *This* was the Mr. Powell she knew. "It's a rather fine start I've made, if I do say so myself," she said sweetly, and fixed him with a well-practiced gaze that blended mild puzzlement with entreaty. "Do I take it that you have some objection to the improvement that I'm making?"

Chapter Five

He might have predicted that the beautiful idiot would end up doing something idiotic while he was gone from the campsite. She was an irritating woman, no doubt about it. A tricky one, too, and he didn't want even to *begin* to respond to the look in her big brown eyes, no sir, or imagine how many men had fallen victim to it. And although he was able to recognize the not-so-subtle manipulative intention of that look, its effect on him was in no way lessened. It reminded him that a year in the field was a long time—

He shook his head to clear it. "I object to wearing a shirt with a bird that belongs on a sewing sampler."

"I think you should know, sir, that this pattern represents a skill level well beyond that of the sampler. It is found on parlor pillows in the best houses and on napkins, *linen* napkins."

"Especially a bird that's surrounded by all those curlicues."

"Those are to become mimosa flowers," she informed him. "I have hardly had time to finish the entire pattern, so perhaps it's premature of you to judge it at this stage. The pink of the flowers will nicely complement the golden orange of the bird's body, while the brown of the branch balances out the white and black of its head and wing feathers.''

''Does it have to be so big?''

''Well, this is about the size of the design as it figures on parlor pillows.''

''Ah, but I suppose that on napkins, it would be—'' He broke off.

There it was again, that look. ''You were saying, sir?'' That voice, too. Sweet enough to melt a foolish man. ''Something about napkins?''

This was a ridiculous conversation, and he wasn't going to pursue it. He needed a shirt, and it looked as if he was going to have one with an orange bird, surrounded by pink flowers, poised to chirp its silent song across several square inches of his upper left breast. He exhaled gustily, slipped the suspenders hanging down at his sides over his shoulders and rose to his tender bare feet.

''Let me know when the shirt's ready,'' he said. ''You can eat whenever you want.''

He retrieved his moccasins and was at the edge of the campsite when she stopped him with the words, precisely enunciated, ''Do you mind telling me where you are going, sir?''

Yes, I do mind. ''Is there a specific reason why you need to know, ma'am?''

''Since I wish to bathe at the spring, I would like to be assured that we do not get in each other's way.''

He should have guessed. ''I'm going to check out possible wagon tracks and trails. Since I can't move out in the open for any considerable length of time, I'll be gone several hours at least, but won't be able to cover much more than a mile or so.''

"And if the prairie wolf comes, should I chip stones again?"

He nodded. "Keep the fire going, too, or start another one for practice. Remember never to make two fires in one place. That will make it easier to cover our tracks before we move on out of here later today."

As he was leaving the campsite in a direction away from the spring, he heard her say, "If you're worried about not quite striking the right fashion note with a beautiful oriole on your shirt, I might remind you that your present outfit is far more stylish than the one you were wearing when I first saw you."

He crunched his way through the trees, grumbling to himself. This was hardly the best start to a day that was sure to be as grueling as the one before. He was in better shape, though, much better shape. After the beautiful idiot had fallen asleep the night before, he had boiled some water and put some snakeweed in it. Then he had soaked his feet in the concoction and slept with his soles wrapped in sage leaves. This morning, although his feet were far from healed, they were no longer stabbing him with pain. Since he wouldn't be doing much walking today, mostly waiting, he figured his feet would be even better by the time of the evening's trek.

As a man from everywhere and nowhere, he liked to plot people and places in precise positions on the various mental maps he held in his head, and he knew just where to put Miss No-First-Name Harris with her postures and her pretenses and her embroidery scissors. He knew her type. Hell, he had been given birth by her type. The lack of physical resemblance between Miss No-Name and his mother wasn't going to mislead him, and he'd have to remember his mother's jet black hair and sapphire eyes every time he looked at Miss No-Name's golden curls and twist-a-man-around-her-little-finger brown eyes. He indulged fellow feelings for the poor fool who had extended her the supposedly excellent offer of marriage she claimed to have turned down—and even dared to wonder *if* she had received such an offer. But why had a farm girl from the Chesapeake taken a trip to England with a chaperon?

He didn't know, and he wasn't going to spend the day thinking about her, especially not thinking of her bathing in the spring. Better to think of where he was and what he was doing, and that was surveying the one hundredth meridian. Better to find a place to hide in the occasional sprigs of vegetation where he could calculate the slant of the sun and plan his moves to coincide with the slow shifts of shadows. Better to wonder why white men wore black trousers, the kind that didn't blend into any daytime landscape.

Now that his senses were returning, he was interested to find out what happened to his telescope and his chain and his level, not to mention what might have happened in the meantime to the rest of his team of three other surveyors. However, he wouldn't be able to retrieve his instruments in the Sioux camp or restore himself to his team until he had returned the beautiful idiot to her family.

Full circle. Begin by thinking about a woman. End by thinking about a woman. Maybe it had something to do with having been stripped naked, made to face certain death, and then being reborn. But how long was he—were they—destined to survive with almost no resources in the middle of hundreds of thousands of acres of wilderness? Make that several millions of acres. He didn't know exactly how many, and it was the job of the surveying team to establish that number. The odds against him accomplishing his part of the mission now were high, and here he was a good hundred miles east of where he had last seen his team, with no equipment, no horse, and in the company of an irritating woman who seemed to think that their life-or-death circumstances made a good occasion to embroider.

He eventually found a miniature scarp in the seemingly smooth grassland in which he could nestle himself. Lying horizontally, he shared this patch of earth with creeping critters and stared at the sky, which was three hundred and sixty degrees of clouds, packaged like a drawing-room gift assortment of mare's tails and cumulus and cirrus, with an occasional dark storm cloud resting on a silvery gray pedestal of rain afar off to the west. He brought his gaze down to the horizon and chose a fixed point in the middle distance upon which to base his estimates of the wide spaces yawning around him. He took his time and arrived at what he knew would be a remarkably accurate estimate of fifteen miles to the slight rise of land on the western horizon.

This neat trick of spatial approximations was one he had taught himself as a distraction during the regular beatings he brought upon himself at the military academy. Over time, he discovered that he was good not only at the small-scale calibrations he had performed in the confines of the Correctional Chamber but also at the mapping of larger spaces, where plane geometry no longer applied and the curvature of the earth came into play. When he had surpassed his cartography teachers in precision, the beatings stopped, and he was sent to the War Department and the Bureau of Indian Affairs in Washington, D.C.

He calculated and waited, moved and calculated, waited some more and moved again. He spied what might have been fresh wagon tracks, but didn't risk following them. Instead he simply calculated their direction and figured in the possible ground that had been covered in the past forty-eight hours. The possibility danced around the edges of his busy brain that Miss No-Name's family had back-tracked to find her. However, it seemed more logical, since she was the one who had been spared from attack, that her parents would do their best to arrive at the next meeting point and wait for her there.

That is, if they were still alive. And if they weren't, he was stuck with her.

He had seen what there was to see, so he headed back to the campsite. This took enough time to imagine a variety of scenarios for how she had spent her day, which included her being foolishly preyed upon by the prairie wolf and bathing in the spring. The image of her bathing in the spring seized hold of his imagination but was instantly replaced, upon his return to the camp, by the combination of her with the prairie wolf.

He came upon the campsite from the direction he had left it, and the first thing he saw was Miss Harris standing in the center of the little clearing with her back to him. Her spine was rigid, and she was looking straight ahead of her. She was wearing her bonnet, and her clothes looked fresh but slightly rumpled in a way that suggested that she had washed them and dried them in the sun on rocks. Across from her and facing him was the prairie wolf, who had ventured right up to the edge of the opposite side of the campsite. He was a scruffy, pitiful excuse for a wolf, but he was more than a match for a human. His ears were cocked, his right foreleg was raised, and he had a wary look in his eye, as if he was waiting for his best moment to pounce. Or was he, incredibly, about to retreat?

In that first half second Powell realized that the beautiful, blessed idiot was trying to stare the damned prairie wolf down. In the next half second, he realized that she was winning the war of nerves.

The scene unfroze. Powell moved forward. The prairie wolf turned tail and ran. She whirled at the sound of his footfall behind her and clutched her heart.

"Oh, it's you!" she exclaimed under her breath. "You scared me!"

"*I* scared you?"

"Sneaking up on me like that. I didn't hear you."

"A wise man doesn't announce his arrival anywhere in these parts," he replied, "but as for being scared, I would have thought our mangy friend did that for you."

She let her hand fall to her side. "He was playing a game of hide-and-seek with me on the edges of the trees there for a good long while. I picked up my rocks, and I would have thrown them at him if I had had to." She gestured to the rocks at her feet. "I decided not to go on the offensive, recalling what you said about your feeling, so I dropped them and figured that my best strategy was to stand my ground here in the center."

"Why did you figure that?"

"To let him know that I knew he was there and that I wasn't moving. I've been standing here immobile for an age and am heartily sick of it."

He controlled himself to say levelly, "Since his teeth are much bigger than yours, that was a risky strategy to pursue."

"What would you have had me do instead?"

"Climb into the safety of a tree, to name but one idea."

Her brown eyes flashed with magnificent scorn. "I will *not* be treed by such a mangy creature, as you so aptly described him! I had no assurance that you would return to deliver me from the branches, and so I made my decision to die standing up. You will grant me that measure of dignity, surely, even in these thoroughly undignified circumstances." With a lofty gesture toward his bed of leaves, she informed him summarily, "I have finished the embroidery on your shirt. I am quite pleased with the result."

He wasn't going to argue with her astonishing success in staring down that peculiar prairie wolf, who was either unusually cowardly or remarkably wise. He himself remembered that discretion was the better part of valor and concluded that he didn't want to mess with her while she was in this mood any more than did, perhaps, the wolf. Nor did he think it wise to comment on the brilliantly hued bird that now adorned his shirt, so he put that piece of clothing on in silence.

At the moment he decided it was time to find some food and moved away from his tree, he was jumped on from behind. Writhing vigorously, he put his attackers to the test before his mouth was gagged and his arms were wrenched and tied behind his back. In his twisting and turning, he was able to see that Miss Harris had been set upon by three men, Indians by their dress and hair, and that she was being bound and gagged, as well. Their eyes met briefly. Hers flashed with surprise and terror. Raging against his helplessness, he redoubled his efforts, but he did not effect his release, since he had determined that not three but rather four men were holding him.

He strained to catch words or phrases from the language the Indians were speaking to one another. They hadn't said enough for him to know whether the Teton Sioux had finally caught up with him, and he hadn't had a close enough look at the warriors following him three days before to know whether they were the same ones now. All he could think was that either he had been careless and had led them straight to the camp or the prairie wolf had somehow alerted them to this human hiding place.

However the Indians had tracked them down, he and Miss Harris were in for it now. He was being pushed and pulled around the spring, and made to stumble up the rocks and over a ridge to where the Indians had left their horses. He wished he could see how it was going for her, but she was being kept out of his sight range. The Indians mounted their horses. One end of a rope was tied around his waist, the other end around one of the horses, which meant that he was going to be forced to trot along on the ground beside the rider. He imagined that Miss Harris was subjected to this same unhappy means of travel.

The party took off, seven men on horses plus a man and a woman on foot. Powell regretted that he wasn't wearing the boots he had retrieved from the dead man. He regretted that she wasn't wearing her ankle boots, even without the laces. He regretted that he hadn't at the very least had the foresight to make them two new pairs of moccasins.

Because he knew how to survive pain and suffering, he feared for her more than he feared for himself. What he was experiencing now wasn't anything compared to the treatment he had endured the few days before, when his hands and feet had been bound, and the Sioux braves had been set to find out how tough a man he was. They had begun by stripping his clothes off and staking him out in the sun. They had hung a water bag close to his head with water dripping from it drop by drop within inches of his mouth, but they'd given him none of it.

The youngsters around camp and some of the squaws had come around and thrown dirt in his face or beat him with sticks, sometimes for a half hour at a time. All they got out of him was a far-off gaze, so they decided to try something really good. While they were sitting around the fire talking it over, he had kept himself busy.

One of the youngsters had dropped his stick when he got tired of beating the prisoner, and it lay across Powell's chest. By humping himself up, he slid the stick down toward his mouth, got it into his teeth and tilted it up until the drops from that water bag were coming down it toward his mouth. At first most of the drops fell off onto the ground, but he had hung on to that stick like a bulldog, and after a while some drops began to get into his mouth. It wasn't much, but it was enough to have sustained him.

All of a sudden one of the braves noticed what he was doing. He called the others, and they gathered around, pointing and laughing. It was a new thing, and they had admired their prisoner for being game, but that didn't change his status much. After they had all seen it, one of the braves reached over, jerked the stick from his jaws, then kicked him.

He lay there all night, staked out on the dirt with no water and less hope, calculating every square inch of that village and the night sky. In the morning they untied his feet and led him to an anthill where they had stakes driven into the ground, and he could see what they were planning. Of a sudden there was a yell, some moaning cries, and every Sioux brave in the lot jumped his horse and rushed off after whatever it was.

And when they lit out, Powell did likewise.

He had run and run and run until he could run no more, and then he had run some more. He had run until...

Until he had splashed down the river and seen her. Hiding conspicuously in the little glade of trees. That was what had stopped him running. The combination of water, shade and a beautiful woman. A corner of paradise. Or almost. The woman in the glade, instead of suffering from

Eve's desire to know too much, was ignorant of everything and seemed to be proud of it. No, more than ignorant. Idiotic. Hadn't she just proven it by standing eye to
eye, almost nose to nose, with a hungry prairie wolf? No,
idiotic didn't cover the half of it. So how could she possibly be taking this punishment?

He tried to see her. In vain. He had long-term training
in survival, and he kept a part of his mind on himself. He
knew how to pace off distances as accurately as he could
calculate them with his eye, and he had retreated to that
clean part of his mind that he reserved for emergencies.
Since they had set off in a northerly direction from the
hollow, he had been keeping track of the distance he was
covering on foot. Evening came with her shadows, then
the night with her stars. He kept counting. The devil of it
was, they were moving north and slightly east, as well.

The yards and the miles, he covered them step by step.
When he had calculated an inhuman number of miles to
cover in a trot, he covered some more. Before daybreak,
he must have almost passed out, because some semicon-
scious part of him recognized that he had been slung
across a horse's rump, and now he absorbed every dark
mile in his gut before it jangled through the rest of his
body. At daybreak he passed out completely. When he
came to, drenched in sweat from the unmerciful heat, his
first conscious thought was for the pace of the horse, the
height of the sun, the time that must have elapsed since
he had quit counting, and the distance they must have
covered in the meantime.

When the sun was sinking, they were still heading
north, and there was still no sight of Miss Harris. He assumed, no, he hoped, that she had gone beyond the excruciating pain of the sort he was feeling and died.

As the miles passed, it came to him slowly, then surely,

that they weren't in Sioux country anymore. Not that their previous location had been controlled by the Sioux precisely. Rather, it was more infringed upon by them, hotly contested and coveted by them, such that white man and red man alike traversed it at their peril. The idea that his captors weren't Sioux spun out to him as the thinnest thread of human hope. It was almost a cruelty that the thread was there, tantalizing him, just beyond his reach, like the placement of the Sioux water bag by his mouth.

The sun was sinking when his swimming gaze perceived on the horizon a river with mounds before it. Mounds of mounds. Beautiful, sensual shapes, these mounds, like full breasts rising from the earth, all clustered together. No longer on the horizon. Right in front of him. All around him now. Large mounds, forty, sixty feet in diameter. He could see that at a glance.

No, not mounds. *Lodges.* They were lodges. He was in a village, one very different from the Sioux camp. He felt the thread of hope thicken and stream toward his fingertips so that he could almost grasp it and pull himself up by it, back to the land of the living. His brain slogged through the implications.

River Dwellers. Mandans.

Relief. Perhaps premature.

And Miss Harris?

Hardly had he posed the question than the horse he was on came to a halt, and he was released from its rump to slither off onto the ground in a heap of worn-out muscle and tired bones. Lying on the ground, he looked up at a circle of cedar posts, then higher into the sky at long, long poles topped by scarecrows or effigies of some kind. He didn't have any experience with the Mandans, but he had heard that they were far kinder than the Sioux, and this was a fact that was confirmed with his next vision.

It was of Miss Harris. She was astride a horse, sitting behind the rider, against whom she was slightly slumped, but she was very far from dead. She didn't look fresh—how could she after the night and day they had just endured?—but she was no longer bound or gagged as he was, and she didn't truly look very much the worse for wear. It occurred to him that she had ridden from the beginning, and he wondered if, in his next life, he could return as a beautiful woman.

The horse she was riding came to a stop beside him. When the rider got off, she fell ungracefully to the ground. The fall couldn't have felt good, but still she was able to stagger to her feet within the minute. At her full height she swayed slightly. Or was his vision wavering?

His senses swirled with exhaustion, tried to settle down. He figured that they must be in the center of the village, and he was aware that the villagers were congregating around them, exclaiming over the newcomers. He maneuvered himself to a sitting position and nearly slumped back down with the effort of keeping his head upright. With the endless bouncing of his lashed wrists against his back, the bindings had loosened, but not enough to be able to free his hands on his own.

For all her idiocy, Miss Harris had a sense of decency and the dramatic. She stumbled over to him and bent down, nearly keeling over with that simple action. Then she picked the knots behind his back, ungagged him and offered him her arm. He looked at her gratefully, unable to speak. When she returned his gaze, he realized that she, too, would be able to speak only with difficulty. Her expression, grave and closed, suggested that, in her own way, she had suffered as much as he had this night. He took the arm she extended him, but he did not use it for support, for he guessed she had no strength for his weight.

When he wobbled to stand on the soft pincushions that had once been his feet, two curious things happened at once. First, the villagers who had pressed up and around them suddenly stared at him, eyes popping, and fell back almost as one. Then a hush came over them, and the crowd—he was unable to distinguish man from woman from child—parted like the Red Sea.

Through the pathway shuffled an ancient man. His skin was burnt red. His face was a geological formation of wrinkles. His chest was painted and tattooed. He wore five precisely positioned feathers around his head, strings of beads and charms around his neck, and buffalo skin breeches, fringed down each leg, from the waist of which hung an entire fox pelt, head and all. On his feet were a pair of the most magnificently beaded moccasins Powell had ever seen, and to the heels were attached bushy foxtails. In each hand he carried a fan of eagle feathers, along with beribboned canes. This man was undoubtedly the medicine man, and he was to decide their fates.

The ancient man stopped within three feet of them. He regarded them at length, his expression inscrutable. His gaze came to rest on Powell's upper left breast. A tuneless chant rattled deep in the medicine man's throat, and the next sounds he made came in the form of the remarkable words, "Shirt. White man shirt. How make that shirt?"

Powell wasn't sure what the medicine man was asking. Nor was he sure that it was a friendly question. However, he didn't have an opportunity to fashion a response because his companion took a step forward. Despite the scratch in her voice, Miss Harris struck what he might call the tone of social nicety and said, "I am so glad you asked about the shirt, sir. Now, I did not make the shirt, but I believe that you are particularly interested in the embroidered bird. It is a Baltimore oriole, and it is a species commonly found far to the east of here in a state called Maryland. I began the composition yesterday morning and achieved it sometime yesterday afternoon, and I must say that I am rather proud of it, given the deficiencies of my working conditions.'' She smiled politely. ''Regarding the bird, then, I will take full credit for it. Or blame, as the case may be.''

No hint of a change of expression crossed the ancient man's features, but Powell would have said that a kind of understanding of that remarkably inappropriate and foolish speech was registered. Without turning around, the medicine man began speaking, causing two large braves to come forward and to stand on either side of Miss Harris.

The braves were not as elaborately dressed as the medicine man, but they wore fearsome necklaces of eagle talons and buffalo teeth. They reached up and took Miss Harris's bonnet off her head, causing her tangled mass of hair to fall down her back, scattering what was left of her hairpins. They put their hands at the beaded sheaths at their waists and withdrew broad knives with elk-horn handles.

Miss Harris didn't flinch. Her back remained straight, her expression polite. Powell reassessed her speech to the medicine man and her encounter with the prairie wolf. It was then that he realized that the beautiful idiot wasn't made of foolhardy fluff. She was built of rock-solid courage.

Chapter Six

When her bonnet was taken from her head, Sarah stared straight ahead into the setting sun and rapidly made her peace. She murmured a silent goodbye to her mother and father, to her sisters, to Mrs. Ross. She prepared to meet her Maker and wondered if, at last, she would meet the General, her guiding light. When the braves on either side of her unsheathed their knives, she hoped against hope that it wouldn't hurt too much to have her throat slit. She figured the worst would be the exact moment of contact, blade to tender skin, and imagined that the actual passing from one world to the next should not be so bad. She swallowed hard and consoled herself with the thought that this would be a more dignified end than being mauled to death by a mangy prairie wolf.

She swallowed a second time and realized that she was still alive and in one piece. She had the oddest impression that her hands, which she must have clenched at her sides, were being pried open and raised into an upturned position. Something was laid across each palm. She looked down and saw two wicked knives lying innocently in her very own hands. She had no more idea what this was about than anything else that had happened in the past

five minutes or twenty-four hours, but she did not think
a brush with death justified a lapse from good manners.

She croaked a polite "Thank you."

The old man standing before her spoke again, his words
bringing forth from the crowd two squaws, who came to
stand on either side of her. This time Sarah felt far less
threatened by what might happen next, for she was now
holding two big knives and the squaws carried between
them a harmless, beaded leather band stuck with feathers
similar to the headdress the old man was wearing.

With a leap of new life, Sarah realized that she was
being given gifts. How wrong had been her vision of her
fate! Nightlong and daylong, riding on the back of a horse,
she was sure the Indian man who had claimed her cher-
ished evil designs on her person. Thus, when she had
arrived in the village, she was sure that she was facing
either degradation or death, and likely both. But now she
felt her spirits rise, as if carried on the wings of her embroidered oriole, and she put her hands together in front
of her, palms still upturned and forming a cup, so that the
squaws could lay the offering of the headband across the
knives.

Her soaring spirits changed course abruptly when the
squaws, instead of draping the headband over her hands,
proceeded to tie that dirty strip of leather around her forehead. This was certainly better than being slain, but she
didn't want some unsanitary piece of animal skin further
mussing her already very tangled hair. Now that her life
seemed to be out of immediate danger and she was in the
position of a guest receiving gifts, she determined that
what she needed most was a comb and brush.

She was about to formulate a request for such useful
items, but then the old man began uttering more phrases
on subjects, she guessed, that were entirely irrelevant to

her needs, and here she was the honored guest. Not to mention the fact that poor Mr. Powell had been brutally ill-treated throughout the night and day. He should surely be shown *some* consideration for wearing the shirt upon which she had embroidered the bird that was apparently so important!

She glanced at Mr. Powell. Although he was still standing and even seemingly alert, she saw that he was suffering, and she was suddenly struck by an inspiration to revive his spirits, just as hers had been revived. Powell turned to meet her regard. She nodded graciously to him, then proceeded to offer him the knives she held in her upturned palms. She knew how much he had felt the lack of such over the past few days.

When he accepted the knives and thrust them into the waist of his trousers, a collective gasp rose from the crowd, and as one they fell to their knees. Sarah looked to the crowd, then back at Powell, puzzled by this new turn of events. She didn't interpret this as a bad turn precisely, but still she had the vaguest sense that she had traded away perhaps more than she had intended. She could not gauge his reaction, because he lowered his remarkable blue eyes and turned away from her to face the crowd. She had a sneaking suspicion that he was concealing a smile, haggard though it might have been.

Then all was noise and movement. She was swept up and into a tangle of bodies and voices crying out—she wouldn't dignify the raucous sounds by calling them *singing*—and regretted that she had foolishly given away her only protection. She closed her eyes and feared that now she would be trampled to death.

But, no. She opened her eyes and saw an evening sky streaked orange and pink and black, the very colors of her pretty little oriole, and she was hoisted up above the crowd, held aloft by many brick red arms that carried her around the village square—or circle, as the case was. She craned her neck and saw that Mr. Powell was being given the same treatment. She disliked in the extreme being carried this way.

"Put me down!" she cried, heedless of the strain on her poor parched throat, heedless of the fact that she could not be heard above the din. "Put me down this instant!"

She was obeyed. Abruptly. And found herself once again in an unladylike heap on the ground. She was back where she had started in the center of the village circle, her legs collapsed beneath her, her skirts and petticoat flurrying immodestly above her knees.

Enough was enough. "Do you intend to honor me or to kill me?" she demanded angrily. She tried to rise but her heel caught in the hem of her skirts, and she plopped down on her bottom. "Either way—honor or death—is fine with me, but I will *not* tolerate this continuing indignity!"

Although she didn't think she had truly made herself understood, she felt a little better for having vented her ire. It was roused again the next moment when Mr. Powell was set down next to her, and he managed to remain standing on his own two abused feet. She looked up at him. His spine was straight, his head was erect, and he seemed to be receiving the homage from the surrounding crowds to which she, in truth, was entitled. He didn't even look down at her or offer her a hand to help her up.

She scrambled to her feet.

"Mr. Powell," she said, "I would like to know if you have any idea what is happening."

He didn't look at her and rasped a harsh "Go with it."

"As if that explains anything whatsoever! Mr. Powell, what I would like to know is—"

"Go with it," he repeated, cutting her off.

"Go with what?" she demanded impatiently. "If you can't tell me what is happening here, you might tell me instead why you didn't help me up just now, when I so kindly performed the same service for you not ten minutes ago!"

His voice scratched. "If I move an inch...one way or the other, I am...not likely to remain...standing." He glanced at her out of the corner of his eye. "Adjust your headband."

She did so for the good reason that she didn't want to look more ridiculous than absolutely necessary, then asked, "Is that better?"

He didn't look at her when he replied, "Your bravery...won them over. Now's...not the time to let...your brave face slip."

Her eyes widened. "Paying me a compliment, Mr. Powell? You needn't sound so reluctant!" She smiled. "And don't think it will divert me from the *real* issue, namely that the bird I embroidered on your shirt just may have saved our lives!" Her smile widened. "But I don't intend to gloat."

His glance traveled past her. "Don't gloat...yet."

She followed the line of his gaze, and the fear that had gone to sleep inside her wakened to new life. About twenty feet away an enormous bonfire had been built and was now being lit. Little tongues of fire were beginning to lick the wood, crackling and snapping as they grew into flames.

She was aghast at the implications. "I had determined that we had not fallen among the hostile Sioux. Was I mistaken?"

He shook his head minimally. "Mandan...I believe."

"But do you think— No, really, it can't be that—"

She was unable to complete any of her thoughts. "Surely we aren't to be—"

"I cannot tell...our fate," he said without emotion.

There was no doubt in her mind that having her throat slit would have been far preferable to being burned alive. Still, she struggled against the apparent logic of the situation. "I have the oddest notion that we are being hailed as something special, out of the ordinary. We have been given gifts, and I believe that we are considered honored guests, no?"

"Some honors...are better...not to have."

That was all too true. If they were to be a burnt offering to some Indian god symbolized by the Baltimore oriole, she would grant that Mr. Powell would have just cause to be mighty aggrieved with her. She appreciated the fact that he didn't waste his breath on futile reproach, but neither did he truly have the voice for it or the opportunity, for just then two squaws came to him and led him toward the bonfire.

Two braves approached Sarah and led her in Powell's wake. With each step, her vision of her fate grew more grisly, and she determined that now, *now* she was destined to die. About five feet from the fire she was stopped so that she was standing next to Powell. A large animal skin was laid down on the ground before them, and they were gestured to sit on the skin facing away from the fire and toward the center of the village circle. Then two bowls of food were set before them, along with two large gourds filled with water.

She sat down next to Powell, and in wordless agreement they began to drink. After a while, Powell pronounced in a voice resonant with satisfaction, "I was expecting whiskey, but I'm glad it's not." He sighed deeply. "Best water I ever drank."

She picked up a yellow item from the bowl before her and bit into what she identified as a cornmeal ball stuffed with sunflower seeds. "Best food I ever ate," she agreed. A thought inevitably occurred to her. "Do you think that we are being fattened up for sacrifice?"

Powell, who was now chewing on a piece of jerky, was visibly restored by the water and the meat. He paused long enough to say, "I'm guessing the evening will offer entertainment of a different sort," and continued to further restore himself.

Sarah noticed that the villagers had dispersed to rim the edges of the village circle. Some were standing. Some were sitting. Some were eating. Some had even climbed onto the domes of the three or four large mounds nearest the central circle, as if positioning themselves to witness some forthcoming spectacle. Most were talking and laughing. The occasion did not have the look of a solemn sacrifice. Even the medicine man, who stood not but a few feet from them by the bonfire, did not seem to be actively interested in his two honored guests—or sacrificial lambs—but had fixed his attention beyond them on the village circle.

Since she was able to face death only so many times in so many ways and in so many minutes, Sarah decided to do as Powell did, namely eat and drink and watch whatever diversion was to be offered them. The entertainment came soon enough, announced by the rumbling of drums and the shaking of rattles. Then six pairs of men, scantily clad, came hopping and jumping into the center of the circle from different directions, all wearing grotesque buffalo skins, heads and all. They carried elaborately decorated spears, and they began hooting and hollering in a way that drew seemingly approving yips and yaps from the audience.

The dance was remarkable not only for its repetitive length but also for its riveting effect on its audience. After the first half hour or so, Sarah was far from rapt herself and rather more bored, and preferred to watch the stars come out and the moon rise. The air was clear and turning chilly, but the dying bonfire behind her kept her warm. She was well fed and no longer thirsty, tired but not really sleepy. Her overriding feeling was one of pleasurable surprise to have survived another day, no doubt the strangest of her life.

While the dance was still in full pitch, the medicine man summoned the two braves and the two squaws back to the honored guests. She and Powell were bidden to rise, then escorted around the edge of the crowd to the nearest of the large round structures that were heaped together to form the village. Its entrance looked directly onto the main circle, which was still lively with activity.

The exterior of the structure was very unpleasant to Sarah, and she would not be surprised to learn that it was made entirely of dirt; its entryway, fashioned from wood posts, looked like the opening to a mine shaft. Since the squaws and braves were behind her, she had no choice but to follow Powell and the medicine man into the structure. After taking several steps in, she stopped next to Mr. Powell and looked around. In contrast to the exterior, her initial impression of the interior was of neatness, comfort and spaciousness. The whole glowed, moreover, with moonlight, since in the center of the timbered dome was an opening about three or four feet in diameter. Sarah saw that the opening served as both chimney and skylight.

The top of the dome must have been some ten or twelve feet high. In the center of the enormous circle was an open, cubed structure of eight-foot beams, which seemed to support the dome in four places, and in the center of that on the floor was the sunken, circular fireplace, in which soughed a gentle fire. The overall effect was welcoming and cheering. The floor itself did not seem to be made of earth, because it looked so clean and polished. Yet Sarah could not imagine what substance it could have been other than dirt.

Thick mats of willow boughs were slung over the timbered beams of the central cube, pots were stacked neatly around the fireplace, and in their midst squatted, incongruously, a European-style kettle. On the timbered walls were hung pipes and spears and shields, along with trinkets and ornaments of every conceivable size and texture. At the periphery on either side of the center were what Sarah guessed to be two large bedsteads. They were lower to the ground than a European bed, and they were formed from sturdy poles lashed together, across which a stripped skin, probably buffalo, was stretched. Other furs were piled atop these skins, and the beds looked soft, even luxurious.

The medicine man walked to the fireplace. He took a pouch out of his breeches and sprinkled some powder into the fire that made the low flames sparkle and leap before settling back down. Then he threw his head back toward the skylight and crooned at the slice of moon it framed. When he was finished, he commanded the squaws and braves to leave, then walked toward his honored guests, pronouncing yet another incantation. He took some more powder out of his pouch and dusted them liberally with it, bringing both her and Mr. Powell to fits of coughing.

The old man bowed and said, "This house, you house." He pronounced the English words with effort. "You house this."

The old man was looking straight at her, so Sarah ventured, "This is our house?" Her gesture encompassed herself, Powell and the space around them.

"Two people, this house, man, woman," the old man repeated, affirming her inference. He thumped his chest. "Many spirits." He thumped his chest again, either for emphasis or from indigestion, Sarah was not quite sure, but she was coming to the happy conclusion that she and Mr. Powell would have comfortable beds for the night and a certain amount of privacy.

The old man bowed a second time and began to shuffle out of the structure. Before he reached the door, he turned back toward them, pointed toward the bed positioned along the lefthand wall and said, "Spirit bed. No you." He referred to the bed on the righthand wall. "You bed this. You bed. Two people, man, woman." His voice was stern. "No spirit bed."

Then he was gone.

Sarah and Powell exchanged a long regard. She was aware of the drums continuing to beat outside their door and the accompanying merriment of the villagers. She was aware of the change in atmosphere around her, causing a slight prickling of her skin, making her feel uncomfortably warm. A change seemed to have come over Powell, as well, a sharpening of the glint in his eyes, a tightening of a muscle along his jaw and his neck, a shifting of his shoulders and hips. Perhaps it was only the effect of the moonlight and the firelight and the soft shadows that flickered and layered down in successive circles of darkness around the walls.

Powell broke the silence between them. "You seem to do better than I at interpreting the medicine man's statements. What do you think he was telling us?"

She looked away. "That we're not alone here. It seems we have Mandan spirits for company."

"And the sleeping arrangements?"

"I think he meant that the bed over there—" she pointed to the left "—is sacred. Not to be used by mere mortals."

"That's what I thought he meant."

She dared to look back at him and fought the blush that crawled up her neck. She dropped her eyes and fixed her gaze on the absurd bird on his shirt, which had caused them so much trouble and confusion. She felt suddenly uneasy about spending the night under the same roof as Mr. Powell and the spirits. She suspected that their privacy was not going to be quite what it could have been.

"Well, at least our throats weren't slit," she said in an attempt to avoid the real problem, "and we weren't trampled to death or offered as sacrifice. We have a house to ourselves—to share with the spirits, of course—and we're still in one piece."

"With one bed between us," Powell said, stating the problem directly. "I suppose I should be chivalrous and offer it to you."

She lost the fight with the blush. "You mustn't!" she objected, feeling her cheeks suffuse with heat. "You've had a much rougher time than I during the past night and day, and I won't deprive you of the rest you deserve. I'll take the floor."

"I'll have to take the floor, here and now, if you don't help me to the bed," Powell said. "You see, I'm at the end of being able to walk on my own. I got this far, but can go no farther."

"Oh!" she exclaimed, her embarrassment evaporating, and offered him her arm. "I had forgotten how bad your case must be, because you were moving with such ease."

"I didn't think it wise to show my weakness until we knew our fate."

"Do we know it now?"

"We're still in one piece, as you've observed."

He leaned heavily against her. His weight communicated to her just how spent were his energies. She led him slowly toward the bed on the right side of the house. He was limping badly.

"Your feet are paining you?"

His laugh rattled without humor. "My feet may well kill me if the Mandan don't."

"Do you think they might still mean to kill us?"

"It depends on who they think we are. We're special to them all right, but I don't yet know why."

When they arrived at the edge of the bed, he eased the knives from his waist and laid them on the floor. He groaned with effort as he lowered himself until his back was against the mattress-skin, but then he reared up again and said, "Razor."

She reached around behind him, withdrew the tilt-edged razor from his back pocket and put it on the floor next to the knives. Then he lay down, but his legs were still draped over the side with his feet on the floor. She lifted them and put them on the bed so that he was fully stretched out. He closed his eyes and sighed as he settled his weary bones.

"Heaven," he said simply.

"Comfortable?"

He sighed again, at length.

She arranged some of the soft fur pelts around him, pillowed his head, cushioned his arms and legs.

"My moccasins," he said, "are in shreds." His voice was groggy, his eyes were still closed. "So are yours. Sorry about that. Wish I had made new ones. Could you remove mine for me?"

She was happy to do as he requested, and she inspected

the soles of his feet in the dim light. "I don't see any obvious signs of infection. Would you like me to find some water to bathe them?"

He groaned in consideration. "No. Just let them air out. I'll see what I can do for them in the morning." He paused. "If I ever wake up."

She moved away and wondered what to do next.

His voice came as if from afar. "This bed feels as good as the water tasted earlier. Never lain down in a better one." He sighed again, deeply. "If ever a woman could be sure she wouldn't receive unwanted advances from a man, this is the time." His groan tottered on the edge of consciousness. "It'd do you good to sleep here in the bed."

"I don't think—it wouldn't be—that is to say—"

"You know, Miss Harris," he broke in, his voice shaking with a kind of sleepy humor, "I make it a policy never to be intimate with a woman whose first name I don't know."

After all they had just been through, she regretted her deliberate oversight when she had introduced herself to him. "My first name is Sarah," she said. "Sarah Ross." Then she clapped a hand over her mouth, fearing she might have just offered her availability for intimacy.

His groans and sighs grew deeper. On a faint murmur he repeated, "Sarah Ross Harris."

She dropped her hand from her mouth when she realized that poor Mr. Powell was already fast asleep and that she would be a fool not to get a good night's rest. So she moved toward the empty side of the bed that was made for two and removed her moccasins. As she lay down next to Mr. Powell, she remembered that she was still wearing the dratted headband, so she untied the feathered strip and put it on the floor beside her.

She stretched out and discovered that this was, indeed, the most comfortable bed she had ever been in. She gathered up her portion of the bed furs and snuggled into their softness. Her last waking thought was to curse the drums still pounding outside, but she was pleased to note that Mr. Powell didn't snore. Then she sank into the abyss of sleep like a heavy anchor thrown into the ocean.

Chapter Seven

Sarah awoke sometime later. She opened her eyes. It was still dark outside and in. It wasn't the darkness she first noticed, but the silence. She had gone to sleep to the pounding of drums, but now no noise, human or otherwise, drifted into the house from the central circle. The village seemed to be wrapped in a peace as dense and luxurious as her bed of buffalo skin and covers of animal fur.

She shifted and looked at the fire still soughing softly in the fireplace. She wondered at her carelessness in having neglected to bank it earlier and reasoned that it must have been because the flames had been too low and well contained to worry about before she fell asleep. Since the flames were still low and well contained now that she was awake, she saw no need to get up to douse them. As she lay there gazing at the little flames, she worked through the idea that the untended fire should have consumed itself hours ago. This brought her to the notion that here was the spirits' fire, an eternal flame of sorts, and it was better not to tamper with it.

She wondered hazily what had wakened her. It couldn't have been the silence, and she didn't think Mr. Powell had disturbed her, for he was sleeping the sleep of the righteous. But something had roused her from sleep, and as she wound her regard through the flames to the spirits' bed on the opposite side of the house, she felt drawn toward it. Not that she wanted to get up—she was too tired to move—and not that she needed to distance herself from Mr. Powell. He hadn't twitched so much as a muscle from the moment he had lain down.

It was some movement in the spirits' bed opposite that had wakened her. That was it. No, that was fanciful. She must have simply woken up on her own. Her body felt different somehow. Could her women's courses be coming on? She counted out the days and decided that it wasn't yet that time of the month. Besides, she felt no cramps or bloating. Rather, she felt light, girlish, almost giddy, as if she were anticipating something. It was the same feeling she had had on those beautiful evenings in England, going to fancy parties in the company of Mrs. Ross, wearing a pretty ball gown, wondering if she might be asked to dance by some dashing young man.

That was it, then. She felt as if she might be asked to dance. But only her body. Her soul was to remain on the sidelines.

Strange thoughts. Strange feelings. Then again, everything had been strange since the moment she had laid eyes on the naked man-beast splashing through the water.

Through the flickering flames she discerned another movement. On the spirits' bed opposite. The movement sketched the outline of a body—not of a whole body, just part of one. The partial outline rose from the bed, walked into the fire, stopped. The flames played at the edges of the outline, leapt up, grew big around it. How curious. She should be frightened by this flaming apparition but wasn't, and figured she must have spent her entire budget of fear hours earlier. The outline assumed the fiery form of a man's torso. He had broad shoulders, muscular arms, a thick neck, a flat face with high cheekbones and flamboyant streaks of war paint. Whipping tendrils of flame red hair flashed down the man's back.

She recognized him. It was the Indian who had captured her back at the hollow. So. He had chosen to visit her. Like this. She wasn't surprised, not really, and in a sleepy sort of way his visit made sense. She had a score to settle with him, after all, given the way he had looked at her, the way he had handled her with desire and contempt. She could read that combination of compliment and insult on a man's face in an instant, could feel it in his touch, whether the man's skin was white or red or green. The Indian's eyes had assessed. His hands had possessed. His face and hands had said, *You're mine.*

She had conquered her initial terror and replied with an attitude of challenge and a look that said, *If you dare!*

He had dared. Had thrown her up on his horse so that she rode behind him instead of being dragged along at the end of a rope. Meaning that she had profited, if only temporarily, from his desire and contempt. And at journey's end she had been saved from his clutches only by the miracle of an embroidered bird.

The flaming torso transmuted into the shape of another man. He blazed into existence among the flames as a big and beefy man, well dressed with intricate flickers of flame lace at his neck and wrists. He had a long, thin nose, and he was rich and powerful. Proper to others. Improper to her. She recognized him to be the insufferable Duke of Merton, darling of English society. His fellow aristocrats saw only his grace and charm. She saw only the bully who dwelled behind the smooth exterior. Thus, when the duke had first approached her, she had flirted aggressively, figuring he would back off. However he hadn't backed off, and neither did he lose interest in her when she switched tactics and turned into a coy, colorless thing who sighed and simpered.

At one of her pretty balls, she learned that the duke had discovered the secret of her tainted birth. Too late one night in the wilds of a lush garden, the duke told her that he knew that her father was the illustrious British General Robert Ross, who had lost his life in the wilds of Maryland in 1814. This self-satisfied son of a dozen dukes before him thought he had a right to make a conquest of the glorious general's bastard daughter, whether she was willing or not. It didn't matter that she was being passed off as Mrs. Ross's respectable goddaughter from America. He knew a loose woman when he saw one.

And so he had told her while she had tried to fight him off in the bushes.

The flames replayed the hateful scene. The sickening rip of the delicate cloth of her bodice. One beefy hand on her breasts, the other bunching up her skirts above her knees, high on her thighs. Her back on the damp ground. His weight on top of her. His arousal. Her feelings of fear and shame and a hideous sense, deep down, that she had brought this on herself, that she deserved it. Her flailing hand bumped up against a rock. Grasped it. Knocked the bully out.

Then William James. This sweet paragon of Baltimore society flamed up and out of the ashes of her near defeat at the duke's hands. William had soothed her lacerated feelings in the wake of the disgrace the duke made sure she endured. William had paid her respectful court. He had made so bold, three or four times, to hold her hand. He had pecked her twice on the cheek. He had touched her lips once with his. Nothing. Not even tepid feelings of affection. William had put her so high on a pedestal that she could not take a step without grinding him beneath her feet.

However much William had been a balm to her wounded dignity, William's mother had dealt it a nearly mortal blow. In the days after refusing William's proposal, Sarah had learned that Mrs. James was widely known to have said that even if Sarah had accepted him, the marriage would have never taken place. The son of the best family in Baltimore would not marry the love child of an invading enemy officer, and Mrs. James wasn't going to believe for a minute the rumor that Sarah's mother had not willingly submitted to the handsome British General Ross. Why, everyone knew that Sarah's mother had been a wanton beauty in her day, too. Such a family, that Harris family, and Morgan Harris's former life with a savage woman did not bear speaking of!

The flames turned around an image of a man who would offer her a much different kiss from the one William had ventured. The image flamed and formed from a part of every man who had ever coveted her, and there had been many. Morgan Harris had always done his best to protect her, but Morgan Harris could not live at her side all day long. So she had learned what kind of power a woman could wield in the world of men, how to flirt with them or flatten them, as the occasion demanded.

Now the flames in the fire suggested a different kind of power, more dangerous and complex, ultimately more effective. The flames twisted, oddly, into the form of a Baltimore oriole, then transformed into a hoot owl. The owl spread its wings and soared high in the sky until it was lost from sight. Then, out of nowhere, an eagle swooped down and asked her body to dance while her soul sat watching, breathless, on the sidelines.

* * *

Powell awoke during the night. He couldn't say what had awakened him, but something had. A feeling, perhaps. A kind of lightness that wasn't really a lightness because it was accompanied by a surge of strength.

He lay still and didn't open his eyes. He felt good, strangely good. Head to foot. Top to toe.

Foot. Feet. Toe. Toes.

He wriggled them.

And was amazed that instead of excruciating pain, his feet felt whole. Hale. Healed. Healthy.

How odd.

He must be dreaming.

Or flying.

That was it. He was flying.

Ah. He *had* turned into a bird, just as he had wanted to the other morning when he had woken up and his feet were killing him with pain and distorting his perceptions. During that agony-crazed fantasy, he had evolved from a plant to a snake to a fish to his final form as a bird, who could take flight anytime he wanted and spare his feet his weight.

What an exquisite feeling, this flying. And what a difference a gourd of fresh water, a meal of meat and corn and a few hours' sleep on a delightful bed could make. Why, he felt—he felt—

Like a man.

That fine strength surged through him again, distributed itself, circulated in his blood. It flowed through him like liquid iron, hot and metallic. This is what it felt like to be alive, to be a man, to be in bed with a desirable woman.

Woman?

He opened his eyes and propped himself up on his elbow. A woman was curled next to him, lying on her side,

facing away from him. Her hair tumbled down her back.
It was a tangled cascade, but still beautiful. In fact, everything he had seen and imagined about her was beautiful. She was wearing all her clothes, but he could change
that easily enough. Wanted to change that right now, with
some sense of urgency.

He groaned. He couldn't be wanting a woman after
having drawn back from the brink of death, could he?

Yes, he could, and that was exactly what he wanted.
There was no mistaking his desire, which was becoming
ever more evident by the second, and why shouldn't he
desire her? Her face and body were beautiful, and she had
a way about her that was arousing. No, really, she was
downright irritating—that much about her wasn't beautiful—but why should he care about that? She was in bed
with him, and she had been lured by his most effective
line to date.

*If ever a woman could be sure she wouldn't receive
unwanted advances from a man, this is the time.*

He'd have to remember that one in the future. Whenever he wanted a woman, all he would have to do was
walk up to death's door with only one bed available for
them. The trick was to sound sincere about his impotent
exhaustion. The next trick was to wake her up and per-
suade her that it was a wicked waste of time to be in bed
with him and sleep. He raised himself up off his elbow
and surveyed the curve of her body as she lay there. She
was sleeping soundly, that much he could tell, but he'd
be damned if she didn't look alluring, even when she
wasn't trying.

He smiled when he realized that he had a name to put
to her. A prim and proper Sarah conjoined to an odd Ross.
It made him think of something. He didn't know what and
didn't care, because he was intending to sweet talk and

sway Miss Sarah Ross Harris in a way she'd never been sweet talked and swayed before.

He reached out to put one hand on her shoulder and another on her hip so that he could turn her toward him and bring her gently to consciousness. Just as he spread his arms out in either direction, he was distracted by a movement he caught out of the corner of his eye. He glanced up and across the horizon of her body and looked into the flames still flickering in the middle of the lodge. Through the flames, he could see the empty bed opposite, the one reserved for the spirits. It wasn't empty now, and it wasn't occupied by a Mandan spirit. Instead he saw the outline of a woman reclining there, artfully undressed, limbs disposed for maximum exposure of flesh.

He was surprised, and yet not surprised, to recognize Amanda Clarke, the lonely, lascivious wife of Senator Clarke of New York. She rose from the bed, assumed a fiery form. Moving toward the fire, she smiled at him, beckoned to him, promised him whatever he wanted. He responded. His arms sprouted into powerful wings, and he flew straight into the flames, where he met her. On wings that could bridge both time and space, he and Amanda returned to Washington, D.C., to those first few weeks he had spent there after being shipped off from West Point.

No, no, he hadn't been shipped off from the military academy. He had, in fact, been properly graduated. He had been the number one cadet in his class, and the authorities knew that gross unfairness toward one cadet was bad for the morale of all. Besides, his stoicism in the face of repeated and often unjust punishment had won him the respect of not only his classmates but several of those in command, and so singling him out for dismissal would have meant double trouble among the lower ranks. Even so, those officers whose respect he had won weren't inclined to intervene in the regular schedule of beatings he was so prone to receive. And since he had the glorious military name of Powell but no lineage, any officer who had ever been crushed under his father's severe thumb could pick on his illegitimate offspring with no fear of reprisal.

At West Point he'd been beaten, but never broken, and he'd been shipped off a year early. His talents were needed to carry out the vast project of surveying the lands made newly available in the southeast under orders from President Jackson and the Indian Removal Act. He was expected to keep a low profile in Washington, but it wasn't easy. He was the spit and image of Jackson's secretary of defense, Major General George Washington Powell, well-known as the randiest man alive and the true "father of his country"; and even if Wesley's mother hadn't boldly slapped the surname Powell on him at birth, it wouldn't have been very long before someone of the major general's wide acquaintance in the small world of Washington would have added two plus two and arrived at the sum of Wesley Powell's parentage.

Amanda Clarke hadn't known and hadn't cared who his daddy was when she first set eyes on him. They met late one chilly autumn evening by accident, although the word *accident* didn't do justice to the series of circumstances that had sent Powell to the White House to drive the unattended among the senators' wives to their homes at the end of a state dinner. Although the charge of escorting ladies fell far outside his normal duties at the Bureau of Indian Affairs, he had accepted it on the off chance of glimpsing his father. Major General George Washington Powell must have known that the unacknowledged fruit of his loins had been assigned to the bureau.

The major general may even have approved of the assignment, but he made no effort to seek out his son, and if he saw Wesley that night tooling an official carriage up to the north portico of the White House, he gave no sign of it.

The major general's son attracted immediate attention from one of the senators' wives, and she made sure that she was the last one to be squired home. Amanda Clarke had had a little too much to drink and needed help into her house. Needed help into her bedroom, too, and after he stoked the fire in her grate, he stoked a fire in her bed. Young Wesley Powell spent the next few years mapping the coastlines and inland waterways not only of every state from Maryland to Georgia but also of every married woman in Washington, D.C. When finally reminded by one of his superiors that he had been strongly advised to keep a low profile, Powell replied that he could hardly keep his profile any lower.

It wasn't long thereafter that the authorities decided Powell needed a larger scope for his surveying genius, namely the whole of the continent west of the Mississippi. Thus he became the fourth in a team of crack surveyors, the other three being far in advance of him in age and experience, and he couldn't help but suspect that this extraordinary promotion had been sanctioned by his powerful and distant father.

On magic wings he returned to his bed of buffalo skin, where he saw the succession of his amorous adventures ignite and extinguish in the flames of the fire flickering in the center of the lodge. He drew his eyes away from the fascinations of the fire and looked down at the woman slumbering in the bed next to him. He puzzled through the notion that in Washington he hadn't needed to lay smooth-talking lines on women to get them into his bed.

Rather, he had needed fancy-edged lines to keep them out. So that he could finish his calculations and lay precisely drawn inked lines on curling charts. Enjoy an evening with male friends and colleagues. Sleep in peace.

He didn't want to sleep in peace now. He wanted one of his lusty Washington wives, and at this point it occurred to him that Sarah Ross Harris was not a Mrs. but a Miss. He spent a full ten seconds wrestling with his conscience over the impropriety of despoiling a virgin, then cleared it on the perfectly good grounds that they were sleeping in the same bed and would be condemned for the crime anyway, even if they didn't commit it. So—

He spread his wings again toward her, with intention, with desire, and then he noticed something odd. It was the dead of night, and the fire in the fireplace was burning at the same low rate it had when he had first entered the lodge, hours ago already. He stared into the flames and saw exactly what he wanted to see, namely a vision of himself wrapped and happy in the fleshly folds of sweet Sarah Ross. He also saw himself being seen by the Mandan spirits.

Then he understood.

They were being watched. Not by dead ancestor spirits, he guessed, but rather by very alive human eyes. He had wondered in what way he and Miss Harris were special to these villagers and what they might be expected to do for the villagers as a result of their special status. As he lay next to her, desiring her, considering that they had been fed and entertained and given the relative privacy of a comfortable bed, he realized that what they were expected to do was precisely what he wanted to do—what he wanted to do ever more desperately with every passing moment.

Which was odd, given the fact that his best instincts

warned him that she was the kind of woman a man like him should avoid at all costs; and which made him wonder what magic medicine might have been put into their gourds of water—into his, at least—to have made the pain in his feet disappear and to have drenched him in a sexual desire for her that he hadn't felt before. Not to this degree, that is, for he admitted to himself that, in some corner of his exhausted being that had still pulsed with life, he had wanted her from the moment he had set eyes on her. And if he was admitting this only now, it was because his condition no longer allowed him to repress the knowledge that he could have slipped into her beautiful body anytime during these past few days and died a happy man.

Thoughts of sex and death pricked his spine with alarm, and a creepy feeling came over him that the moment he might finish making love to her, he would die. As if the oriole he wore on his shirt was the sign of some exalted Mandan bird spirit above. As if his sole purpose was to couple with her, to impregnate her, at the exquisite point of which he would be killed—an honor, no doubt—by those with the watching eyes, so that he could fly heavenward and join the bird spirit. As if her sole purpose was to bear his child, after which she would be killed—another honor, no doubt.

He was thinking crazy thoughts again. He had no reason to imagine such a far-fetched scenario. He must be wrong. All he had to do was wake her up, sweet talk her, sway her—

But the moment he moved toward her again, the flesh on his back crawled with warning. In his mind's eye, he relived all he had suffered in the past days to stay alive. The heat, the pain, the thirst, the muscle-quivering depletion of energy, the bone-wearying need to stay alert. That same alertness cautioned him to suffer a little more in order to continue to stay alive.

He lay back down. For now, it seemed better not to touch her. If he was wrong in his interpretation of their purpose in the village, he had nothing to lose but a night's pleasure. Surely that wasn't as bad as being stripped by the Sioux, staked out in the sun and beaten with sticks. Surely, surely…

Surely not. After several interminable minutes, he decided that the denial of desire wasn't as bad as any torture the Sioux had devised, it was perversely worse. And there was still half a night to endure.

He lay there with his eyes wide open, a variety of violent thoughts colliding in his brain, the overall gist of which was *Just my luck!*

Chapter Eight

Sarah awoke with a curious feeling that was both heavy and energetic. She didn't want to get up because it felt so lovely to lie there, lusciously fleshly, wrapped in sleek buffalo skin and furs. Still, her blood was humming with too much energy for her to lie there any longer like a sleepy, sultry slug.

She sprang out of bed and stretched deliciously, this way and that. She reached up, trilling her fingers at the skylight, through which pale yellow sunlight was streaming. She arched her back, moaned with pleasure, curved her spine sinuously. She put her hands on her hips. She closed her eyes, let her head fall back, thrust her breasts forward. The movement felt unexpectedly good on the backs of her thighs, so she held the position, feeling her hair fall in a tangled mess down her back. Knowing that she would have to find a way to untangle it before the morning was over. Knowing that she was being watched.

Watched? She snapped her head up, opened her eyes and looked around. Mr. Powell was squatting on his heels before the fire in the fireplace, which was burning at the same low level that was apparently kept constant. His forearms were settled lightly on his thighs. His upturned palms balanced the two broad knives with the elk-horn handles. He was wearing Indian breeches, no shirt and a pair of fine, new moccasins. His hair was slicked back, and he was clean shaven. His head was turned toward her, his eyes resting on her. Although he was bathed in a shaft of sunlight, his expression was dark and unsettling and reminded her of the way the prairie wolf had looked when he had sized up his chances for pouncing on her. As she held Mr. Powell's gaze, she discovered that she had no desire to stare this wolf down, no desire to scare him off. Instead, she wanted to challenge him, to bring him forward, to see what would happen if he did pounce.

She blinked and looked away, vaguely embarrassed but not completely so. She wasn't sure what had just happened, but she was aware again of the energy flowing through her blood. Like the foaming effects of a glass of champagne. As if she might do or say something she might regret.

She turned her back to him. "You're up," she commented. She began to fuss with the bedcovers to give herself something to do.

"For several hours already," he replied. He didn't sound happy about it.

"It's late?"

"Not much past seven o'clock, I reckon."

She was surprised. "It's early, then. You've eaten?"

His grunt resembled assent.

When she figured she was in control of herself again, she turned back to him and glanced around the fireplace, looking for the remains of breakfast. "Was food brought inside?"

He shook his head. "I ate outside. Some of the braves from last night never left the central circle, and bowls of jerky and corn balls are still being passed around."

She raised her brows. "They're still there? The drums stopped hours ago."

"Jugs of firewater are circulating, too, if I'm not mistaken. So, even if a man remained in condition to play the drums, he might meet with strong resistance from any of his fellow revelers whose heads are already pounding with the drums of a hangover."

"It seems to have been quite some party. Have you discovered yet the reason for the celebration? Beyond the mere fact of our arrival, that is?"

He shrugged, his expression unreadable.

"And your clothes?"

He rose to his feet, causing a fluid line of fringe to ripple down each long leg. He thrust one of the knives into his waistband, began to flip the other in his left hand. "I awoke this morning to discover these breeches and moccasins by the bedside. As for my black trousers and the shirt with the magic bird, those items are gone."

She was rather pleased with herself. "Yes, the magic bird. Our salvation." She smiled at him, primly. "You have yet to thank me for having embroidered us into good food and lodging."

"That's right," he said with a distinct lack of gratitude, "I have yet to thank you," and left it at that.

She could see that he meant to be difficult. Perhaps he had not slept as well as she had. Then she frowned. "But how did it happen that you went to sleep with your other clothes on and now don't know where they are?"

He shrugged again. "I was awake for half the night and couldn't have dozed off for very long during the wee hours. Whoever took my clothes off was very careful. I didn't feel a thing."

So he hadn't slept well. That would certainly account

for his grouchiness. "Did your feet pain you and keep you awake?"

"My feet," he said, "have never felt better."

"Oh."

For some reason her embarrassment returned, and she plucked at her blouse and skirts to assure herself that she was still wearing her own clothing. It was uncomfortable to imagine that someone had come in and undressed him during the night, but she had to admit that he looked good. Really good. The way the sunlight chiseled the bones in his face, strengthening its attractive, masculine edges. The way his muscles were layered across his shoulders and down his chest and roped around his arms. The way those breeches fit him in the hips and thighs—

She dropped her eyes to his feet. It was less embarrassing somehow. Or less dangerous. His moccasins were expertly sewn, and from the relaxed way he was standing, she guessed that his feet must have, indeed, been miraculously restored overnight. Her eye caught on the glint of metal next to his foot at the edge of the hearth; it was the razor he had already used to good effect this morning. Then her heart leapt with joy to see what was lying in a basket next to the razor.

"A comb and brush," she breathed reverently, walking forward. "A real comb and brush set. I don't remember seeing them there last night, and I can hardly believe my eyes now."

"They were there when I got up this morning," he said, stepping away from the hearth, from her approach. "My guess is that they were brought when my clothes were exchanged and when these items were delivered." He gestured to one of the willow mats, which had been unrolled and placed on one side of the fire.

Her attention diverted, Sarah moved toward the willow

mat, amazed to see spread out upon it a beautiful dress
of cream-colored satin elaborately beaded at the neckline.
When she knelt down to touch the garment, she was almost more amazed to discover that it was made of something more like deerskin. Next to the dress was a long,
woven leather belt, and next to that sat a pair of dainty
moccasins, seemingly in her size.

"Do you think I'm supposed to put these clothes on?"
she asked.

This time his grunt was noncommittal. He turned away
from her and moved toward the door. At the entryway,
he stopped, propped an arm against the timbered door
frame, fixed his gaze toward the outside. She understood
that he was giving her privacy to change, if she so chose.

It was hard to resist the appeal of such a beautiful material, especially since her own clothing was torn and trail-
dirty. To shed it came as a relief, but out of modesty she
kept her percale chemise and pantalets. Soon her ragged
European cottons and cambrics were in a heap on the
floor, and the soft deerskin had floated over her head to
settle around her in a snug hug. She pulled her hair out
from the back and secured the belt around her waist. She
bent down to tie the moccasins—pretty little kisses of
rabbit skin—around her feet, then reached eagerly for the
comb and brush. They were silver-chased, obviously of
European descent, and she resolutely turned her thoughts
away from contemplating the fate of the woman who had
originally owned them.

After the first few scalp-tingling tugs through the tangles, she huffed and spoke her thoughts aloud. "I may
have to cut it all off yet."

Powell didn't move. His voice came as if from very far
away. "You're not serious, are you?"

"In a way, yes," she replied, struggling with the mess.

"My head had become so hot and itchy under my bonnet yesterday that I was dreaming about cutting it all off the whole time we were traveling to the village. Last night when I took my bonnet off I felt better, but already this morning I was thinking that it might just have to go."

To this Powell said nothing.

She bent down and fished among her old clothes to retrieve her reticule and discovered, glory be, that it held what she was looking for. "You see," she said, "I still have my scissors." She pulled the blond mass over her shoulder and put the winking blades to the thickest part. "It's a temptation, I own."

At that Powell dropped his arm from the frame, turned toward her and bit off a sharp "Don't."

Although surprised, she decided not to let his grumpiness get to her. She said, pleasantly enough, "I don't know how I'm going to deal with this otherwise."

"The scissors are so small," he snapped, "that it would take you as much time to hack it all off as to comb through it."

It was true that the tiny blades would make the cutting process slow going. It was also true that her problems would be greatly reduced if Mr. Powell would stand behind her and comb her hair for her. However, something in the way he was looking at her stopped her from asking for his help. She entertained the notion that perhaps he found her hair as beautiful as other men had found it and didn't want her to cut it off.

She was disabused of that intriguing notion when he added in a milder tone, "If you're determined to cut it off, at least wait until tomorrow, when we're gone from here."

She lowered the blades, picked up the comb again. "We're leaving?"

"If possible."

"Is there a hurry?"

"Yes."

"Do you think—" She choked on the horrible thought, then composed herself. "Do you think they mean to sacrifice us today?"

"It's not the day I'm worried about, but the night."

"I see," she said without seeing anything at all. "What do you think will happen during the day?"

"Not much. I may have to go hunting. You may have...to do whatever it is the women do."

"I take it you mean for us to sneak away?"

"More or less."

"On foot?"

"I'd like to steal a horse or two. We'll just have to see."

"And the hurry about leaving before the night?"

"You know that it's best to travel in the dark," he replied, which was not an answer to her question. She was about to ask him more pointedly about the hurry, but he diverted her by offering to fetch her some food and water.

"Food, yes, thank you," she said, touched by his consideration, "but don't bother with the water. I notice there's a full jug here by the hearth."

He reverted to his sharp tones. "Don't drink it."

"Oh? Why not?"

"Just don't."

"It's not fresh?"

His expression stony, he repeated the simple, insulting command, "Don't drink it."

By now she was downright annoyed by his grumpiness, by his bossiness, and saw no reason to do what he said just because he said it. In fact, she had a good mind to do the opposite, so she put scissors and comb in one hand, picked up the jug of water with the other and took a healthy draft. Then she sighed with satisfaction and said in all sincerity, "That is the *best* water I've ever tasted!"

His displeasure was visible and tinged with a hint of grim amusement.

She chirped on. "I don't know what it is about the taste, but you mentioned it last night. It's as if the water is sweet," she said, taking another sip, "but that's not quite it, either." She considered. "Of course, it's impossible to describe a taste, and water has none anyway. Nevertheless, it's delicious." She held the jug out. She offered, she taunted, "Want some?"

He paused, narrowed his eyes speculatively. Then he gave his head a shake, as if tossing off a thought. He looked oddly thirsty when he said, "Drink all you want, but stay away from me."

She could think of no better invitation. She put the jug down, began walking toward him. She grabbed a hunk of her hair, held the scissors up to it. She smiled and teased, "Snip, snip."

As she approached, he moved into the doorway. His back was in full sunlight. His front was shadowed by the interior. "Because my requests have only—"

"Your requests?" she echoed sweetly. "Don't you mean your commands?"

"Have only provoked in you the opposite response, I can't do more than entreat you—"

"Entreat?"

"Not to do anything to arouse suspicion. It would be best if you didn't alter your appearance, beyond changing your clothing, or act any differently today than you did yesterday."

She came to a halt right under his nose. She lifted her

lashes to him, smiled her prettiest smile. She cooed, "You request. You entreat. But you don't intend to explain yourself."

He met her gaze. She saw resolution steel his blue eyes, felt the force of it emanate from his body, all muscle and sinew. He returned her smile with a sly smile of his own. He shook his head slowly. "No, Miss Sarah Ross Harris, I don't intend to explain myself."

Then he was gone.

Her first thought was *I don't think he intends to return with food for me.*

Her second thought was *My, my, that was fun!*

It had been fun to walk right up to Mr. Wesley Powell and to bait him. Yes, it was more fun than walking all over William, who worshiped her. It was much more fun than having to fight off that insufferable duke, who scorned her. Why, she liked seeing a man back up for once instead of her; and once he had backed up, she liked the fact that he had stood up to her, that he hadn't caved in. So, what was it about Wesley Powell that had made the encounter particularly enjoyable? Was it his strength? His resourcefulness in the wilderness? The possibility that he was attracted to her but was—charming thought!—a man of integrity?

She returned to the hearth and took another swig of that yummy water. She decided that what she enjoyed most about her encounter with Wesley Powell were his muscled chest and the way those breeches fit him.

At the very moment he said, "Don't drink it," Powell had a sinking feeling about what would happen next.

Still, he hoped that she would accept the unexplained wisdom of his command, because hardly the minute before, when he had told her not to cut off her hair, she had obeyed him. However, her obedience in that case might have been explained by the fact that she would be loath to part with such a glorious asset. On the other hand, for her to have even entertained the idea of cutting off her hair suggested that she wasn't as vain as he supposed her to be, just as he had discovered last evening that she was not so much foolish as remarkably brave.

He nipped these musings in the bud. Now was *not* the moment to be endowing her with any attractive personal qualities.

Especially not the moment when she picked up the jug and—*please don't!*—took a good long swig—*damn it!*—of water that he guessed to be spiked with an aphrodisiac and—*oh, shit!*—pronounced it the best she had ever tasted. Even more ominous was the expression on her face when she put the jug down and began to walk toward him, testing and teasing. Her voice, whose tone had always previously annoyed him, fairly cooed and cajoled, and its effect on him was nowise lessened by his knowledge that it wasn't her but the magic that was talking.

He had no choice but to beat a retreat, for if he stood his ground and let her come any closer, he didn't think he could withstand the honey in her voice, the look in her eye, the smile on her lips, the sway of her hips. Not to mention the fact that he had just spent a year alone in the field, on top of which was the ongoing temptation of having spent the past four days and four nights in her company. Her mere approach reactivated the surge of liquid iron that had flowed in his veins during the night, and he wasn't quite sure that he could resist her if she actually touched him. She looked so sweet and sultry and seductive that his resolve was already softening....

He gave his head a decisive shake and reminded himself that he wanted to live to see the dawn of another day.

Then he blabbered something to the effect that she shouldn't do anything to arouse suspicion and got himself the hell out of the lodge. Once in the relative safety of the village circle, he took several deep breaths, looked around to get his bearings and felt pretty sure that he had just avoided a mighty powerful, possibly fatal trap. And not by much.

His sense of narrow escape was heightened when he spied a pole planted atop the roof of his lodge at the edge of the skylight opening. From the pole was waving the shirt embroidered with that god-awful bird. The mystery of why he had been undressed during the night was solved, and his overall assessment of the part he was supposed to play in the village was confirmed. Since he hadn't performed his sexual duty while his veins were foaming with desire and he was wearing the shirt, someone must have decided to take the shirt off and put it outside the lodge. Perhaps it was intended to serve as a beacon to the god it symbolized, to draw its spirit down from the heavens and into the lodge so that the spirit could incite the white man to action the next night.

Perhaps the spirit had already entered the lodge. Perhaps the spirit had seen the need to tempt him more forcefully. Perhaps the spirit had taken human form and now inhabited the sweet body of Miss Sarah Ross.

He was having crazy thoughts. Again. He didn't believe in spirits, certainly not Mandan spirits, and especially not ones symbolized by a ridiculous Baltimore oriole. It was all *her* fault, this mess, start to finish, but there was no point rehashing that now, when it was far more important to set his sights on devising their escape from the village.

Running, running, he had been running forever, it seemed. And just as he had run *to* her as if his life depended on it—that vision of a beautiful woman standing in the midst of a shaded glade—now he wanted to run *away* from her, knowing that his life *did* depend on it. But first he would have to check out where the Mandans kept their horses and stash some provisions for their night-time flight.

He made his way through the village, circling first this way, then that, around the huddle of huge earthen-mound lodges. Life within the village was active but unhurried. Naked children played everywhere. Idle hunters and warriors lounged and sunned themselves on the rounded roofs of the lodges. Women went about their work, which seemed to consist of hauling water, weaving, gossiping, carrying bowls and baskets filled with food and armfuls of animal skins.

The villagers appeared well dressed and well fed, but Powell wondered whether they didn't have a wary edge and a worried look about them. Although no one opposed his progress through the village, everyone seemed to be regarding him with a certain expectation. Or was it merely suspicion? He couldn't help but think that here were a people who expected a miracle and who looked to him as the miracle worker. And if it was only a figment of his warped imagination that he thought he was being seen as a magic baby-maker, then that was reason enough to get out of this place before he lost what was left of his sanity.

Walking north, he reached the outskirts of the village and met open plain. About a half mile off to the west he spied an odd rock formation that looked like the geological fossil of the droppings of some gigantic bird. A gift from the heavens, compliments of the almighty Baltimore oriole, perhaps? He kept his eye on the rock formation a moment longer and reestimated its distance to be more like a mile away. He decided that the morning shadows had thrown his initial calculation off, and the more he looked at the rock, the higher he realized it must be. The squat shape of its outline had at first fooled his eye.

He shrugged and headed east until he came to the banks of a wide river. They had not traveled far enough north or east to have encountered the Missouri, so he figured this to be a significant tributary, perhaps the Elkhorn. In any case, women were there, gathered in clusters. The ones closest to him stood on the bank and called both to women on an island in the river and to women who were floating in tubs on the river, apparently ferrying a variety of goods from one bank to the other. Then, too, there were women washing clothes at river's edge, and beyond them, half-tucked away in a pretty little inlet, were women bathing.

That caught his attention, and he paused to look at the naked women. Fans of long black hair floated on the surface of the water, and long brown limbs rose on occasion from its depths, then sank back into it. He must have been staring at the women long enough for his presence and his interest to have been noticed. One of the women, young and pretty, lifted herself ever so slowly from the water, teasing him, turning away from him so that only the curve of one hip and one breast were visible to him. Her skin was the color of creamy peanut butter. She looked at him over her shoulder. Her features were well-defined and pretty. Her eyes were large and dark. She flicked him a glance filled with sultry speculation.

He'd been the recipient of hundreds of such glances. Knew just how to read them as both an invitation and a dare. Knew just how to respond to them. Starved as he was for feminine flesh, he felt—

Nothing. Nothing at all.

After that nothing came an unpleasant tingle down his spine. Was that blasted magic water he drank in the lodge one of those desire-the-first-woman-you-see type of potions he'd read about a long time ago? As an unmothered kid he'd read everything he could get his hands on, and he remembered running across stories about magic potions and star-crossed lovers, but they hadn't held his attention at the time. He had far preferred reading about geography and studying maps of faraway places.

He turned south, wending his way along the riverbank at the eastern outskirts of the village, and began to wrack his brain—not that he really believed in any of this nonsense, any more than he believed in Mandan spirits—to remember what he'd read on the subject of magic potions and such. He couldn't remember much, but he had a vague feeling that the magic produced only mischief.

The most important question he entertained concerned whether or not these potions tended to wear off, and he decided, emphatically, that they did. So it was only a matter of time before he could safely return to the lodge and interact with Miss Magic. However, since he didn't know how much time was necessary for the effect of the potion to lessen, or where Miss Magic would be spending her time, he decided to keep outside the village for the better part of the day, as well. He figured to put his time to productive use by devising the plan for their eventual escape.

He headed west at the southern boundary of the village for the simple reason that a lesser creek flowed into the river at this point. Taking the well-worn path that ran alongside the tributary, he mulled over possible escape plans. He moved through the high grasses, following the sinuous bends in the tributary, without paying much heed to his surroundings until he came upon a sight that made him think that, at long last, his wretched luck had finally changed.

Before him was a large, secluded corral in which grazed a dozen horses or more. He approached the rough-hewn log fence, and his optimism grew when one fine stallion, a hefty-haunched gray about sixteen hands high, pranced over to him, either just plain curious or eager for a treat. He wished he had an apple for Lucky Liberty but decided that some friendly chat with the old boy would just have to do. However, before Lucky could get close enough for him to rub his neck and make friends, Powell saw another sight that spelled trouble just as surely as if it were written in bold letters across the sky.

A group of four braves—had they tracked him in his progress around the perimeter of the village?—emerged from the trees on the edge of the corral opposite where he was standing and began walking toward him. Powell put one moccasined foot on the lower bar of the fence and leaned his forearms casually against the upper bar. He didn't reach out to the stallion when Lucky sidled next to him on his side of the fence, but he hoped his relaxation communicated itself to the horse and established some kind of a bond.

Powell figured the four braves to be a subset of the seven Indians who had originally captured him and Sarah. The one in the lead had harsh features and skin the color of a dull penny, and he looked somewhat familiar, but Powell couldn't quite place him. Then, his mind's eye rotated his perspective on the brave's face, and he remembered that he had gotten a good look at him when he had first arrived in the village. He had been lying on the ground, had looked up and had seen the rider with the dull-penny skin, whose horse had carried Sarah through the night and day. Powell guessed that it was only the intervention of the embroidered bird that had saved Sarah from that man's bed.

Dull Penny made swift progress around the corral, and the look of challenge etched upon his face said something to the effect that if Powell wasn't prepared to do his manly duty by Miss Magic, Dull Penny would, and he was happy to prove himself the better man.

In having left the lodge to escape Sarah's seduction, Powell had a stunningly clear sense of the expression Out of the frying pan—

Chapter Nine

Powell discovered soon enough what kind of fire he'd jumped into.

Once Dull Penny had come within fistfighting range, Powell straightened from his lounging position and met his opponent eye to eye. Dull Penny gave him a contemptuous once-over, then consulted with his sidekicks, all three of whom wore bows slung over their shoulders and quiver straps across their chests. He turned to Powell and spoke.

Powell didn't need to understand a word of Mandan to know what was up. He put a hand on the handle of one of the knives at his waist. The elk horn felt smooth and reassuring. He thought it safe to respond.

"Whatever you say, my man. Just show me the way."

Dull Penny responded to that by gesturing elaborately, then disappeared into the high grasses between the corral and the tributary. Powell followed. He was sandwiched from behind by the Trusty Trio, who were, he suspected, supposed to keep him honest. He gave no thought to slipping away or otherwise weaseling out of whatever competition Dull Penny had in mind. This was not because he imagined Dull Penny's intentions to be friendly.

Rather, with all the unspent desire pumping through his veins, he wasn't unhappy about the prospect of working some of it off. Since he wanted to stay away from the village and Miss Magic for most of the day anyway, he hoped that his challenger had planned a full schedule of trials.

Dull Penny had, and hunting was on his mind. Big game. Little critters. Close range. At a distance. Open plain. Underbrush.

Powell moved easily into the rhythms of a day sustained by long, observant pauses and punctuated by brief, active exclamation points. He had first begun to cultivate an Indian's patience as a boy on his grandmammy's farm in Tennessee. There he'd spent vast stretches of time alone, roaming the hills and pitching stones at hoot owls until he discovered it was more interesting to communicate with them.

When his grandmammy died and he was shuttled off to his aunt's austere family in Virginia, he was marked from the start as an outcast and entertained himself at length with geography books. When they felt they'd done their Christian duty by this child of a wicked fallen woman, he'd been shoved on to a cousin's family in Delaware. He'd always suspected that his very own mother had gained him entry to West Point, and he had exercised his hunter's patience in the Correctional Chamber. He had perfected it during the year he'd spent in the field making painstaking calibrations and drawing detailed maps.

He didn't know what the past few days of fighting to stay alive had done for him other than make him appreciate the miracle that he was still walking the earth, breathing in, breathing out. He was content to hold back, to stalk at a snail's pace, to aim and shoot, to lunge and chuck his spear. His well-trained eye was unerring. His fine moccasins and buckskin breeches moved like a second skin. His elk-horn knives handled like beautifully scanned lines of poetry. The bow and arrows lent to him by one of the Trusty Trio were serviceable, but he doubted he'd been given the use of the best-balanced bow or the finest notched arrows. Still, he matched Dull Penny squirrel for squirrel, raccoon for raccoon, deer for deer.

They played fair, these Indians. Dull Penny didn't cheat, nor did any one of the Trusty Trio lend Dull Penny an unfair hand or thwart Powell's success. They played their roles as impartial witnesses. They gave him food and drink, too, throughout the day, no more and no less than they gave to his opponent.

For having jumped into a fire, Powell figured this wasn't a bad one, but there were dimensions to it he didn't yet understand. Since this challenge seemed to be private, played out behind the medicine man's back, he couldn't yet guess if Dull Penny truly expected to win sleeping rights to Sarah or not. And he wasn't at all sure where he would be, win or lose. As the day wore on, he felt doom close in on him, but that weighty sense of impending death had become so familiar that it was indistinguishable from his equally vibrant sense of being alive.

Animal for animal. Pelt for pelt. Skin for skin. He had been keeping pace with his Indian counterpart all day, and when Dull Penny finally accepted the fact that he wasn't going to get the better of him, Powell noticed that the path of their hunting was leading them back to the village.

When he came within sight of the first lodges at the northwest corner of the village, he perceived that a crowd had gathered, and he began to doubt that this had been an entirely private challenge. It might have begun as such and become public when the villagers noticed that neither

Dull Penny nor their magic baby-maker was around. Whatever the reason, a goodly crowd was there.

The Trusty Trio arrived first. They were walking Indian file, linked by two long sticks hung with the carcasses of the day's hunt, which they carried across their shoulders. They laid the long sticks down on the ground before the villagers.

Powell arrived in Dull Penny's wake and saw that the villagers, who were crowded around the sticks and speaking volubly, had determined that the catches were equal. So, even if they hadn't known about the hunting challenge before it occurred, they had figured it out by now. They had declared it a draw, if Powell was any judge of the murmurs and the half-speculative, half-admiring glances thrown his way. He searched the crowd for Sarah, but didn't see her. Nor was the medicine man in evidence.

Whatever Dull Penny's intentions had been, they had not been fulfilled. The Indian didn't say a word to defend himself, but Powell observed that he rapidly sized up the situation, came to a decision, then claimed the attention of the rather dissatisfied crowd. He spoke, and when he was finished, approving noises rose up from the crowd. From the gestures that Dull Penny made, Powell inferred that one last trial was being proposed.

Powell smiled to himself that the final contest seemed to be a footrace to the top of that mountainous mess of bird droppings and back. He squinted into the sky and reckoned it to be five-thirty, white man's time, and he'd be damned if the afternoon shadows didn't make that rock formation look as if it loomed a mere couple hundred yards away. For all his fair play, Dull Penny seemed to have one trick up his sleeve, and Powell set his surveyor's sights in action for the second time that day. He compensated for the distortions of the light and calculated a distance of one mile, give or take, confirming his estimate of the morning.

Once the race got under way, Powell began to pace out the distance precisely, and he and Dull Penny were taking off over open plain, heading north and west into the setting sun and the lengthening shadows. Powell could have taken a much bigger lead because Dull Penny was holding back, apparently depending on the likelihood that Powell would mistake the overall length of the race course and be fooled into thinking Dull Penny the slower runner. So Powell kept ahead by only a few paces and was determined to maintain this lead. He knew that this race wasn't being run on the flat surface of the ground but rather on the trickier terrain of their minds.

His legs consumed the yards at a regular rate, eating up the first quarter mile, then the half mile, then the three-quarters. He kept the pace and the lead, all the while calculating the exact distance he covered on the ground and at the same time estimating the exact height of the mountain the closer he came. Then he was flush with rock and ran the numbers through his head. A mile and a fifth plus half a foot, and now all he had to do was zigzag his way to the top of the sacred bird droppings. This activity would be less an exercise for his leg muscles and arm muscles and more a game to see if the height he had estimated fell neatly within the foot or if he had slacked and been off a yard or more.

Coordination of limbs. Upstretch. Pause. Upstretch. Pause. Hands gripping. Feet gripping. Breathing in. Breathing out. The same two paces ahead of Dull Penny. Feeling like a jackrabbit without an ounce of fat left anywhere in his body. Only hard bone and red blood and lean muscle. Scampering. Darting traps. Reaching the top.

Confirming the height within the foot. Good job. Starting down again.

The descent brought consideration of inevitable consequences. The thought came to him and stayed that, win or lose, he was to die. White man win, he'd spend another night with Sarah, be expected to do his duty, then be sent to the spirit world. White man lose, he'd be sacrificed on the spot, and the red man could step into his moccasins with no accompanying sentence of death.

Since his capture by the Sioux, his life had been reduced to bare-boned existence and revealed as little more than a race toward death. He ran toward the village, two steps ahead of Dull Penny, two steps closer to death. He despaired not of his end, but of the thinness of his life as he had lived it. He faced his fate, he faced his regrets, and then a miracle happened. Feelings thick and fine and human wedged through the sorry surface of his despair, and he entered the landscape of his dreams. He almost didn't recognize this new geography, for he had hardly ever acknowledged his dreams. But now, as he ran through life, as he ran toward death, he let his dreams engulf him.

They were surprisingly simple and seemingly unattainable. He wanted a woman. A shy and retiring woman. Quiet, obedient, unspoiled. A gray sparrow or maybe a mouse. In any case, a woman who would not be coveted by other men, perhaps not even noticed by them. He wanted children. Three, four, five children. He wanted a house in town, crowded up against other houses, and a community of friends. He didn't want to sleep under stars and run endlessly over open plain. He wanted a job at a desk, enclosed in four sturdy walls. He wanted to wade knee-deep in curling sheafs of paper, to plant neat rows of maps and files. He wanted to die an old man in his bed.

The earth lodges grew before his eyes. The mass of villagers watching the race separated into distinct bodies. Individual faces emerged. Expressions came into focus. A path opened for his triumphant finish, and he entered the village proper, but he wasn't going to stop before he got to the center circle. He turned this way, that way, spied the spirits' lodge and saw Sarah standing before the entry.

She shimmered like a beautiful vision in her deerskin dress. Her hair was tamed into two thick braids that trailed over her shoulders and breasts. She reminded him of the woman he had seen in the shady oasis when he had been running through the river. That woman had sustained him then, and this woman would sustain him now. To stay alive, he would have to reach out to her. To really live, he would have to put this beautiful illusion aside and reach to his true dream beyond.

Sarah figured that no good could come of this contest between Powell and one of the braves.

She had gotten wind of the proceedings toward the end of the afternoon. She had followed the line of curiosity seekers toward the northwest corner of the village, where she had arrived in time to see two runners recede into specks on the horizon. With everyone's attention on the race, she returned to the village circle and entered the lodge. She fetched her bonnet and stuffed it with what she could, acting on the ominous noises Powell had made that morning about wanting to leave before nightfall. She wanted to be prepared, but for what she wasn't sure. She went back outside to find out.

She had a good long time to wait. Long enough for the medicine man to make his silent, disapproving appearance at the village circle. Long enough to imagine a hundred horrible possibilities for her fate and to picture them twice. When she arrived at the conclusion that Powell would *never* return, she glimpsed him weaving through the path between the earthen mounds. Several paces behind him was the brave she recognized as the one who had taken her up behind him on his horse. She began to fear the worst, no matter what the outcome of this race.

The line of Powell's gaze was pinned directly on her. His body was strained but in graceful motion, his muscles gleaming, his long legs striding. She didn't see him as the young buck who had been so much fun to tease this morning. Rather, something in his expression reminded her of the first time she had seen him splashing through the water. This time, however, instead of hoping that the man-beast wouldn't see her, she was standing in full view of him and telling him with her eyes, *You can do it!* and, *Don't give up now!* She put all her mental effort into reeling him in to the finish, to her.

She was peripherally aware that the two runners brought in their wake a rowdy crowd of villagers. Others were whooping and streaming into the circle from all directions, while still others swarmed onto the roofs for the best view of the action. Out of the corner of her eye she caught the motions of a bonfire being laid. Evening was staining the sky in startling colors and seeping through the village in stealthy, shadowed patterns.

In a situation where anything could happen next, what did happen exceeded by far her wildest imaginings.

Powell was in the lead, running toward her, dead-on. When he was close enough to her to slow down, he didn't. Nor did he stop, and before she knew it, it was too late to get out of his way. At the very moment it looked as if he was going to run her down, he scooped her off her feet and kissed her. This was no chaste peck of greeting, but a real lips-to-lips, man-woman kiss that took her by surprise and tingled from the top of her scalp to the tips of her toes. Wrapped in strong, slick muscles, engulfed in a mist of clean-scented sweat, she felt herself being swept toward the spirits' lodge.

When her feet touched the ground again lightly, she realized that they were moving slowly through the shadows that crowded up and around the entrance. Her body still met his in an embrace of legs, arms and lips. She almost dropped her bonnet, but hung on to it. She could feel the overall pulse of his blood beating from his exertion, the heat and quiver of muscles and breath. The very unlikeliness of the passion heightened it, and she was put in mind of the intriguing thoughts she had had that morning. A flame flickered to life inside her.

"Stay with me...on this," he murmured against her lips.

"Oh, yes," she replied.

"I mean it."

"Oh, yes."

He brushed his lips across her cheek to her ear. "Do you know...what we're doing?"

He was kissing her with an intensity she'd never before experienced, but his odd question interrupted the mood. She felt the passion ebbing. "Well, I thought—"

"We're making our escape."

"Escape?"

"Stay with me, I said.... Don't stop kissing me. That's better. Mmm. That's right."

She noticed that instead of going into the lodge, they were moving around the entrance, keeping to the shadows, edging away from sight of the main circle.

"This is our escape?"

"Mmm-hmm," he answered against her lips, "and it seems...to be working."

"It does?"

"How anyone could think…I'm up to this now…is beyond me. Maybe they…really do think…I'm a magic baby-maker."

She wasn't sure she had heard him aright, but this wasn't the moment to question him. They were moving faster now and more awkwardly. Her legs were tangling in his. They stumbled, lips still locked, but managed to stay upright. He grunted with effort, with exhaustion.

"You're tired," she said.

"If I stop running now…it's over for me…and maybe for you, too."

When they rounded the wall of the lodge just beyond the entry, he broke the embrace, grabbed her hand and pulled her into the blackness away from the main circle, where the bonfire was beginning to blaze. One hand clasping his, the other clutching her bonnet, she hurried behind him as he threaded them through the maze of earthen mounds and plunged them into the tall grasses at the south edge of the village. The moon had risen to hide itself behind a thick cover of clouds. She began to think that he had lost his mind to imagine they could simply run away, but then she saw a corral materialize before her in the dimness.

Powell whistled softly and began removing the upper log of one section of fence. A huge gray trotted over to them. Powell patted the stallion's flanks, stroked his withers. To her he said, "Up you go."

The stallion loomed large in the moonlight, snorting and stomping. She shrank back.

"Step onto the lower railing," Powell recommended. "I'll help you the rest of the way."

"You know this horse?"

"Met him this morning."

"He's huge."

"Lucky's a fine fellow."

"How much do you think he weighs?"

"Not more than twelve hundred pounds."

"You should know that I'm not much of a horse-woman."

"You've faced worse."

She wasn't so sure.

"Now, up!" he encouraged. "We don't have much time."

She swallowed her fears and stepped onto the railing. She hitched her deerskin dress, reached out to the stallion's neck and swung a leg over the brute. Powell propelled her rump. Then he coaxed Lucky to step over the lower railing and replaced the upper railing while she hung desperately on to both her balance and her bonnet. Then he settled himself behind her and prevented her from sliding around on Lucky's back with his arms and chest.

He heaved a sigh of satisfaction and relief. "For the moment at least, our diversion seems to have worked."

"You mean they think we're in the lodge...still kissing?"

"Right, but I doubt they'll think that for long."

She peered around in the darkness, saw nothing. "How will they know otherwise?"

"They spied on us last night. My guess is that they intend to spy on us tonight, as well."

"What makes you think they spied on us last night?"

"The water," he replied. "The damned magic water."

"The magic wa—" she began, but was jolted from speech when the horse reared up.

Powell quickly slipped his arms around her sides to grasp Lucky's neck, spoke into his ear, and—miracle of miracles, terror of terrors—the stallion seemed eager to be off.

Sarah felt twelve hundred pounds of horseflesh curvet along the path by the tributary, slide down the shadowy embankment to water's edge, carom over stones and roots, and suck hooves from soggy mud. Although she was steadied by Powell's embrace, her poor, scared brain stuck on the idea that she was heading for a horrible, bone-crushing, blood-spurting death far worse than any the Mandan might have devised for her.

After several jarring minutes Powell informed her, "We'll cross at the first shallow place."

"Then what?"

"We'll head south and west."

"Do you think they'll come looking for us?"

"My guess is yes."

"We'll be leaving an easy trail to follow, no?"

His grunt suggested another yes.

"And if they catch us, do you think that then, *then* they mean to kill us?"

"Not right away, and if they do catch us, I think we'll be able to make it through the night—or what's left of it. The effects of the magic have surely been wearing off throughout the day."

"The magic?" she echoed. "Wearing off?"

He had been leaning forward, his bare chest pressed against her back, his crotch nestled against her butt, but at her questions, he eased away from her. When he continued, his voice rumbled in a lower register. "You're right. These aren't the ideal circumstances to discover whether or not those effects have worn off."

Before she could respond, he plunged the horse into the water, and they were splashing across a sandy bar in the tributary. Lucky heaved them up and over the opposing bank, and then they were cantering across the plains under a sky that was becoming darker and lower with every passing furlong.

At one moment he turned around to look behind him, then turned back and said into her ear, "Don't see a thing. Can't see a thing. Which means they can't see us, either. All for the good."

All for the good. She felt the stallion's hooves chewing the ground like a train crossing a bridge collapsing in its wake, as if each pace churned the space behind into an abyss no pursuer would be able to cross. She sensed that the village was vanishing into a distant dimension of time and space, and with it receded the comforts of a luxurious bed, a fine roof, good food…and magic water?

Bones jangling, thoughts jostling, she tried to focus all her attention on the desperate effort to remain astride the thundering beast, but she kept getting distracted by her awareness of the man behind her. She felt the crack and sizzle of liquid heat curl around the narrow space between her back and his chest, tingling her spine, shaking her joints. The crack and sizzle between their bodies jumped up into the heavens and returned to earth in the form of lightning bolts that flashed out from all corners of the dark space through which they were riding.

The sensations swirling through her body and through the sky turned heavy and humid. She blurted out, "What's all this about magic water?"

Just then the heavens opened up, and rain poured forth in a sudden, stupendous gush.

He whooped joyously and laughed out loud. "Magic water?" he shouted against the rain and into the night. "*This* is magic water, and it will cover our tracks! We're saved!"

Chapter Ten

Sarah had gone on a pleasant outing into the countryside with some of her friends. She must have become separated from the group because she was aware that she was alone. No, not truly alone, for she had a vague feeling that she was in the company of a young man. A suitor no doubt. However, he wasn't paying her court. This was most proper, and so she wasn't displeased, and yet, she wasn't entirely pleased, either, since the young man wasn't even paying her any attention. In fact, it seemed as if he was deliberately ignoring her. Keeping away from her. As if she was bothering him somehow. Annoying him.

Well, she certainly wasn't going to waste her time worrying about some inattentive, inconsiderate, most probably *ineligible* young man who didn't know how to behave around the most sought-after young woman in all of Baltimore. Or was she in England now? No matter. The day was fine, the surroundings amenable, and she was determined to enjoy herself. But she was eager to return to her group so that she could tell light and delightful stories of how she had spent her afternoon wandering among the hills and lazing beside the waterfall.

The waterfall. She was seated—or was she reclining?—

by a cascade. In fact, it was more like a roaring cataract, and she had been there all afternoon, it seemed, with the water rushing and pounding—mostly pounding—over the rocks and in her ears. It was creating such a heavy mist that her pretty day dress was getting sprayed. At least she had her parasol with her to shield her delicate skin from the rays of the sun. But why had she taken off her bonnet? And why was that young man so disagreeable? It made her want to flirt with him, to show him what he was missing, to make him declare himself.

But, no. If he was as ineligible as she was beginning to suspect, she didn't want to receive a declaration from him that she would only have to spurn. On the other hand, why not? If she was being honest with herself, she had to admit that she took pleasure in receiving offers she disdained. It made her feel important and in control. Even more, it made her feel accepted. Acceptance was fine for a start, but she really needed to feel something more than mere acceptance. She needed to feel desired. Yes, desired. Truly, madly, deeply desired, so that she could be assured of the man's interest and attention, even though she did not reciprocate those feelings. Particularly if she did not reciprocate those feelings, because if she did, she would be at risk.

At risk of what?

At risk of nothing whatsoever, and she refused to consider uncomfortable topics when she was part of such a special outing. Exclusive, really. Attended by only the most socially acceptable people in town. Baltimore? London? Meaning that she must be a member of the high-toned set. Meaning also that she should not have been paired off with this strange and brooding young man who, she was beginning to think, was not a member of the group but the worst of all social creatures: the encroaching mushroom, the party-crasher, the *one who did not belong*.

She needed to rise, to return to her group, to find for herself a suitable young man who would adore her, but not let her walk all over him. Who would desire her, but respectfully, acknowledging her true inner worthiness and legitimacy. Who would want to marry her and to secure for all time her acceptance. Surely there must be one such man in the group. Maybe several. She needed to rise, to get away from the waterfall, for her dress had become thoroughly soaked. She needed to rise so that she could return to her group and find that impossibly perfect man. It was her dream, after all, to arrange the world as she liked.

Her dream? No, no and no. If she didn't wake up, she could remain in the lovely countryside. If she didn't open her eyes, she wouldn't have to face—

She opened her eyes, then shut them to recapture her dream, but it was too late. The pleasant illusion was dispelled, and she had bodily returned to a damp, inhospitable world. She cracked her eyes again. Through the filter of her lashes, she beheld in the wan daylight a moving screen that resembled a stream of polished rice. When she opened her eyes fully, she more rightly perceived a shower of pelting rain that hung about the earth like a thick curtain of dirty gauze. No sight could have been more depressing than the reality that surrounded her.

And no position could have been more uncomfortable, lying as she was on the chill, soaked ground, waterlogged in skin and spirit. She lifted her head, stirred her stiff spine and uncramped her arms and legs just enough to creak to a sitting position. Taking stock of her situation in no way raised her sodden spirits.

She was seated, facing west more or less, under a half

ring of outcropped rock, which provided shelter by a spare foot of overhang. Powell was seated about five feet away from her, his knees drawn up to his chin, his arms wrapped around his legs. His face was in profile to her, and he was looking through the dirty, wet curtain into the infinite emptiness before them. Perhaps sensing her glance, he turned his head to look at her. He didn't speak or even change his expression, but some flicker in the depths of his rain-clouded blue eyes informed her that she looked like the bedraggled wretch that she felt.

He, on the other hand, did not look so bad. Relatively speaking, of course. He was wearing a day's growth of beard, but she had become accustomed to seeing him like that, and his black curls were plastered away from his face and against his head in a way that suited him. His buck beige breeches and moccasins had turned to mahogany with their soaking, and since he had no shirt to wear, his chest and shoulders and forearms, once burnt, had burnished to bronze and blended to the color of his breeches. He looked like a statue of oiled wood or glistening topaz.

But he was not made of wood or of stone. She wondered how he felt with no defensive line of shirt between his upper body and the elements. Since he wasn't shivering, or showing gooseflesh, she decided not to ask him if he was cold. In these meager circumstances, she rightly feared the power of suggestion.

Beyond him, next to the rock, stood Lucky. Of the three creatures, Lucky looked the least abashed by the rain and the fate that had marooned him in the middle of a vast nothingness with two pitiful humans who needed warm, dry clothing and a hearty meal.

She remembered her bonnet and revived at the mere thought of it. She reached out eagerly to that puddle of cloth as if it were a precious treasure chest.

"Food," she said. "I have food."

Though his eyes still rested on her, Powell's expression darkened slightly, as if he was concerned for her sanity.

She plopped the melted bonnet in her lap and began to pick at the ties. She opened it and withdrew some very soggy cornmeal balls, which could not have looked more appetizing. She counted out eight, put five in one palm and handed them over to him.

His eyes narrowed, and he regarded her outstretched hand for several seconds. Then he shook his head at her unequal offer and took but four.

"No, take them all. You did more work than I did yesterday, and you'll probably do more today, too, if there's any to do."

"I was well fed yesterday during the hunt."

"So was I in the village. Please," she said, still holding out the fifth yellow ball. "I have some jerky in here, too, so you needn't think this is all there is."

His expression lightened. "Jerky?"

She fished in her bonnet and pulled out several strips of dried buffalo meat, which she added to the lonely cornmeal ball in her palm. "I've got about ten more strips in here, so at least we're set on sustenance for the next little while."

He took the jerky and the remaining ball with a word of thanks. Biting into a strip of jerky, he nodded at her bonnet. "What else do you have in there?"

She noticed that his voice rasped lightly, like fingernails on a soft filing board. It was a worrisome sign for the state of his health, and she wished her bonnet was more like a magician's hat from which she could pull one of the bed furs that had cuddled them night before last. Alas, all she could produce were the remaining strips of jerky, the comb and brush—which had seemed more important when she had stashed them than they did now—the tilt-edged razor and her reticule with its embroidery scissors, pins, needles, threads and useless coins. From the bottom of this pouch she also withdrew the pieces of iron pyrite he had given her. When she held these up for his inspection, the look she gave him was a little pitiful; there would be no possibility of starting a fire this day.

"Not much, I'm afraid," she said sadly. "How I regret not stuffing your shirt in here. Of course, I would have had to mount the roof in order to retrieve it, although what it was doing up there, I'll never know!" She held up a hand to stop the speech he gave no sign of delivering. "And I *do* remember that you said it's better not to think of all that's been left behind—"

"No, better not to think of it."

"But it's hard *not* to think of it. My skirts and blouse. Your shirt. Not to mention my petticoats and shawl and hairpins, which are, at this point, long gone."

He chewed thoughtfully for a moment or two, then said, "Look at it this way. I'm wearing better breeches now than the previous two pairs of trousers I've come across this week past. We both have decent moccasins. I have my razor, and you have your comb and brush." He gestured to the two elk-horn knives stuck in the ground beside him. "And these beauties are worth quite a lot more than we've lost."

She wasn't entirely sure she agreed with him. When she thought of the lodge with its furs, food and fire, it seemed to her like a world of comfort and plenty. In light of her present impoverished circumstances, she was inclined to wonder whether her stepbrother Laurence might not have had a more abundant background as an Iroquois than she had previously imagined. However, this was hardly the moment for grand insights or moral reevaluations of cultural differences.

Instead, she asked, "What was the hurry to leave the village?"

He returned his gaze to contemplate the watery nothingness. "I can't say for sure," he admitted, "but I do know that yesterday's competition with Dull Penny was no good omen for your fate or mine."

"Dull—" she echoed. "Oh, yes, *him.* I, too, was troubled enough by yesterday's events to fill my bonnet with what I could, just to be prepared. As it turns out, I suppose I should be glad we got away with this much."

She began to nibble at one of the cornmeal balls, enjoying it despite its sloppy consistency. Her thoughts fell first on the aptly named Dull Penny, then tangled when she tried to imagine what specific negative outcomes for their respective fates Powell might have had in mind.

She asked, "What do you think would have happened to you if you hadn't won the race?"

He shrugged minimally. "Perhaps my encounter with the Sioux gave me the wrong notion of how low the Indians regard the white man. Nevertheless, I can't help but think that Dull Penny was counting on winning the footrace and demanding my immediate death."

She eyed the half-moon that remained of her cornmeal ball and ventured, "What about me?"

He swung his gaze toward her. His brows quirked a hint of *Need you ask?*

She felt her cheeks blanch then flush, but she didn't look away. "The medicine man didn't hand me over to Dull Penny, as you'll recall. He paired me with you."

"Paired," he repeated. "That's right. He paired me with you."

"Which makes it likely that the medicine man wasn't

necessarily pleased with Dull Penny's challenge, if Dull Penny's goal was to eliminate you and be...paired with..." She didn't finish the thought either in words or in her head.

"Right again. The medicine man might not necessarily have been pleased by the challenge mounted by a brave who didn't like the way the spoils of their capture were sorted out. If Dull Penny had bested me in front of the entire village, the medicine man might have had to grant his wishes. But Dull Penny didn't win, and I deployed the only diversionary tactic available to me, in case his honor was so compromised that he felt compelled to kill me anyway."

His diversionary tactic had been to kiss her in full view of everyone, and it had worked. They had made their escape because the villagers had figured they had gone into the lodge to continue kissing. Although she still wasn't ready to acknowledge what the passionate conclusion to the kiss might have been, neither could she drop the topic.

Circling around the problem, she asked next, "Did you determine what role the Baltimore oriole played in all of this?"

He shook his head. "Who knows? Most likely it symbolizes some important Mandan spirit."

"I saw a beaded version of the bird on the medicine man's headband," she offered. "It was so tiny that I didn't notice it at first, but it was there in the center of the band, above a rising sun. Or perhaps the sun was setting."

"There you have it, then."

She did have it, and she didn't. Not yet. He was holding something back, but she wasn't quite sure what. In the past few days the usual distinctions had blurred between waking and sleeping, between dream and nightmare. Her sleeping, dreaming self knew what he meant, but her waking self did not. So, she did have it, and she didn't. Not in so many words.

She kept at it. "You said that we were spied on the other night in the lodge."

"I did."

"And you said something about the water. The magic water."

He did not immediately respond.

She gestured to the wet gray gauze shrouding them. "When you first mentioned the water, I don't think you were referring to the possibility of a magic downpour to drown out our trail."

He stood up, flexed his back muscles, turned away from her and the rock. He went to Lucky, rubbed the old boy's neck, leaned against his flanks, possibly for warmth. He didn't react to the rivulets of water that were streaming through his hair and tracing slow, sinuous paths down the bones and over the muscles in his back. He shifted his weight from one foot to the other and squared his shoulders. That most minimal reframing of his back and hips and legs altered the field of energies within the semicircle of the rock. It charged the dampness, made it heavy with more than humidity.

He didn't turn around to face her. "True enough. I was referring to the water that was both in our gourds at the bonfire and in the jug in the spirits' lodge."

Oddly enough, this is what she thought he had meant. She felt a crack sizzle up her spine similar to what she had experienced the night before but without the answering lightning in the sky. "What was magical about it?"

He paused at length. "The water was sweet. You said you'd never tasted better." He paused again. "So did I."

"The water was sweet," she acknowledged, "but it wasn't magical. At least, not as far as I know."

"Well then, how much do you know?"

"I know that the water came from the spring at the edge of town and that it tasted just as delicious straight from the source as it did from either the gourd or the pitcher. Everyone in the village drinks it." Still speaking to his back, she added, "One of my duties yesterday was to toss the old water and refill the jug. I went to the spring with the other women, did my job and replaced the jug with the fresh water by the hearth. Where was the magic in that?"

He turned, aimed his blue gaze at her. "Where did you toss the old water?"

"On the seedlings in the field by the source, just like all the other women did."

"And after refilling the jug and replacing it by the hearth, did anyone besides yourself enter the lodge?"

"No, I stayed in and about the lodge all day, except for the few minutes at the end of the afternoon when I went to the edge of the village to see what all the commotion was about."

"And the medicine man? Where was he during that time?"

"Watching the footrace himself. Did you fear that he would poison it...poison us?"

"No, I didn't fear poison." His gaze, resting upon her, momentarily intensified.

She felt a stab of emotion that sliced a fine hair between pain and pleasure. She breathed in and caught the sour-scented tang of wet earth. She breathed out and felt drifts of heat warm the small space. She hoped it was the effect of the rising sun, which was thickening the runny rain into a foggy stew.

He swung his gaze away and turned his back to her
again. She breathed more easily. Her deerskin dress
clammed against her breasts and arms. When she pulled
at it, it made a sucking noise. Then she rose to her feet,
nearly clunking her head against the overhang, and stood
in the stew. She unstuck her dress at her waist, hips,
knees. She felt the ropy mess of her braids and wondered
what it would be like to be cozy in the lodge, seated at
the hearth, brushing out her hair, drinking delicious water.
She imagined looking into the depths of the flames, seeing
playful pictures come to life, just as they had come to
color her dreams the night before last.

She glanced at Powell's back, studied its strengths and
contours. Her languorous, sleeping self yawned and
stretched and came awake. Oh, yes, he was holding something back, and now she knew what. So he thought he
could get away with ignoring her, did he? She decided
that the inattentive Mr. Powell—her unlikely squire on
this most unlikely outing—should be brought to his
senses. Even better, he should be brought to his knees.
Preferably at her feet.

What a diverting thought!

A deep voice broke into her unexpectedly pleasant reflections. "We're not going anywhere today, I fear."

She could hardly enthrall him with her present rag-doll
appearance, so she wasn't sorry that he was rude enough
not to face her when he spoke to her.

"We don't travel by daylight anyway," she replied.

He grunted meditatively, then spoke aloud as if he was
speaking to himself. "I don't like our position here. We
couldn't press Lucky for more than twenty miles or so
last night, and I can't be sure we didn't double back at
times. I have little idea of where we are, but I don't dare

leave our stronghold—such as it is—until I can see the sky, whether it be day or night.''

"We'll travel during the day, then, if the rain lets up?"

"Yes," he replied. He must have given this a second thought, for he added on a more tentative note, "We'll see."

She smiled. She sensed that he wanted to get away from this tiny shelter, away from her. But whenever he would get on the move, she'd be coming with him. Poor man! She contemplated the figure he cut and felt him back up, metaphorically speaking, just as he had backed up when she had toyed with him the morning before in the lodge. And what had he said to her then? *Don't drink the water.... Just don't.* As if it contained some magic that made him feel what he didn't already feel or desire what he didn't really desire? As if it contained some magic that would make her—oh ho, he flattered himself!—want to seduce him?

Now, what was he afraid of, Mr. Wesley Powell? He looked like a big, strong man who could take care of himself. He looked like the kind of man who liked women, too. She could tell that. In fact, she knew it in her bones. Well, she'd just have to see how far she could poke him and push him. She didn't want to seduce him, God forbid, and end up suffering what she had suffered at the hands of the Duke of Merton. No, she just wanted to have a little fun!

She could hear her mother's voice say, *You will simply have to stop teasing these poor men!*

To which she silently replied, *I don't have anything better to do!*

Not a blessed thing better to do, given that she was clammy from wet and creaky from a night spent on the ground. At least they wouldn't starve to death anytime soon, and there was no lack of water to sustain them. So, she may as well amuse herself by plotting her strategy for Powell's amorous downfall. She may as well plan for the future, which could only get better, since things couldn't get any worse.

The gods chose to punish her for this unwise thought by opening the heavens and pouring sheets of rain upon them for the next eight hours straight, rendering it progressively more difficult to attend to any conscious thought beyond the need to survive from one miserable minute to the next. To add to their misfortune and her worry, a cold front moved in during the midafternoon. At first it felt good to feel relief from the steam bath, but then she realized that this sudden shift in temperature could do no good for Powell's scratchy throat.

By late afternoon, the sky had cleared so quickly and completely that the magnificent sunset seemed to mock their perceptions of what they had just endured. Only their still-soaked clothing and the mucky ground bore witness to the full day of unrelenting rain. Powell wasted no time and fewer words getting them on the trail.

In the early morning, when she had still been able to weave pleasant webs for Powell's undoing, she had imagined tormenting him with her body while they rode together to their next destination. However, now that it was late afternoon, she was rather more worried about keeping her spine erect and her wet dress away from his exposed chest. The warmth of the full sun had come too late in the day to chase the chill, and with the night coming on, she didn't want to further endanger her companion's possibly fragile health. As frightening as she had found the experience of riding bareback on Lucky the night before, the threat of being stranded with the care of a very sick man was even worse, and so she did her best to keep her seat without sapping Powell's strength the way she had done the night before.

They rode through the night, heading south and west—not that she was a judge of such matters, since she could set no course by the constellations above. However, she was sure that Powell could, given that he would pause on occasion, scan the sky, then adjust their course. She was also sure that his health was deteriorating. In fact, with every passing mile she became ever more alarmed by his physical condition. She was downright cold in her still-damp dress, but she still had the wherewithal to generate her own internal warmth, while Powell, already pushed past his limit, had no resources left with which to fight.

At one point, she heard his teeth chattering, felt his body shivering, and wished she could have given him half her warmth, but her dress was still too cold with damp to have imparted him any comfort. Not much later, she felt radiate out from him a heat that was very different from the kind that had crackled between them the night before. Even before shifting to look at him, she knew that he was burning with fever. She turned at the very moment he slumped forward. His forehead sizzled to her touch. His chest and sides had broken out into an ominous sweat. His responses to her anxious questions were incoherent mumbles.

For the next few interminable hours she plodded forward with Powell's weight against her back, letting Lucky put one hoof in front of the other, not knowing what else to do but stay the course. Powell's case was grim as he cycled through perilous spirals of sweating and shaking. Black despair saturated her innards just as the rain had saturated her skin. So despairing was she that she no longer feared the great dark masses of sleeping buffalo they occasionally encountered. She came to pray that any next step would pitch them into the abyss that surely lay beyond the crest of this low-grade rise they had been climbing for ever and ever and ever.

The sun squeezed up over the horizon and rose behind her. When she could see out over the top of the hill, she looked down upon no cruel abyss, only another slope as gentle as the one they had just mounted. And in the valley that flowered before her were one, two, three, four, five, six, *seven* white sails schooning through the prairie grasses in the soft breezes of the morning.

She could hardly believe her eyes. Her thumping heart flushed her body of its black despair, pumped red blood of hope and happiness. She was looking down on her wagon train—or what was left of it, anyway. She was soon to be reunited with her parents! With her sisters! Even that horrible Mrs. Fletcher would be a welcome sight!

She hugged Lucky's neck with one arm, twisted the other one around Powell's unconscious body and began the descent toward the wagon train. She had to restrain herself so that she didn't lose control of either horse or patient, but it was hard not to let Lucky kick up his heels and fly. *This time* they would be saved! Well and truly saved!

As the tiny wagons grew bigger, one word echoed through her brain and that was *Joy!*

Chapter Eleven

Sarah angled into the wagon train at a perpendicular, coming up alongside the middle wagon—pulled by a team of mules—at the head of which sat a man and a woman. When Sarah was close enough to distinguish their faces, her joy turned to confusion not to recognize them, and she was further confused not to be recognized by them. She had expected welcoming signs of relief or shouts of happiness at her reappearance, but was met only with measuring regards and silence. It wasn't until much later that she realized what a sight she must have presented astride a huge gray stallion, with her pantalets exposed beneath her Indian dress and a man in buckskin breeches slumped behind her.

She opened her mouth to identify herself as Sarah Ross Harris, daughter to Barbara and Morgan, sister to Martha and Helen—those brats!—who had no doubt found some poor soul on the wagon train to plague and pester in her place. She opened her mouth to remind everybody who she was, but what came out were odd scratching noises. It seemed that her throat no longer worked properly.

Neither did her ears. The woman on the wagon turned to the man, and Sarah could not believe that she heard the woman say, "Mr. Wilkins, do you think this poor woman speaks English?"

"I don't know, Mrs. Wilkins," the man replied. "Her hair is blond, and her eyes are brown, so she might well speak English, for she does not look like any Indian I've ever seen."

"Indeed not," Mrs. Wilkins agreed, "and it's not as if she looks dangerous, but rather more...disreputable."

Of course I'm not an Indian! Sarah tried to say. She didn't think she managed to get the words out because Mr. and Mrs. Wilkins continued to look at her with equal parts curiosity and suspicion. *And I'm not disreputable!*

"Yes, disreputable," Mrs. Wilkins continued, "careering about the wilderness with a half-naked man who might well be an Indian."

"In a Christian spirit, Mrs. Wilkins," Mr. Wilkins said, "we cannot judge whether she herself is a heathen or whether the half-naked man is past saving. So we must..."

Sarah didn't even try to understand the rest of this strange conversation. She gestured to Powell's unconscious body, so that Mr. and Mrs. Wilkins could see that he was in desperate need of their Christian aid, if it came to religious principles. She tried words like "please" and "help" and "thirsty" and "riding all night long," but succeeded in capturing their attention only with her clear articulation of the word "Baltimore."

By that time, another man, most likely the wagon master, had ridden back to the wagon to size the situation up. Drawing next to her, the man on horseback asked, "You're from Baltimore, ma'am?"

Sarah nodded vigorously, croaked some more, and knew how Powell had felt when he had first splashed through the water and had come upon her. "And Washington," she managed next in reference to Powell. "Government. Surveyor."

The wagon master, a big, ruddy man, raised bushy brows. "A surveyor, then? Well now, ain't that a coincidence! Do I take it he's been wounded?"

She shook her head emphatically. "Sick. Very sick. Fever."

The wagon master reined his horse a pace or two away. "What kind of fever? I cain't compromise the health of this wagon train with no kind of pox or cholera."

She had regained a tenuous hold on her voice. "He lost consciousness a few hours ago," she croaked. "The fever came on him only this past night, as a result of heat and cold and the exhaustion of our escape."

"That would be escape from the Sioux?"

She shook her head again. "Mandan."

The wagon master pushed his broad-brimmed hat up off his forehead and frowned. "You say he's a surveyor for the government? And you've been captured by the Mandan? What's his name?"

"Powell. Wesley Powell."

He considered the information, then grunted a hefty "Huh. Don't recall the name, nosiree." He fixed her with a curious stare. "And you would be Mrs. Powell?"

She slid Mr. and Mrs. Wilkins a glance and noticed that Mr. Wilkins wore stiff black clothing and a white parson's collar. She gathered what was left of her wits and said, swallowing hard, "Yes, I am Mrs. Powell, and my husband is very sick. He needs help. Please."

The wagon master pondered the situation, then came to a decision. He swung off his horse, reached for Powell's body, which slithered from the stallion and crumpled on the ground. After helping Sarah down, the wagon master knelt beside Powell's body and raised one of his eyelids.

Apparently satisfied by this glimpse of blue, he looked up at Reverend Wilkins and said, "Help me make a place for this man in the back of your wagon. I ain't saying this adds up to the reports I heard, but now's not the time to be jawing when a white man is burning with fever. When we've fixed the surveyor in your wagon, I'll tie this here horse to the last wagon." He eyed Lucky appreciatively. "Fine animal, mighty fine, but blown to bits! You rode him hard, Mrs. Powell, and here you was coming at us from the east." He shook his head. "Don't make a durned bit of sense!"

The wagon plowed and pitched a slow path across the pockmarked prairie, but Sarah was grateful to be sheltered from the sun, grateful to be cradling Powell in her arms, grateful to have a supply of fresh water at her disposal. She was tired, but not so tired that she would consider stopping, even for a minute, bathing Powell's forehead, shoulders, chest, arms, hands. Over and over. Cooling his burning skin. Giving him comfort.

Bathing, stroking, cooling. She wanted to believe that their lot in life had improved, but she couldn't quite convince herself of it. Sure, they were heading west, but at such a pace that they'd never catch up with her family—not that she even knew in which direction they had fled or if they were still alive—and she hadn't realized until now, with Powell's life in perhaps graver danger than it had been all week, which was saying a lot, how much she had linked her happy reunion to her family with Powell's ability to return her to them. Then, too, she couldn't quite shake the uncomfortable feeling that Mr. and Mrs. Wilkins still disapproved of her, even though their initial impression of her as a blond-haired heathen had been corrected.

In their eyes she was a respectable woman married to an equally respectable government surveyor. So why did she continue to feel so disreputable bumping along in the back of the Wilkinses' wagon, holding Powell in her arms? Was it because she had told Reverend Wilkins and his wife a lie? No. Her lie had been justified, and she was sure that if she and Powell had been separated, no one would have given him the kind of care she was giving him. Bathing, stroking, cooling.

If only his skin did not look so wan beneath his tan. If only his body was not so limp and lifeless. If only his soaring fever would break.

The pain came from the inside, not the outside. That much he knew, but not much more. The pain felt weird, warped. Elongated. As if it were taffy. As if it were being pulled and pulled. As if it were stretching to fill the space. What space? Stretching to fill the universe.

Yes, the universe. Universal pain. Complete. Utter. Nestled in every pore. Threaded through every muscle. Settled in every joint, every separate vertebra, every crook of fingers and toes. Screaming through blood. Screaming toward death.

Why didn't he die? Why wasn't he able—no, then why wasn't he *allowed*—to die, to travel to that wonderful place beyond the body, beyond pain? He was being kept alive by some cruel being. His pain elongated and twisted inside out. It wasn't that he was being kept alive, it was rather that he was being brought to life. Yes, he was being brought to painful life by some cruel being.

This was his birth. The cruel being was his mother. His black-haired, beautiful witch of a mother. Who made her living off men's desires. Who was connected, one way or another, to every powerful man in Washington, D.C. Who had conceived him, then abandoned him. Who had sent money over the years, here and there, to support him. Who had bought his way into West Point. Or had her economic exchange been more direct? It would have been less effort, and amounted to the same thing anyway, to have simply traded her sexual favors for whatever it was she wanted on his behalf.

Washington, D.C. Of all the wanton women in the capital—and he knew the married portion of them—his mother was surely the most notorious. Not that anyone had ever mentioned her name to him. And not that he had ever even seen her. But hovering just beneath the surface of his consciousness, he had always known, somehow, the significance of the pretty brick house on the shady, sedate street in Georgetown. He had always known the men who frequented it, and it was often the very officers and senators whose wives he was comforting. He had guessed she was the magnificent madam who ran that lively, well-frequented house, and he had guessed, as well, that she had known who was comforting her clients' wives. But just how he had been able to make such interesting guesses—and just how he had been able to keep that knowledge hidden from himself—he could not say for sure.

Nor could he say how he had ended up—or, rather, begun again—in his cruel mother's arms. Feeling a pain beyond pain in a body that was fully grown. He cracked his eyes, closed them again, wincing from the shaft of light piercing his pupils. He had glimpsed a wanton witch, but the strange thing was, she wasn't his mother. She wasn't even black-haired.

This woman was blond and beautiful, and she was tending to him. Fragments of memories wisped around his brain that she had tended to him before. Had slept beside him in a luxurious bed. Had beckoned to him, tempted him with her arms. Had possibly caressed him. Possibly not. Was she tending him? Or seducing him? His thoughts were darting off in crazy directions, like kernels of corn yielding to the pressure of extreme heat, popping off all at once like a fountain. He couldn't quite get these crazy thoughts to settle down and behave.

Who was this woman? And why did he think that she was trying to kill him? Or was she trying to save him? Seduce and kill? Tend and save? His conceptual horizon tilted this way and that. At such nauseating angles that the terms jumbled up, fell all over one another, turned upside down. He couldn't map a thing. He tried again. Tend and kill? Seduce and save?

Who knew? Who cared?

These were tricky questions. Sticklers. Too much for his tired brain.

Well, as long as he was in her arms, let the woman do what she wanted with him. He'd know what to do in return. What he always did, in fact. For lonely, wanton women.

His spine tingled. So did the skin at his nape. Warning him that it would be fatal to let her do what she wanted with him. But why? Did it have something to do with a magic potion? Or was it poison? Was she more dangerous than other women he had known and desired? Was she an evil temptress who would lead him astray and rob him of his dreams?

Now the woman had split into two. One part of her was soothing his brow, the other part his feet. His poor, maltreated feet. Lacerated, then healed. Lacerated again, then healed again. How good this felt, this soothing of his feet and ankles and calves and knees. How horrible this felt, this rough stroking. As if the solid mass of pain had fractured into a million particles transformed to metal bits that were ripping through his body from the top of his head to the tips of his feet, like iron shavings to a magnet.

He continued to feel the presence of this double woman. She was both Eve and Mary. The good angel and the bad angel. But which was which? Which part would save him? Which part would seduce him? The one that soothed his brow? Or the one that stroked his feet? Did it matter?

If it didn't matter, he might as well die on the spot.

If it did matter, he was still willing to live.

The pain was tearing through him. The metal bits, already red-hot, turned white-hot. He had endured much in the past week. Searing sun. Sioux sticks. Sexual frustration. But these sharp metal bits set loose in his body were surely the worst. Death would be a liberation.

These past few days had been especially bad, but what about his life from before? Was there anything in it that would inspire him to continue living through this pain and beyond? No answer came to him. His thoughts had nowhere to go, nowhere to call home. He had a few friends—he was capable of friendship—but no family. No love. No reason to live.

On and on and on into darkest night. Ripples of pain, waves of pain, oceans of pain. And then some more.

So, let go. Let go of the rope of life.

Or was it a boot strap? What was it about boot straps? He strained to remember that he was supposed to pull himself up by them. That's right. Maybe he wasn't supposed to let go of the rope that kept him tethered to earth. Maybe he was supposed to pull himself up by his bootstraps, up from the hell that was consuming him, fiery flames and all.

No reason to live. But no reason to die, either. Not yet.

Not before he could attain his delirium—no, not his delirium. His dream. Yes, his dream of marrying a quiet gray sparrow who would bear him five children, who would make his nest near the fields where he would plant his rows of maps. No, he didn't want to die before he could attain his dream.

Something in him rose up to say, "Yes, it matters." Then, again, more forcefully, "Yes."

He opened his eyes. Looked down at his poor feet.

Immediately the beautiful woman's face appeared above him. Her features were drawn and anxious, but as he focused on her, he could see her expression shift to one of question, then acquire a faint cast of hope. Her shapely, half-naked form hovered over him, tantalizing him with flesh and the promise of pleasure after pain. Her blond hair clouded around her shoulders, fell to graze his chest.

She was familiar to him, stirred memories of desire and death. He searched for her name and came up with Miss Magic. But, no, that was a recent name and he had known her longer than that. At least from the time of his first miraculous escape, when a seductive vision had shimmered before him and drawn him into a tiny glade with water, shade and her.

He broke out in a healthy sweat. With a slight turn of humor, he realized that he was still alive and back where he had started with the beautiful idiot.

When she surfaced to consciousness to find herself swimming in a pool of lamplight, Sarah realized that she had dozed off to the glow of firelight outside the wagon, the smell of frying bacon and burnt coffee and the wistful melodies of a harmonica. She was glad to have awakened so that she could resume her task of nursing. She plopped her hand into the basin of water at her side and automatically fished for the cloth.

Before she could continue, an arm reached out to stop her, and a woman's brittle voice whispered, "I'll spell you for a while."

Sarah looked up, adjusted herself to her surroundings. "Thank you, Mrs. Wilkins," she managed to say, "but I don't want to stop."

Mrs. Wilkins hung her lamp from a hook that dangled from the center rib of the canvas roof. The interior came to mellow life to reveal ordered series of pots, pans, buckets, trunks, yokes, chains, kegs of flour and salt, bags of bacon, beans and rice. There was even a stove and a chest of drawers with a matching claw-footed table, which might have to be abandoned later in the journey to lighten the load.

The preacher's wife held up an extra cloth. "I thought you might not want to stop," she said, settling herself on her knees at Powell's side across from Sarah, "so I brought this, just in case. Unfortunately, I've already brought you all the water we can spare."

Sarah nodded, put her hand on Powell's forehead. It sizzled.

"No change?" Mrs. Wilkins asked.

Sarah shook her head. "Not yet." She sloshed the basin closer to Mrs. Wilkins and began to crawl to another position. "If you please, could you work on his head and neck? I'll do his feet. My mother always told me that a fever leaves the body through the feet."

Sarah crossed her legs, picked up Powell's feet, put them in her lap. She reached for the cloth in the basin, wrung it out and began to bathe Powell's ankles and soles. With the smacking lips of the cloth, she kissed each toe in turn, drawing the wet over them, caressing the tips, beckoning the fever with her cloth. Then she smoothed the cloth over his soles, pausing at the arch, concentrating on those tender hollows, beckoning some more. She dampened her cloth again, wrapped it first around one ankle, then the other, skimmed it over his calves and shins, around his knees.

She moved her whole body into the effort so that his feet pressed against her hips, her stomach, her breasts, her arms. She moved like a carpenter bent over her work, plane in hand, shaving the rough spots off a board. She moved like the waves sculpting the sands on a beach. Flowing, ebbing, ebbing, flowing. Back and forth. Soft, soothing wetness against fevered skin.

Mrs. Wilkins did not immediately begin her ministrations. Sarah noticed that the preacher's wife spent a furtive half minute contemplating the body of the strange man who was stretched out on a mattress in the back of her wagon and whose nakedness was hidden only by the sheet that covered him from the waist down. As Sarah ventured her cloth up the backs of his thighs, more of his naked body beneath the sheet was exposed. Sarah didn't care and figured the preacher's wife could look her fill.

Although Powell lay unnaturally still, the lamplight glowed over the muscles of his shoulders and brought his strength into high relief. The light spilled over onto the muscles of his neck and down his upper arms, which cast shadows that curved like finely crafted twists of wrought iron. The sheet meringued around his hips and thighs, peaked at the knobs of his hipbones, spanned the provocative space between them.

His legs, knee to ankle, were well-defined in the light, lifted and extended through the sequences of Sarah's care. They melted into the recesses of her body where his feet touched her, so that in the gliding shadow play writ large across the inside of the covered wagon's canvas, it was impossible to say where his body ended and hers started.

Moving like a carpenter, moving like an ocean, Sarah was aware that she became the focus of Mrs. Wilkins' fleeting attention for the next half minute. She was almost naked herself, clad only in her thin chemise and pantalets. Again, she didn't care and figured the bony-bodied preacher's wife could look her fill. Sarah hardly desired the role of fleshly spectacle for Mrs. Wilkins, but she was not about to put that damp dress back on.

When Powell had been laid out in the back of the wagon and she had been left to tend to him, she had stripped him and covered him with a sheet. Then she had untied her woven belt, peeled off her dress and spread it to dry with his breeches over the top of the table. She had placed their moccasins on the floor next to the two knives and her bonnet, from which she had unpacked the comb and brush and razor and reticule. She had guessed their clothing would be dry by morning—if Powell was to live so long.

In the meantime, she was not going to try to hide herself from Mrs. Wilkins' disapproving eyes. She needed her arms to bathe Powell's body and not to fiddle with the gaping neckline of her chemise, whose drawstring had become undone.

Finished with her critical scrutiny, Mrs. Wilkins took her cloth, let it dissolve in the water, then placed it on Powell's forehead. She stroked the unconscious man's temples, wiped the drops that slid down over his ears, his neck. She was not wearing a night rail but rather a dark, high-necked day dress. She moved as stiffly as the cut of the clothing she was wearing.

After a few minutes of silence, Mrs. Wilkins said, "I couldn't sleep. Mr. Rogers—the wagon master, you know—gave us the use of his tent, while he slept under the stars." She plucked her cloth from the water. "Mr. Wilkins snores. Quite loudly, I'm afraid." She shrugged in acceptance of this routine disturbance. "At least tonight I had something to do with myself. I mean," she amended hastily, "that it was a blessing to be awake so that I could have this opportunity to be useful."

"Very useful," Sarah replied, concentrating on Powell's feet, toe by toe, drawing the fever to her.

"Sometimes when I'm awake at night, I don't always know how best to spend my time, and I have to choose between knitting caps for the poor and reading my devotions. But tonight, well, I knew just what God wanted me to do."

Sarah was amazed. "You knew that God wanted you to do this?"

The preacher's wife's gaze met Sarah's. "It's part of God's plan that I help alleviate the suffering of others where I can. It's part of God's plan that you have come to us so that I can help Mr. Powell recover. Yes, Mrs. Powell, my part in God's plan is to help others." She paused in pious reflection. "And to seek truth, of course."

"If God's plan is to help," Sarah replied, "then I'm glad he's finally thrown a little our way."

"You've had a difficult time of it, Mrs. Powell?"

"To say the least."

"Then your unusual difficulties might account for the discrepancies in the reports."

Sarah looked up in question. She felt an unmistakable charge in the air that was separate from the mounting of Powell's fever and his twitching. Sarah didn't let her strength flag, didn't let her composure dissolve under the continuing disapproval she felt from Mrs. Wilkins, who had once again become suspicious.

The preacher's wife continued, "Yes, the reports. The wagon master, Mr. Rogers, often scouts the territory ahead and exchanges information with any trappers or traders he might encounter. Well! Only day before yesterday he heard that a man was missing from a team of government surveyors."

Sarah took this news in stride. So, Powell was with a team of surveyors. He should have told her as much. "The missing man would be Mr. Powell, of course."

"Would it?" Mrs. Wilkins countered. "The report of the missing man did not include information that he was traveling with his wife."

This gentle ambush made Sarah realize how tired and vulnerable she was, but she wasn't a famous British general's daughter for nothing. Summoning strength from what she imagined to be the steel of her dead father's character, she said calmly, "As you know, Mrs. Wilkins, we womenfolk are not considered to be as important as the menfolk and are often simply ignored."

"However, your presence would have been especially noteworthy in the reports, would it have not, given that it is unusual for a wife to accompany her husband on such a mission?"

"Yes, certainly," Sarah replied, resigned to the fact that one lie led to another. "But we were newlyweds when Mr. Powell's assignment came up, and he demanded that I come with him."

"Have you been married long, Mrs. Powell?"

Sarah laughed low and answered honestly, "It seems like forever, because I can hardly remember what it was like before we were together." While she cooled his blazing skin, she indulged herself. "My husband is very attached to me, you see, and wouldn't hear of me staying behind when his assignment came up. Why, he is so devoted that he doesn't even *look* at other women!'' She favored Mrs. Wilkins with a superior, feminine smile. "He is a most faithful and loving husband. Aren't I fortunate?"

With her own version of superiority, Mrs. Wilkins replied, "In truth, I don't know whether you are fortunate or not, and in order to perform God's work, one must adhere to the truth at all times. At the moment I am concerned only that the report Mr. Rogers heard does not coincide with the story you have told.''

Sarah wondered whether the preacher's wife was as righteous as she seemed or whether she just didn't like Sarah's unbound hair and uncorseted curves. "Do you think that I am not telling the truth?''

Mrs. Wilkins primmed her prunish mouth. "Again, I do not know. I know only that there are discrepancies between your story and the one Mr. Rogers heard.''

At that moment, Powell's agitation increased too much to allow further conversation. Sarah continued to bathe his feet and willed him to keep up the fight to remain on this earth, but she saw him losing it. Feeling despair, she said dully, "I'm not sure the discrepancies in the stories matter anymore.'' She bit her lip to hold back a sob. "It just doesn't matter.''

At that moment Powell's body shuddered with a great spasm, then he lay completely still. For the flash of a horrible second, Sarah thought he had died. The next moment his voice came weakly, but clearly, "Yes, it matters.''

"Can you hear me?'' Sarah asked quickly, moving over him, feeling her dying hope rekindle. "It does matter? It *does*?''

With strength, he repeated, "Yes.''

Then he opened his eyes.

Chapter Twelve

Sarah peered anxiously into Powell's face. She held her breath as he struggled to focus on her. When a glimmer of recognition registered in his expression, relief drizzled through her. Her satisfaction in having helped him defy his brutal exposure to the elements was quickly masked by an anxiety to avoid brutal exposure herself—not to the harsh elements, of course, but to the equally harsh realities of even this modest return to white society.

This was not the moment to lose her nerve. She smiled down at him lovingly. "No, Wesley darling, you're not dreaming, and you're not dead. You're still on earth with me, your own true Sarah."

These soft words, sweetly spoken, certainly captured his wavering attention. His eyes fixed on her.

"Yes, you've just made it through a very difficult time," she continued, "and recovered from a worrisome fever, my darling! Do you remember falling ill after we fled from the Mandan village?"

He considered this information. Considered her, too, for a moment, before mumbling, "But not...exactly back... where I...started...it seems."

She thought it wise to humor this nonsense. "No, not exactly back where you started."

He had broken out in a good, healthy sweat, so she reached across him to the basin of water that was next to Mrs. Wilkins. As she leaned over him, her thinly clad breasts pressed against his bare chest. She dipped her cloth in the basin, let it fill with water, then wrung it out. She straightened, sat back on her heels and began to wipe his forehead.

"We are now in the care of the Reverend and Mrs. Wilkins," she told him, "and they have kindly lent us the use of their wagon." She directed Powell's attention to the woman opposite her on his other side. "My darling, I would like to introduce you to Mrs. Wilkins."

Powell shifted his glance to the preacher's wife. He nodded in acknowledgement and articulated something that resembled "Much...obliged, ma'am."

Mrs. Wilkins replied austerely but correctly, "It has been our Christian duty to give what aid is within our power to you and your wife."

At that, Powell's eyes swerved back to Sarah, alive with question and the word *wife*. She chose that moment to wipe her cloth over the rest of his face, making sure to muzzle his mouth. With great complacency, she said, "Yes, Mrs. Wilkins has been wonderfully scrupulous in fulfilling her Christian duty by helping me tend you." She let her hand fall to his shoulder and squeezed it in warning.

He seemed to have received the essential part of her message. He rasped out, "Have I...been...delirious?"

She didn't think the dryness of his tone was due entirely to the dryness in his throat. "At times you were transported by your fever," she replied in soothing tones. "But

I myself never succumbed to any delirium, or did anything you would not have approved of, I assure you!''

He arched a skeptical brow, then croaked, ''Water.''

''My darling,'' she said, ''water is in short supply on the wagon train, and we've had to use so much to keep your skin cooled. All that we can spare right now is in the basin, and it is no longer fresh.''

Blue glints flashed. He obviously understood her objection for what it was, namely an attempt to keep it difficult for him to speak. When the blue glints became fierce, she decided not to press her luck.

''However, since only you have used this water,'' she conceded, ''I'm guessing that a few drops of it can't hurt you and may well help you, even if it isn't fresh.''

She leaned over him again to reach the basin. This time the contact of her breasts against his chest caused heat to scurry up her front and down her back. The charge that leapt up from his blood and muscle took her off guard. She was suddenly aware that tending a naked man who was unconscious was a very different matter from tending one who was conscious.

A new feeling curled around inside her when she put one arm behind his neck to lift it. She wet his lips with the sopping cloth and squeezed a good gulp of water into his mouth. When she laid his head back down, she decided that she had better stay in control of the situation.

She put her fingertips to his lips and said solicitously, ''Please don't spend your energies trying to speak, my darling. You need only nod your head to answer whether you would like more water to drink.''

He grasped her fingers in his. ''Your concern does you credit, dear wife,'' he said evenly, ''but it is, perhaps, misplaced.'' He released her hand and hitched himself up on his elbow. "You see, my love, that I'm feeling stronger with every passing second."

Her reply was a demure "You mustn't overdo, my darling."

"Since my recovery should be in proportion to my illness," he said, "I'll have a better idea of my limits if you tell me how long I was helpless with fever."

"A little more than twenty-four hours, my darling. By the time I met up with this wagon train early yesterday morning, you had already fallen unconscious. You were put straight into the wagon, whereupon Mrs. Wilkins fetched me water several times during the day, then came to help me bathe you in the small hours of this past night."

He shifted himself toward the preacher's wife. "And your husband is the Reverend Wilkins, ma'am? Do I have reason to thank him for any particular service rendered?"

Which was, Sarah guessed, his way of asking whether the preacher had performed a marriage ceremony in a moment when Powell might have been lucid enough to act the role of bridegroom. Absurd man! As if she truly wanted to marry him and had taken advantage of his weakness to do so! As if, in parading as his wife, she wished to fashion for herself anything more than a shield of respectability!

Mrs. Wilkins told him how Mr. Wilkins, along with the wagon master, had helped him into the wagon and how Mrs. Powell had declined further help after that. "Certain days on a wagon train can be extraordinarily busy," she continued, "and yesterday was one of them. So it was just as well that your wife is such an efficient nurse, because it would have been difficult for us to spare another pair of hands." She folded her lips primly, then opened them again to add, "Not that we wouldn't have found a way to help you, sir, if your wife had been unable to carry through.''

Powell nodded politely, then eased himself back down. He murmured, ''Her strength of character and her fine nursing abilities were the qualities that first drew me to her, of course.'' He slanted Sarah a sly glance before closing his eyes. ''You are quite right, my love, that I should take care not to overdo.'' He sighed wearily. ''I'll take more of that water now.''

So he wanted her to lean across him again, did he? Well, she wasn't going to play games with her imaginary husband, so she asked Mrs. Wilkins to please pass her the basin of water to have it at her side anytime her dear husband should like a drink. Mrs. Wilkins obliged her. Her dear husband did not, for he opened his eyes again and gave her a look of exaggerated exhaustion. In the ever increasing light of day seeping through the canvas, she could see from his expression that, even after all he had been through, he could not have been as weak as he was making himself out to be.

Under Mrs. Wilkins' critical gaze, Sarah was obliged to put her arm under his neck again in order to administer the squeeze of water from the dripping cloth. When she slipped her arm under him, she felt the heaviness of sensual suggestion more than she felt the weight of his head.

He swallowed the water with a soft ''Ah!'' and said, ''Yes, Mrs. Wilkins, you're right about my wife's fine nursing abilities. Her loving concern for others was what drew me to her all those years ago.''

''All those years ago?'' Mrs. Wilkins repeated skeptically. ''Mrs. Powell indicated that you are newlyweds.''

Sarah lay Powell's head back down, figuring that he could get himself out of whatever he had just gotten himself into.

"For years I admired Miss Sarah from afar," he told Mrs. Wilkins, "before I gathered my courage to approach her and court her."

Surprised and interested, Mrs. Wilkins asked, "Are you from Baltimore, too, Mr. Powell?"

He rolled his head to smile dreamily at Sarah, then rolled it back to look at Mrs. Wilkins. "Where are you from, ma'am?"

"Ohio."

"Fine country," he commented. Apparently satisfied that Mrs. Wilkins came from a place conveniently far away, he answered that, yes, he was from Baltimore, then launched into his story. "My wife—" here his tone swelled with pride and importance "—is from the Harris family of Baltimore. The Powells are a far less illustrious family, and thus I was persuaded that I could admire her only from afar."

"Oh," Mrs. Wilkins said, as if impressed, which she was supposed to be. Even more surprised and interested now, she asked, "And what exactly was the nature of your wife's loving concern for others that drew you to her?"

He sighed again, this time in fond memory. "Miss Sarah was in charge of the charitable works at the local hospital. Some years ago I had occasion to visit a sick friend of mine there, and I was immediately attracted to Miss Sarah's competence, her strength of character, her deep caring for others." He regarded Mrs. Wilkins soulfully. "In my eyes at least, her personal, *inner* qualities shone through any, uh, imperfections of her physical self." He turned to Sarah and said, "Not to say that I have not also learned to love your outer self, as well, my dear, since we've been married."

Mrs. Wilkins ran a sharp eye over the all-too-obvious

attractions of Sarah's disheveled voluptuousness and frowned, as if unsure what to make of that last comment.

Sarah knew just what to make of it. She laid a cool hand on Powell's warm brow and said, "I'm worried that a touch of your fever is returning, my darling."

He grasped her fingers, brought them to his lips to pay them tribute, then wrapped her hand in his and laid it on his chest. "No, my love, my sanity is fully restored. I can remember, when I first met you, how I was struck by your becoming modesty. How I was forcibly impressed by your wish to avoid praise for your compassion. How I admired your refusal to be sought after for your family's fortune."

Sarah withdrew her hand from his and chided, "My darling, you are giving Mrs. Wilkins a very odd impression of me."

Powell smiled at Mrs. Wilkins. "You see, ma'am?" he said, as if no better proof of his praise could be found than his wife's resistance to it. "I cannot fail to add that Miss Sarah, as an unmarried woman, did not resort to the usual feminine vanities of dress and coiffure, especially since a little more attention to her personal appearance might have caught the eye of some of the finest Baltimore dandies."

"You are too kind, my darling!" Sarah said in failing accents. "Surely you are finished with this catalog of my virtues!"

He wasn't. "I am convinced that you did nothing to enhance your quiet charms, in the hope that a man such as I would come along and see directly into your soul without being distracted by artificial embellishments designed to attract men of superficial sensibilities."

In the glow of this sweet sunshine, Mrs. Wilkins was thawing. When she looked at Sarah, her lips relaxed into a slight upward movement, and her expression conveyed a kind of ingratiating acknowledgment of the status of the Harris family of Baltimore.

Sarah was doubly disgusted, first by the absurdity of Powell's ridiculous story, then again by her feeling of reluctant gratitude toward him to have won her Mrs. Wilkins' respect. It was certainly a novel experience to be regarded as a virtuous young lady whose birth and comportment were above reproach. She had to admit that it felt rather grand!

Powell was smiling serenely, evidently lost in the pleasurable web of his pretty fabrications. "Miss Sarah's father was, at first, very disapproving of my suit, but over time I convinced him that my love was steadfast and true. Then, too, I think Mr. Harris was a little relieved to get his daughter off the shelf and off his hands—" he winked at Mrs. Wilkins "—given Miss Sarah's modest desire to go unnoticed by frippery men of fashion."

This mild joke drew a look of surprise from Mrs. Wilkins and a soft punch to the shoulder from Sarah. "My father," Sarah said, "thought I had run mad to have responded to your attentions, and he figured that marrying me off to you would cost him less than maintaining me in an institution for the insane."

Mrs. Wilkins apparently knew nothing of teasing, for her severe expression returned. "Surely, Mr. Powell, your father-in-law was persuaded that your position as a government surveyor was respectable and important."

"Yes, Mrs. Wilkins," Powell replied, matching the preacher's wife's serious tones, "you are quite right. Mr. Harris was—I hesitate to flatter myself—impressed with my government work. However, he was less pleased that Miss Sarah demanded that she come with me into the wilds on my latest and most important surveying mission." He paused. "However, you perceive how right she was to have insisted that she accompany me and how well she has put her nursing skills to good use.''

Frowning, Mrs. Wilkins said, ''Mrs. Powell told me she accompanied you because you couldn't bear to be parted from her. So she said just before you regained consciousness.''

Powell reversed himself easily. ''Yes, of course, it was I who insisted on her presence—selfish wretch that I am—but in the end it doesn't matter one way or the—''

''Speaking of what does and does not matter,'' Mrs. Wilkins interposed, ''just as you were regaining consciousness, you said, very clearly, 'It matters.' Your wife and I had been speaking of the report the wagon master heard that a government surveyor had gone missing, and you seemed to understand what we were saying.''

Powell paused a moment before saying, ''I'm glad to hear that my team noticed my absence.''

Mrs. Wilkins did not favor nonsense. ''Of course they noticed your absence, Mr. Powell. What they did not notice was the absence of your wife. There was no mention of her.''

Sarah's stomach turned sick the way it had when she had had to return to the ballroom from the garden after the duke had spread those wicked lies about her. She held her breath, foreseeing yet another ruin—much less magnificent, of course, but hurtful all the same.

Fortunately Powell had recovered all his wits, if not yet all his strength. Without a blink he said, ''From the very beginning, it was agreed that we—the team, that is—wouldn't advertise the fact that I was traveling with my wife.'' He propped himself up on both elbows. ''For all the dangers I have exposed her to, the only one I could prevent was the news that might spread from trader to trapper that a woman was part of our team.''

Mrs. Wilkins, seeker of truth, was determined to pursue the matter. "How many men make up the team, Mr. Powell?"

"Four, including myself."

"Shouldn't four men have been protection enough for Mrs. Powell?"

Powell's smile was apologetic and effective. He took Sarah's hand in his and patted it affectionately. "Our idea was that if her presence was unknown, we wouldn't have to be on constant guard for her safety. Of course, we didn't tell her that such was our plan, since we didn't want to worry her unduly!"

"The report of your disappearance came with the news that you had been captured by the Sioux. Your wife has told us, however, that you were among the Mandan."

To this Powell said, "I doubt we'd still be alive if we had been captured by the Sioux."

Just then a ruddy head poked itself through the canvas flaps at the back of the wagon and said, "'Morning to you, Mrs. Wilkins, Mrs. Powell, and to you, too, man! Glad to see you're once again among the living! I'm Hiram Rogers, the master of this wagon train. What's this about the Sioux?"

"We were just speaking of the report you heard," Powell said, looking down his length and through his feet at the wagon master, "and I was saying that it was fortunate for us that we weren't captured by the Sioux. Otherwise…"

Rogers was still trying to put two and two together. "Do you know if there is more than one surveying team in these parts right now, Mr. Powell?"

Powell said his team was the only one, and when he repeated the explanation he had given Mrs. Wilkins about why Sarah's presence hadn't been mentioned, Rogers seemed satisfied.

However, the wagon master was more concerned to get the Indian part of the story straight, and so he wondered how Powell's team could have so inaccurately identified the Sioux as his captors when it had really been the Mandan. "Them trappers who told me the story—Injuns come down from Canada, they are—swore up and down it were the Sioux!" He frowned heavily. "Stands to reason, too, since this surveying team was camped a good hundred miles and more to the *west* of here as recently as last week."

"Which is exactly why my fellow surveyors didn't guess that the Mandan had moved so far into enemy territory," Powell acknowledged mildly. "Where did you encounter the trappers?"

"Between Windlass Hill and Ash Hollow, day afore yesterday it was, and they had encountered the surveyors the day afore that, traveling east."

"Then we just might run into Grant and Lewis and O'Donnell in the next day or two," Powell remarked.

Rogers's expression cleared instantly. "Yup. Them's the names of the surveyors what the trappers said. Grant and Lewis and O'Donnell, and I'll be durned if the name of the missing surveyor weren't Powell!" The eye he turned on Powell was much friendlier than before. "And I'll be durned if them reports weren't just as unreliable about broken-down wagons ahead of us that were said to have been attacked by the Sioux."

Powell was still holding Sarah's hand. At this last bit of news he gripped it hard to keep her from betraying herself. He asked with proper interest, "Broken-down wagons ahead?"

"Four of 'em, so the trappers said!" Rogers replied.

"Not on the trail, though. Off in the hollows beyond the Platte. Very curious."

"Were there any dead?"

Rogers shrugged. "No doubt, but them trappers were too smart to go and investigate. Didn't want to risk a Sioux ambush, so they kept their distance." The red head vanished abruptly behind the back flaps, then reappeared just as suddenly. "And now the sun is where I like to see it when I give the command to move on for the day. Well, I've less to fear from the Mandan, 'specially this far west, and it's a relief to think them Sioux ain't on the warpath."

Very deliberately Powell said, "Still, it's best to keep an eye out, just in case. Better safe..."

Rogers winked broadly. "And so that we won't be sorry, I'll keep my sharp eye out, yessiree!" At that, Rogers turned and bellowed a "Heave ho!" then disappeared for good.

The next moment, the sound of clambering could be heard at the front of the wagon, followed by the weight of a man settling on the buckboard. Then the Reverend Wilkins ducked his head into the wagon, greeted everyone with decorum and informed his wife that the last of the fried bread was going fast and suggested she get some while the getting was good, for herself and their guests.

Mrs. Wilkins obediently moved to the front of the wagon and made her way out the front flaps, but not before she excused herself very properly from her guests, whom she now perceived as most worthy of her help and consideration in God's plan.

When they were alone, Powell shifted on one elbow to face Sarah. He was still holding her hand but didn't seem to realize it, for when she pulled at it, he released it.

Although he was looking at her, he was murmuring more to himself when he said, "Now, it seems we recovered some of the distance we lost...let me see...four days ago already, because we angled far enough north to have met the Elkhorn, I'm guessing, at about the ninety-ninth...more or less...and now it seems we've cut the triangle, because the pioneer trail angled north after the Platte crossing and we're not far from Windlass Hill, which is lucky...." He stopped and asked, "We still do have Lucky, don't we?"

Sarah informed him that the stallion was tied to a long rope at the end of the wagon train.

Powell nodded and continued to calculate under his breath before he stopped again and asked, "Are you able to calculate land covered on horseback? A rough speed-and-distance ratio of some kind?"

Sarah didn't answer that absurd question. Instead she had a much more pressing one to ask, whose immediacy overrode her fears concerning the news of four broken-down wagons ahead. Glancing nervously at the front flaps of the wagon, she whispered, "Are you married, Mr. Powell?"

"Mar—"

She put a hand to his mouth and leaned down to his ear. "Yes, I asked you if you were married."

The look he shot her told her exactly what he thought of this turn in conversation.

She released his mouth and shot back, keeping her voice low, "The question is not as...as idiotic as you seem to think, sir! First I learn that you were part of a *team* of surveyors, and next I hear an affecting story about your worthy but unattractive wife—yes, *unattractive,* as if I should *care* what she looks like!—and you told the story with such conviction that how should I know that you aren't married?"

"I'm not."

She hardly paused to absorb this information about his marital status because she was too needful of venting the worries that had dammed up inside her in the past days and hours and minutes. She continued swiftly, "In addition to which, I don't even know where you're from. For all *I* know, you might well be from the very undistinguished Powell family of Baltimore!"

"I'm not," he repeated.

"It's something to discover that much about you! Here I was the night long and the day before and—my word!—the night before that carrying you around, practically on my back, not knowing whether you'd live to take your next breath, and then where would I have been? Not to mention, what would I have done with you? Who would I have notified? Remember that I didn't even know you were part of a—"

"If we're going to have this conversation," he cut in irritably, "I'd feel better about it if I was wearing my breeches." He looked pointedly down at the cloth draped across his nether regions. "We seem to have the most annoying discussions when I'm in some disadvantageous state of nakedness." He flicked his fever-bright blue eyes at her. "So, if we're returning to civilization, we may as well do it up right and get dressed."

She was suddenly aware of her own near nakedness with the neckline of her chemise gaping and the cloth completely transparent in the light of day. She was surprised into immobility by a potent, improbable mix of embarrassment and arousal.

"And we might as well have this conversation," he went on, "because I might die yet before it's all over. You, too, for that matter. Now, could you hand me my breeches, if you please? Unless, of course, you want me to get up and get them myself."

She scurried down the length of the wagon on all fours and tossed his now dry buckskins back at him, none too politely. To recover her composure, she said with great dignity, "It's nothing to me whether you want to get up and get them yourself. However, after all I've done to keep you alive, I'm wanting to spare you extra effort until you've fully recovered."

Keeping her back to him, still on her hands and knees, she was testing her dress for dryness when Mrs. Wilkins returned to the front of the wagon and announced, "I've brought your bread, Mr. and Mrs. Powell."

Sarah looked back over her shoulder at the preacher's wife. She saw that Powell hadn't made a move toward putting on his breeches and that his eyes were fixed on her backside.

Chapter Thirteen

Powell had to sit up to catch the breeches she threw at him. The sudden movement caused the blood to drain from his head, and he felt the full force of the weakness in the wake of his fever. As his gaze rested on the back of Sarah's curvaceous hips and thighs, which were covered in the sheerest of cotton pantalets, the blood kept flowing down from his head, down his torso, down, down—

Damn! He wasn't feeling the least bit weak anymore, and if he needed a sign that he was recovered, this was surely it. Not for the first time, either, did he have the experience of shaking off death. Of beginning again. Always with this woman. Going in circles. Starting from point zero—but never quite the same point zero. Which meant that there were as many different forms of beginnings as there were versions of the woman who was swaying pleasingly fleshly hips not far from the tips of his toes. Who was, for the moment, Mrs. Powell.

She was acting just like a wife, too. Taking care of him. Fuming. Fussing.

Well, he was feeling husbandly. Assuming possession.

Figuring his angle of approach. Feeling as grumpy as she was acting.

So they were even.

Sort of.

Then that pinch-faced woman returned before he got his clothes on, and the look his temporary wife cast him over her soft, bared shoulder and through her unkempt curls was going to make it even more difficult for him to pull his breeches on anytime soon. That pinch-faced woman must have reacted to the strong energies darting about the wagon, for she got out of there as quick as she could, mumbling something about being needed elsewhere, and thrust a plate of fried bread next to him.

He had plenty of problems right now, only one of which could be immediately solved by eating. He was hoping that another could be helped if his unwifely wife would just put her clothes on. In a belated attempt at modesty, she had snatched her dress to her breasts when she turned to face him. He looked away from her and busied himself with the plate of food so that she might have time to slip her dress on while his eyes were averted. When her twitchings and little puffs of breath calmed down, he looked back at her, extended her the spattered enamel plate, and decided that, no, one problem was definitely remaining. Seeing her dressed had about the same effect on him right now as seeing her undressed. Seated cross-legged as he was, his only defense was to wad his breeches in his lap over the sheet he had drawn around his waist.

She chose a piece of bread, flipped a tangle of hair over her shoulder like some highfalutin society lady, and sniffed her thanks.

Trouble. Trouble. That's all he had was trouble. She irritated him the most when she was like this. He watched in disgust and fascination as she settled herself next to him, smoothed her skirts and nibbled daintily.

"So," she whispered close to his ear in the false social tones that never failed to grate on his nerves, "it's time for the conversation you and I both agree we should have. Afterward you might consider actually dressing yourself—which was your own very good idea not two minutes ago!—and I shall try to make my hair presentable to the world, although after what I've just been through, I don't imagine it will be easy." Her big brown eyes flashed him a saucy look artfully compounded of derision and seduction. "I might just have to cut it all off yet."

He bit into his bread and wondered if it was laced with magic Mandan water, for he was experiencing the same feelings he had had in the lodge on the morning of their escape when she had walked up to him and gotten right in under his skin.

"You can try and brush it now, if you like," he offered, hoping she'd turn away from him or, better yet, leave the wagon for a while. He had been right to have preferred this conversation with his breeches on.

"No, sir," she said, "I won't be diverted."

He resigned himself. "What is it you want to know?"

"First of all, is your mother still alive?"

"She is."

"Where does she live?"

"In Washington, D.C."

"And your father? Is he still alive?"

"Yes."

"And does he also live in Washington, D.C.?"

"Of course," he said, and smiled inwardly to think that she could make of that what she wanted.

"You see?" she said, satisfied. "That wasn't so very

difficult, was it? Now, what branch of the government do you work for, precisely?''

"The Bureau of Indian Affairs, which is a division of the War Department," he informed her. "So, if you're wishing to report my premature death to the proper authorities, you need only address yourself to the offices on the Mall between the White House and Capitol."

"It would be more proper to address that sad news to your mother.''

His soft laugh was mirthless. "Would it? I'm not sure, but you can get her address from anyone at the War Department. You have only to ask the first man you see how to find Miss Alice." He quirked a smile. "This assumes, of course, that you yourself survive this ordeal, never settle in the Oregon Territory and choose to return to your beloved Baltimore.''

She was unmoved by his irony. "And the full names of your fellow surveyors, in case I need to know?''

"Douglas Grant, Jeremiah Lewis and Sean O'Donnell," he told her, "and you may need to know their names sooner than you think. It's likely they'll encounter us here in the next day or two, unless we move on tonight.''

Her brows rose. "Tonight? You're in no condition to travel tonight.''

"With the stories we've told, we're in no position to remain here beyond tomorrow, unless you wish us to get caught in our bald-faced lies. Figuring imperfectly from what I know about our relative locations, Grant, Lewis and O'Donnell should be meeting up with this wagon train within the next forty-eight hours.''

"Do you think they're still looking for you?''

"Maybe. It's only been a little over a week since I disappeared from camp.''

"Wouldn't they support the story of your being married?"

"They might, but not if Rogers sees them first and mentions that a Mr. and Mrs. Powell are now a part of the wagon train."

This new perspective on their situation succeeded in diverting her attention away from investigation of his life. She contemplated the last bits of bread in her hands for a good long minute before raising liquid brown eyes to him. She asked quietly, "If we leave tonight, can we go first to find the four wagons Mr. Rogers mentioned? I couldn't help but think they might have been a part of my family's wagon train." She gulped. "Where do you think we are in relation to the original attack site?"

"A little farther to the west of the place where we were abducted, which was about twelve miles west of the attack site."

Her eyes beseeched. "Can we go find the wagons, then? I have to see them, you know. Have to see whether—"

"Yes, of course. We'll find the wagons. First thing."

"It's not as if I believe that anything...unfortunate has happened to my family. I'm sure they got away and...and are waiting for me at Windlass Hill, which isn't—" she choked on a sob "—which isn't far away now, is it?"

It was less excruciating responding to her when she was irritating than when she was soft and yielding and in need of comfort. Hearing his own slow, stupid tones, he assured her, "No, it isn't far away now, and I'm sure your mother and father and sisters will be there, waiting for you."

She bestowed on him a rather watery smile of gratitude that perversely underscored the fact that he was lusting after a woman who was worried about the fate of her family and who was far from sharing his erotic turn of mind and body.

When she put a hand on his forearm and offered him a sweet "Thank you," he flinched involuntarily from her touch.

His movement did not prompt her to move away from him but rather to move closer so that she could put the back of her hand to his forehead. At that moment, the wagon wheel hit a rut, and she moved flush against him so that her breasts were flattened against his chest.

She grasped his shoulder to steady herself and said in some alarm, "You're still burning with fever! Lie back down and let me bathe you some more." Fussing again, she tried to push him down. "We won't be going anywhere tonight! Not in your condition, sir. We'll just have to take our chances that your team won't reach us before tomorrow's nightfall. Now, promise me that we'll wait another night and day before we move on."

He resisted her attempt to have him lie back down. "It's true that I need rest," he snapped, "but at the moment, ma'am, I'd rather take that rest alone."

He saw that he had offended her, but before he could make amends, she turned huffy. She dropped her hands from his shoulders, sat back on her heels, then picked up the empty plate. At her prissiest she said, "After the hospitality the Reverend and Mrs. Wilkins have shown us, the least I can do is to clean up after ourselves." She moved toward the back of the wagon, where she picked up her comb and brush and moccasins. Without turning to face him, she said, "And when you're rested, you might be so kind to let me know, so that I might use the wagon to get some sleep myself. I really wouldn't want to disturb you further." Then she hopped out of the slow-moving wagon.

He sat there and considered his new situation. He was tired from his bout with fever, grouchy from the discomforts of his physical condition, and just plain bothered by that woman. He looked around idly, wondering how to distract himself. His eye fell first on his razor, then on the basin of water, and his humor improved to think he would be able to shave himself, at least.

He lay back down, put his hands over the wad of buckskin that still protected his lap, and wondered why he couldn't be drawn to a quiet, obedient, God-fearing woman like Mrs. Wilkins. He soon discovered that prolonged thoughts of that lady's pinched face had one direct benefit. He could slip his breeches on without impediment.

Sarah considered it beneath her dignity to return to the interior of the wagon anytime soon, and she was happy to find a variety of things to do. She should have been dead tired from nursing a man who was *plainly not worth her time and trouble,* but she was not. She felt rather more full of energy. She knew that part of that energy came from her anxiety about learning of four more ill-fated wagons. However, not all of her energy derived from that source, and she was unwilling to examine too deeply where, in fact, the rest of it came from.

She cleaned the plate and returned it to Mrs. Wilkins, who was seated next to her husband on the buckboard. She then went to check up on Lucky, who had been tended to by the wagon master. Walking along beside the last wagon, she combed her hair, and since this took quite a bit of time, she got to know the family traveling in that wagon rather well. They, too, were from Ohio, and they, too, were fired by the conviction that they were fulfilling God's plan by moving west.

For the first time in her adult life, she was walking out under the sun wearing no bonnet. In the past few days the bonnet had been stained and battered beyond repair, and it didn't go with her outfit anyway, so she was just as well without it. She was just as well without her boots, too, for her Mandan moccasins were a delight, and she took pleasure in striding along in them. As for her deerskin dress, it fit and felt like a dream, and she was going to have a hard time returning to European cottons and petticoats.

When she conquered the last of the tangles with her comb, she brushed her hair vigorously, then secured it in two thick braids. She tucked her comb and brush into her leather belt and sauntered along with her braids bobbling over her breasts and the ends of her woven belt flapping against her thighs. The sky was big, bright and blue. The trail rolled easily. The surrounding prairie was dotted with reassuring signs of green. The food at the midday break was decent and plentiful. This was the best she had felt since standing at river's edge, hearing wild war whoops and seeing a man-beast splash through the water heading straight for her.

With her thoughts bumped up against the disagreeable Mr. Powell, she resolved not to think about him, and it didn't count as thinking about him to determine that his uncharacteristic sympathy and understanding of her desire to inspect those four wagons was due to the fact that she had just saved his life. Not for the first time, either, because she'd been saving his life almost since the moment she met him. More times than he had saved hers, if they were to tally up the score, and she really wasn't going to count in his favor the way he had played along with her story of their marriage. Her life hadn't depended on that story, only her reputation—as if a young lady's reputation

had any value whatsoever out here in the middle of nowhere! Besides which, she had claimed him as a husband
primarily to be able to tend to him properly. So there!

She wasn't going to think about him, no she wasn't. As
long as she *wasn't* thinking about him, she decided that
she might as well return to the Wilkinses' wagon and bask
in some of the admiration due her as the respectable Mrs.
Powell, formerly known as Miss Harris of the illustrious
Harris family of Baltimore.

She caught up with the middle wagon and saw Reverend Wilkins handling the reins alone. He informed her
that Mrs. Wilkins was on one of God's errands and invited
her to climb up. When she was seated next to him on the
buckboard, the reverend told her that her husband had
been sleeping like a baby the day long.

"He needs his rest," Sarah said, trying to inject some
warmth into her voice, although she didn't care a jot
whether Mr. Wesley Powell slept a wink or not.

"Surely now, he does," Reverend Wilkins agreed.
"And you, too, ma'am, after all you did for him this past
night."

"Oh, I'll sleep later," she said airily. "It was enough
that I stretched my legs this morning and combed out my
hair."

The reverend looked down at her and remarked, "You
look more like a heathen squaw than a Christian woman,
sure now, Mrs. Powell, except for the color of your hair.
Did the heathens who captured you steal your wedding
rings?"

Since she hadn't come to tell more lies, she said the
first thing that came to mind. "I don't think I care to talk
about it."

"I'm sorry, Mrs. Powell," the reverend replied instantly. "It must have been a painful passage for you, and

one you'd like best to forget. However, God was truly watching over you to have delivered you from the heathens and to have sent you to us. Mr. Powell will survive, and now you will go along better. I've asked Mrs. Wilkins to fetch you a spare dress from among our fellow travelers that might fit you, so that you may change into it as soon as she returns to us.''

This prospect did not cheer Sarah, but she supposed she was to thank her host for the consideration, and so she did.

''Think nothing of it, Mrs. Powell,'' the reverend replied, ''for it's only our Christian duty to help where we can.'' He smiled piously down at her. ''And to seek the truth.''

''Oh, yes,'' she agreed, wondering where the truth lay in the tangle of her relationship to Powell.

''We'll find your husband a shirt and jacket, too, and then you'll be back to your proper selves, with no more embarrassment of indecency between you.''

''Embarrassment of indecency?'' Sarah echoed a little weakly.

Reverend Wilkins chuckled indulgently. ''Mrs. Wilkins told me that when your Mr. Powell came to himself and you were alone, he was speaking—and quite rightly, too—about the clothing he didn't have and that man has needed ever since Adam was banished from Eden for his sins!'' He cast a disapproving glance at her deerskin dress. ''So, naturally, Mrs. Wilkins and I saw our duty to fetch you what you need in the way of clothing. Your husband is a fine man, doing God's work for the government and wanting to dress himself as is proper.''

She preserved a silence, thinking that she hadn't come to hear either the reverend's disapproval or praises of her husband.

"And you are a fine woman, Mrs. Powell, coming as you do from the Harrises of Baltimore! So Mrs. Wilkins told me!"

That was better. Much better.

"Which is why," the reverend said, "we are determined that you be clothed in the decent way to which you are accustomed. Now, I am not faulting you for a moment, Mrs. Powell, for having to wear a heathen dress fashioned of animal skin! However, since it is well-known that women are the weaker sex in every respect, it can only go better for you, and then for your good husband, if you were to find yourself once again dressed in the way fitting for a lady of your birth and upbringing. It is a question of seeing one's way clear on the issues of dress and comportment, even in the least promising circumstances."

Remarkably, during the last part of this improving speech, Sarah did, indeed, see her way clear on several matters.

She raised her eyes to this vigilant moral advisor and smiled soulfully at him in a way that tended to drive men, even very pious ones, to distraction. "You are right, Reverend Wilkins," she said sweetly, "that I should dress in a way fitting to my birth and upbringing." She stifled a yawn and stretched a little. "I believe you are also right that I should rest after all my hard work last night tending to my dear husband. I confess that I am much more tired than I previously admitted!"

The Reverend Wilkins' face, whose jaw had gone slack, might have been expressing surprise that this fine young woman had responded so readily to his thoughts and precepts, but Sarah didn't press him for a verbal response. Instead, she took the opportunity to stretch again and to declare her intention of climbing into the back of the wagon, where she hoped to get much needed rest.

"Yes, yes, my dear! Oh, yes!" the reverend blustered as she disappeared behind the flaps.

Once inside the soft glow of canvas in the afternoon, she discovered her would-be husband perched at the back of the wagon with his back to her and his long legs, which were once again encased in buckskin, hanging outside. He was holding up a mirror and had the basin of water at his side. At her entrance, he turned and lowered his razor, and she saw that he was almost finished shaving. She smiled at him, and he turned back around to continue his task. Perfect!

She knelt in the middle of the wagon where he had lain, positioned herself three-quarters away from him and stretched sinuously. She moaned a few tiny, tired noises for good measure, then began to unplait her hair at her leisure. She slipped her comb and brush from her belt, which she untied and let fall away, then began to brush her hair.

Without looking back at him but knowing that she had his complete attention, she proceeded with great deliberation to lift the hem of her dress and draw it over her knees, her thighs, her hips and up, up over her head. She tossed the deerskin aside thinking that respectability, for all its pleasurable novelty, was really not all that grand, and that the conditions of her particular birth coincided better with *un*dress rather than dress.

When she began to stretch again, Powell's words rumbled softly across the small space. "Just what do you think you are doing?"

She turned to meet his snapping blue eyes and smiled sleepily, languorously. "Getting ready to rest. Why?"

"I thought you meant to wait until I was finished here."

"Oh, am I disturbing you?" When he didn't answer that, she continued guilelessly, "But you're finished, aren't you? I mean, you're dressed—'' She ran her eyes over the muscled planes of his torso turned toward her. "That is, you're more dressed than you usually are, and you've finished shaving. So I didn't think I was disturbing you by wanting my turn to lie down." Her smile was especially warm, even melting. "Did your rest restore you?"

The look he gave her suggested that he had been restored to health but not to serenity.

"Hungry?" she asked next. She relished this teasing, testing, pushing, prodding.

He opened his mouth, glanced beyond her to the flaps at the front of the wagon, then thought the better of what he was going to say. His eyes narrowed, and she had the most scandalous sensation that he had just stripped her naked.

"Yes," he said, "I'm hungry. Very hungry." Then he turned away from her, pushed himself through the back flaps and out of the wagon.

Sarah lay down, savoring the satisfaction to have a man—this man in particular—dangling at the end of her string. She nestled into the sheet, rolled on her side and placed her hands prayerfully under her head. She sighed deeply at the thought that it was lots of fun playing with fire. *And I'm not likely to get burned with Reverend Wilkins seated hardly five feet away!*

Tired as she truly was, she was asleep before she knew it.

She was awakened hours later by the shaking of her shoulder and the tickle of buckskin fringe on her cheek.

A man's voice whispered into her ear, "It's time to move on."

Still cradled in the heavy arms of sleep, she murmured, "Haven't I heard that line somewhere before?"

Her question was answered by a spank on her lightly clad butt and the curt command "Now."

Chapter Fourteen

"You've got one minute to get up and dressed," Powell said, pushing deerskin in her face.

She had a groggy recollection of having had this conversation before. "You can't be serious."

"I'm very serious."

She cracked an eye to utter darkness, closed it again. "What time is it?"

"Around midnight."

"Give me another hour to sleep," she moaned, "and I'll be fine."

"You've got one minute, or I'll leave you to your own idiotic explanations of who you are when Lewis, Grant and O'Donnell happen upon this wagon train tomorrow."

That sure sounded familiar. "We *have* had this conversation before," she said, struggling up on one elbow. "That day in the glade after I had just spent hours running to your commands while you lounged, you decided that it was time to move on. Now here you are again, deciding it's time to go, after I spent the last night nursing you and the night before that riding with you collapsed on my back. Well, I'm not going anywhere, and I'm not doing anything but sleeping."

"Lucky's ready to go, and I'm trying to spare you difficulties by catching up with my team before they catch up with us."

"Oh, well, if it's on my account..." she said drowsily, lying back down until a further thought occurred to her. She sat bolt upright. "You promised we wouldn't travel tonight. You promised you would rest."

"I never promised." He grasped her arm by the elbow. "We have about five hours of darkness ahead of us, and I want to put all of them to good use."

"What is it with you and night travel?" she complained.

"We've had this conversation before, too."

She was on her feet, not by her own volition, and not happy about it. "We can never stay *anywhere* for a decent night's sleep." The enforced slipping of her dress over her head muffled her testy whispers. "We had a truly wonderful bed in the lodge that we ran away from for no reason beyond your ravings about magic water. Now we're in the relative safety of a wagon train, and although our present comforts fall far short of those we enjoyed in the lodge, here we are running off again!"

After her dress fell into place, she was kept silent by the jerk of her woven belt around her waist, the thrust of her packed bonnet into her hands, and the clamp of his hand across her mouth. She was forcibly removed from the wagon, then heaved over his shoulder. In this undignified fashion she was whisked away from the circle of wagons dotted with sleeping tents and transported a good hundred yards through the tall grasses where Lucky was waiting, and on whose back she was tossed.

Powell settled himself behind her on the brute and put his arms around her to grasp the stallion's neck. In a provocative tone not calculated to improve her mood, he said,

"You can vent your spleen now that we're out of ear-shot."

She spluttered as Lucky took off, gobbled some half-finished phrases about ill-mannered ruffians, then settled on the threat, passionately delivered, "If you have left my excellent moccasins behind, you'll be sorry, Mr. Powell!"

"They're in your bonnet, Miss Harris, along with your comb and brush and coin purse."

Since she didn't have to maintain her balance because his arms were guarding her, she untied the strings of her bonnet and found her moccasins. She was torn between happiness at finding them and irritation that she couldn't stay mad at him on that score.

The night sky was a cloudless curve of lapis lazuli adorned by the hard silver disk of the moon and twinkling stars. The air was cool, not cold, and except for her toes, she was warm. Surprisingly warm, in fact. It was then that she realized Powell was wearing both shirt and jacket.

Powell had set Lucky on a leisurely pace, so she was able to turn toward him without losing her seat and to rally him with the words, "What a change it is to see you completely dressed!"

He had been surveying the surrounding landscape over the top of her head, but at that comment he looked down at her. His eyes were as dark and blue as the night sky, and the planes of his face were cut from shadows. His lips curved up, bringing long furrows in his cheeks into high relief in the moonlight. She was amazed to discover that he had dimples.

"Mrs. Wilkins rustled up a shirt and a jacket," he said, "from a widow who had brought along her late husband's clothes in case they might prove useful to someone sometime. It was widely agreed that in God's plan I was that someone." His smile spread. "I'm not complaining."

She ran her eye across the expanse of his shoulders, then turned forward again. "The shirt and jacket seem to fit."

"Too short in the sleeves but long enough to cover my heathen self. Or so the good reverend said when he saw me at dinner this evening. However, he did not approve of my decision to continue wearing my heathen breeches simply because the late husband's trousers didn't fit me."

She laughed, then breathed one wistful word, "Dinner!"

He fumbled a moment in his jacket pocket, then offered her a white cloth. In it were wrapped two pieces of bread, which held beans and a hunk of unidentified meat on which she began to munch. She thanked him with a full mouth.

"Pretty soon we'll have fish to eat," he said, "and that will be a most welcome change."

"You know where we are?"

"The landscape is beginning to look familiar, and it's a wonderful feeling to be mounted again. That is, mounted and conscious, instead of collapsed across your back."

She bit into the bread and beans. "You were in such a worrisome state that I didn't really know if you'd make it. As I've already said, I would have preferred to have taken it easy one more night so that your strength could return."

"I would not have preferred it, and my strength has returned in full measure."

"I'm glad," she said, but the moment she said it, she began to wonder whether she should be so glad.

The bit of food in her stomach freed her attention to attend to other aspects of her survival, and she was aware of being both protected and trapped by the circle of his arms. She recalled having teased him—well, all right, she had *flaunted* herself in front of him this afternoon in the wagon, and she had enjoyed herself immensely. The prick up her spine and the tingle down her arms made her realize that he, too, was recalling that little incident, and now the enjoyment was all on his side.

The present occasion struck her as markedly different from her previous experiences of traveling through the night with him. Perhaps this was because he was no longer at any disadvantage and was riding, well fed and fully clothed, into country he knew well. Perhaps this was because he had carried her bodily off and away from the restraining forces of white society. Or perhaps this was because she knew him well enough now to guess that he was going to tease and test her in return.

She finished her tidy little meal, then dared to ask where they were headed.

"To the hollow where the four wagons were sighted," he answered. "The report the wagon master heard was actually rather precise about the location. When he described it to me this evening as we sat around the campfire, I had a pretty good idea of where it must be."

She was almost happy to have her thoughts diverted from consideration of her own possible predicament to wonder about the fates of the owners of those four wagons, and she focused all her energies on willing her family to life and health.

For most of the night they were crossing dry tableland, where time and motion both seemed to stop. Lucky's steady pace seemed to make no difference. The bowl of dark grass around them and the sky above them were stuck and did not move. Then came a steep hill, the steepest yet, one that would prove a challenge to mules pulling wagons. Since they were not so burdened, Powell led Lucky up the hill without incident, and soon thereafter they were picking their way down the other side. They were moving toward what looked to be, even in the waning moonlight, a beautiful meadow.

At the base of the hill, Powell did not head into the meadow but skirted around it in a northerly direction. He poked Lucky's head into this nook, into that cranny, and when the sky flushed rose and gold in the east, they came upon that-which-they-were-looking-for-but-didn't-want-to-see. The remains of four wagons, of which only two were still covered by their original canvas, were crashed up and against an isolated cluster of ash trees at the very edge of the meadow.

Powell slid off Lucky's back, his face grave, and wordlessly raised his arms to receive Sarah. When her feet were on the ground, she thanked him for his help just as silently and just as gravely. He stood by Lucky while she surveyed the wreckage. The week before at the first scene of destruction, the bodies of the Kellys and Clarks had been sprawled on the ground in plain sight. Here, however, there were no dead bodies, and Sarah supposed that those poor unfortunates were probably lying miles and miles back on the trail. The wagons had gotten this far, no doubt, because the driverless mules had plunged ahead, stampeding in their haphazard pack.

The mules were long gone, either freed from broken yokes when the wagons finally crashed or taken by the Sioux at the end of their wild ride. As before, these wagons had been picked clean of possessions, so it could not be by the contents that Sarah would be able to identify whose wagons they had been.

She eyed each wagon slowly and with detachment as she tried to conjure images of the individual characteristics of the various wagons that had been in her train. One she could discount as having belonged to her family because it had no utility box under the buckboard; another she knew was not hers because it had a sidebox where hers had had none; and a third had been carved with the family name across the back. The fourth...

The fourth gave her no clue to whom it had belonged because it looked like almost any other wagon to be seen, utility box and all. It was one of the two whose canvas covers were still there. She climbed in it, empty though it was, and her heart jumped with a mix of joy and grief to find a pink baby bootee, so sweet and tiny and helpless, caught in one of the corners. This must have been the wagon of the MacDonalds, a young family with a pretty baby girl. She gave herself over to the shudder that wracked her as she imagined that baby's fate.

She picked up the bootee and climbed out of the wagon. She crossed to Powell, holding up the knitted sock, and said, "My luck has held, but I fear hers hasn't."

"You're confident you know who owned these wagons?"

She nodded and tucked the bootee into her belt. "Seven wagons down, only three to go. So far my family's safe." She shook her head and corrected herself. "I mean, so far I don't know that my family is not safe."

"It's the best you could hope for, without actually finding them."

The morning was upon them. The day dawned warm and promised heat. She sighed and asked, "Now what?"

"This is where I wanted to be by now, so what's next is proper care of Lucky. We're almost at the North Platte."

Instead of mounting the beast's back again, Powell put a hand to Lucky's neck and led him back where they had come from. They followed the eastern edge of the meadow heading south, met the North Platte and followed the riverbank until they came to a lovely nest of leafy trees. Those they entered and were immediately surrounded by a corner of Eden. The shade was welcome even this early in the day, and they were drawn deeper into the trees by the refreshing scent of cool water, which suggested a hidden spring.

They found the perfect spot to stop, a generous dish of earth with just the right combination of sun and shade, hard rock and soft sand. One side of the dish sloped down and opened onto a vista of the landscape, while at the same time they were protected from sight by the thicket of trees. The other side of the dish sloped up and over to the spring below, so that the running water could be heard but not seen from the center of the spot, where a natural terrace of stone and boulder formed an ideal theater for a fire.

"I'm taking Lucky to the water," Powell said, looking around with satisfaction, "where I hope to tickle some fish for breakfast."

"Tickle?"

He laughed. "I'm too hungry to bother making a fishing pole at the moment, so I'll just stick my hand in the water and hold it there until a fish nudges up against it and I can grab it. It's not the most refined angling, but it's effective. In the meantime, you can start a fire."

"I?"

He nodded at the bonnet in her hands. "You still have the iron pyrites, don't you? Well then, it's high time you learned the art, since you've wanted to know from the beginning how to make a fire in the event of my death."

She recognized his deliberate provocation for what it was and decided that she wasn't going to take the bait. She preserved a superior silence.

"And there's plenty of firewood around," he said, before turning away and leading Lucky up and over the slope.

She sat down on a serviceable rock in front of the place where she planned to make her fire and opened her battered bonnet, out of which seemed to come all the luxuries of the universe. The comb and brush she put aside in order to dig into her reticule for the precious pyrites. Holding these in her palm, she gathered up her firewood and, after several unsuccessful tries, got a small fire going with just enough time to spare before Powell returned. He was looking very happy with himself and the world. In one hand he was holding a sturdy twig on which two fat fish had been speared. In the other he carried a cupped rock filled with water.

"I'm dying for something other than meat to eat," he commented as he picked a deft path among the rock and slipped inside the circle.

"Jackrabbit and dried buffalo have their limits," she agreed.

He flicked a glance at the fire, but since he did not offer her a compliment on her fine industry, she would not lower herself to ask for his praise. He first gave her the water to drink, then in mute challenge handed her the twig with the fish ready for roasting. She quivered this into the ground, and with her hands free built a little spit from loose rock. He made himself comfortable by taking the two Mandan knives out of his waistband and laying them on the ground, then slipping off his jacket and folding it over a boulder and flipping back the cuffs of his shirtsleeves. He stretched his long legs out in front of him and seemed content to let her prepare the meal, such as it was.

She fiddled with the kindling, fanned the flames here and there, twiddled the stick as the fish cooked.

He leaned back against the boulder, scanned the trees

above. "If I had my hat and boots now, I'd be whole again," he said dreamily. "And my rifle, of course. How I'd love to be holding my rifle in my hands again."

"Better not to think about what we don't have," she reminded him.

He brought his gaze down to focus on her. "It was the feeling that I was coming close to the point where I was ten days ago that gave me the idea I could have it all again." He smiled slightly, but not enough to bring the dimples out. "Taking my own good advice, then, I should say that I'm happy to have this jacket and shirt—" his brows quirked "—which have no rips or rents that need your mending."

This time she wasn't going to let the provocation pass. Not bothering to suppress her huff, she rejoined, "My embroidery just may well have saved our lives, and you well know it."

"How easily you rise to the fly," he mused.

She cocked him a quelling eye and drew her dignity around her. "I will not be drawn further into unwise retort, sir. However, permit me to tell you that if your aim is to annoy me, you are succeeding."

He transferred his attention to gaze through the clearing in the trees, which opened onto a view of an opposing ridge. "Even at my worst," he commented in a lazy voice, "I'm not half as annoying as you, ma'am."

She arched a supercilious brow and snapped, "Sorry you didn't throw me to the prairie wolf when you had a chance?"

At that he sat up. "I'll be damned," he murmured, staring into the distance, "if our friend isn't still with us."

"The prairie wolf?" she breathed in surprise, and turned to follow the line of his gaze. "The one with the cropped ear?"

"See that ridge yonder? Now, look to the left, by the rock. Yes, about two feet from that lone tree. He's standing perfectly still and blends into the background of the scrub growth. I'll bet he doesn't go near any bushes so that he won't be seen against the green."

"You're remarkably sharp-sighted to have even perceived him," she said in amazement, "much less been able to see his cropped ear from so far away,"

He shook his head. "I can't see the ear. Not at seventy-five yards, which is what I reckon the distance to be."

"Are you sure it's him, then?"

"No, but he's got that same pitiful look to him. Then, too, I can't imagine any other prairie wolf being interested in us."

"I, on the other hand, can't imagine that mangy animal has followed us over all these miles!"

"It's strange, I own."

"Very," she agreed. "Do you think he means us harm?"

He shrugged. "No more than he meant us before, and we're safe enough here, in any case, since he's apparently clever enough to remain hidden against a background into which he blends. Here we would be able to see him with plenty of time to defend ourselves against him." He paused, then added with satisfaction, "And now we have two knives."

"You'd kill him?"

"If I have to," he admitted, "but I'd rather not have to."

She nodded, then turned the fish on their spit. Once she overcame her initial astonishment about the return of the prairie wolf, she was rather happy that the animal was still with them. It seemed a hopeful sign, somehow, although she couldn't say why. As for Powell, it seemed that he, too, was pleased to see the critter again.

She lifted the stick from the fire, handed it over to him with the words, "It's roasted to a turn, and it smells much, much better than burnt tree frogs."

He accepted her offering with a grin, slid one fish off with his knife. "Being an amiable fellow, I will agree and note how my life has improved since the morning I feasted on that French delicacy."

She smiled at that.

Without wasting further words, they ate, savoring their meal and their relief at not having to fight so hard for survival.

When they were finished, Sarah expressed her desire to spend some time at the spring. She did not say the word *bathe,* but she held up her comb, and it was clear enough what she intended to do. Powell announced his intention of taking Lucky to graze, thereby suggesting that she would have her privacy, but he told her to wait a moment before going to the spring so that he could fetch her something he said would be a "surprise."

He left the campsite, then returned not too many minutes later holding a handful of what he identified as yucca pips. He told her that she could crack them and use the oil inside to untangle her hair. She thanked him for his thoughtfulness. Soon she was naked and wading into the water of the spring, which was every bit as fresh and delicious as she had anticipated.

The next hour or so was glorious, with her hair clean and feeling like a heavy skein of silk down her back— thanks to oil from the yucca pips—and with her skin and muscles soaked free of sweat and grime and weariness. She paddled around the basin, which was so deep in the center that she could not touch the bottom with her feet and propelled herself with her arms above her head and fluttering her feet. She paddled in and out of patches of sun and around boulders slick with moss.

The dappled greens surrounding the spring cradled her. She floated on her back and watched the silent sky above, filigreed through the swaying leaves. It was of a blue so intense that she had to close her eyes. Her spirit—pinched from its cares and worries of the last week and before that by all that now seemed to be most irrelevant—relaxed.

At length she emerged from the pool, donned her chemise and pantalets, which she had washed and left to dry in the sun before taking her bath. She left her dress off so that it could air out some more. From among the cluster of rocks that ringed part of the pool, she found one that had a clever curve in it that was shaped like a reclining chair. She sat like a lizard and sunned herself. She mused and dozed and dreamed. When the sun shifted, she welcomed the shade. Her bones melted. Her reverie lengthened. Her dress lay forgotten. She shifted and sighed, sighed and shifted, and never wanted the moment to end.

A voice, quiet but firm, threaded its way through her pleasant dreams. They turned dark and were shadowed with vague threat. She didn't know why she should be bothered when she was perfectly safe and happy.

The voice spoke again. It came from above and behind her. This time she registered the words.

"Don't move."

Something chilling in the soft command prompted her to obey it. Without moving her arms and legs or head, she opened her eyes. They widened. The longest, fattest, meanest, ugliest-looking snake she had ever seen was coiled up not more than two feet away and looking for all the world as if it had found its next victim.

Before she took her next breath, she saw something

bright flash before her eyes, heard a neat *thwack*. She saw the snake bow its head and crumple into a lifeless length of patterned rope. One of the elk-horn-handled knives was sticking straight up from the serpent's neck, just behind its pointed-snout skull.

Sarah felt like crumpling herself, now that the shock of terror was unblocked by a strong wave of relief.

Powell bounded down from the rock above her, landed at her side.

She turned to him.

He opened his arms to her.

Chapter Fifteen

Powell's arms went around her in comfort and protection. She buried her face in the folds of his unbuttoned shirt, clutched at his neck. Responding to his strength and the steady beat of his heart, she shuddered several times, then sighed at length.

"Are there any more of those awful creatures around here?" she asked, settling her cheek against his shoulder.

"I don't think so. I checked the spring earlier for signs of snakes and found no holes or nests. This one must have gotten lost and was lured here by the scent of water."

She heaved a sigh. In so doing she became conscious of the way her breasts rose and fell against his chest, and she reveled in the warmth of his skin, which penetrated the thin cotton of her chemise. She became aware, as well, of the change in the rate of his heartbeat. Or was that her heart that was suddenly jumping and bucking like a frisky pony? Pressed to him, she could feel the subtle changes in his body when he shifted, so that the slope of a thigh muscle covered in buckskin would ripple against her hip and abdomen, heightening her awareness of him and her own near nakedness.

She gasped, realizing what was happening. She didn't

move away from him, but unclutched her hands from his neck and slid them down the lapels of his shirt, which she grasped lightly. She drew her head away, dared to look up at him. She nodded at a point beyond his shoulder. "What were you doing on that boulder in the first place? Spying on me?"

He looked down at her, his blue eyes stained black. "Looking out for you," he corrected, "and it seems my precaution was justified."

"I suppose I should thank you."

"I suppose you should."

She didn't say a word, only continued to hold his gaze.

"As for spying on you," he said, "I'd already been doing that this hour past."

She raised her brows in inquiry.

His lips curved up. "While you were dozing on the rock, I bathed. Shaved, too."

She ran her eye over the smooth cut of his jaw and chin. "Did you have a nice time in the water?"

"I had a nice view."

She felt a blush rise up from her breasts to her cheeks, but it was less of embarrassment than of pleasure.

"I was sleeping," she said.

"I know, and while I was waiting for you to wake up," he replied, "I got out of the pool and climbed around on the rocks. Then just now I picked up the path of our slithering friend."

She shuddered again with delicious, conflicting emotions, and when he moaned in response to her quiver, her emotions took a deeper, more delicious turn. He put one hand at her nape and grasped the thick fall of her hair. He cinched his other hand around her waist and drew her even closer to him. With intention. With demand.

When he bent his head toward hers, she said, "What are you doing?"

"Obliging you."

"Obliging me?"

"By giving you what you've been asking for," he replied, "ever since you first laid eyes on me."

She jerked her head away, but didn't get far. "When I first laid eyes on you," she retorted indignantly, "I didn't even think you were human!"

"Ah, that's right," he said, as if suddenly recalling this important point. "In that case, it's more accurate to say that I'm giving you what you've been asking for only since yesterday afternoon in the Wilkinses' wagon."

She was about to take issue with him, but he cut her off. He continued seriously, "If you were driven to the point of displaying yourself so openly yesterday to get my attention, that means you must have been asking for it even before then, and I was too dull to realize it."

"You, sir? Too dull?" she echoed, with heavy irony. "I can hardly credit it!"

He ignored this. "Back at the lodge," he said, maintaining his serious demeanor, "you remember the morning when you smiled at me so prettily and walked up to me? But perhaps I misinterpret...?" He shook his head, as if to clear it of confusion. "And then again when we were drenched in rain and stuck for the day, I had the feeling that you had rather specific designs on—I hesitate to say—my manly charms, but I was not then ready to say for sure, and in fact it only came to me in full clarity yesterday."

"And you call yourself dull?" she murmured.

He smiled. "I call myself cautious, too. One of the first things you told me about yourself was how you spurned an excellent marriage proposal." His demeanor changed, and he took on a wounded look. "I'm sure that I'm every bit as sensitive as that poor fellow must have been and fearful of being rejected."

She recognized this for the shameless pandering that it was. "That is difficult to imagine, kind sir," she said sweetly, "because I've often had the feeling that you don't particularly like me."

"I don't dislike you any more than you dislike me," he answered promptly.

Her eyes widened. "You dislike me that much, then?" Her voice rang with exaggerated surprise, but it was a shaky humor. She moved within the circle of his arms but did not try to break free. Her big brown eyes pleaded. "Then, why...why this?"

His expression softened. "We're alive today and may not be tomorrow."

"It would have been safer to stay with the wagon train from Ohio," she argued.

"I wish them well," he replied, "but they're no better off than we are, and perhaps a deal worse since they're a large target for any hostile Indians whose paths they may cross."

"It's hard to imagine that we're better off on our own for ever and ever."

"If it pleases you to imagine a future we may or may not have, I will remind you that we're trying to reunite you with your family." He had the tact not to add *If they're still alive*.

"And in the meantime?"

"In the meantime," he said, placing his lips against her neck, "I'm living the life I have now and can't abide the thought of a future, even a very short one, where you continue to tease me."

Her past lay on an ever receding shore, whittled minute

by minute, eroded in the tide of a life lived from one breath to the next. Her future, of whatever length, was uncertain at best. Her present was her only security, and it lay in his hands. In his arms. Next to his body. Wrapped in masculine scent. Surrounded by sinew and sleek muscle.

Sarah put her lips to the sun-kissed skin of his shoulder. Tasted salt and musk. He was all that she had, might ever have. He was her strength, her warmth, her comfort. Her companion in misfortune. Or, perhaps, simply her companion in fortune, pure and simple. No possessions beyond body and soul. Hers and his.

"And I think," he said, hooking a finger in the loop of the frayed drawstring tie at her breasts, "that your underclothes have outlived their usefulness."

They were the last of the possessions that she had started with, save her needle and threads, and it no longer felt like a loss to shed her poor, abused cottons. It was rather more like a liberation to feel the thin material yield to his touch, give way to parting at the light pressure of his hand, be brushed away like powder dusting a treasured object. She was backed up against the reclining seat of stone. She was wedged between the rock and the hard places of his body, pushing his borrowed shirt off his back, feeling buckskin nestle up against the pantalets, which were sure to shred next.

He finally gave her what she had indeed been asking for, what he had been wanting to give her. He put his lips to hers and kissed with an irresistible combination of desire and respect. With lips and tongue and teeth and breath, he pressed and nipped and molded his mouth to hers. With his kiss, he acknowledged the desire between them that had been there from the beginning.

What had begun as a brittle clash of conflicting forces

had grown thick and more pliant with every test of survival they had passed together. However, since the night in the Mandan lodge, those thick and resilient forces had also grown a callused skin. Those very self-protective instincts that had kept them alive had also kept them apart, but with this kiss, the rough skin sloughed.

Her chemise assumed its ragged existence on the rock against which they lay entwined. His shirt had billowed off his shoulders to smother the flimsier cotton. His arms grasped her fullness. His forearms lodged in the ridges on either side of her spine. His fingers spread themselves through her hair, tangling the well-combed masses.

Her breasts were pressed to his chest, which was delighting her with tingles that turned taut when he ventured his chin down her throat to kiss them with tongue and teeth. Her hips cupped his, twisted legs around twists of fabric. One of her knees was bent, and the sole of her foot was flat on the hot rock, flashing sensation in the form of pleasure up the back of her calf, her thigh.

She was aware of the warm shade and the warm breeze in this corner of paradise. She was aware that this place, for all its idyllic splendor...

Was very, very hard.

"My poor bottom," she complained, trying to shift to find a more comfortable fit on the surface of the rock.

He slid one hand down her back to her buttocks, to cushion her seat, and when he did so, he grasped the cleft at the juncture of her thighs and, lifting her hips up and toward him, spread her legs to form a dainty Y. The desire that had filled her arms and lips and breasts flooded to her belly and below, and she had her first taste of erotic appetite.

"Better?" he queried.

"Almost," she breathed in return.

Some expression of surprised discovery must have been in her face and voice, for he relaxed his intimate hold on her and lifted himself up a fraction. "You've never done this before, have you?" he asked slowly. He was coming to his own surprised discovery, which was less a surprise at her virgin state than a discovery of her passion, which he had known in other forms as her courage and stamina and sheer will to live.

"We can try it here later tonight," he said with a warm light in his eyes, "when the air is cool and the rock is still warm. You and your bottom will appreciate it then. Right now, I'd like to take you to the place I had in mind all along."

He took her forearms and lifted her up, grabbing shirt and chemise and tossing these across his shoulder. He led her around the pool and the deflated serpent. "I'll come back later for the knife," he said, skirting the lifeless coil still stuck to the ground, "and we can surely use the skin for something. Slippers for the lady, perhaps?"

She laughed and declined the treat of snakeskin slippers and said he could make himself a belt. She batted her eyelashes provocatively and favored him with one of her melting looks. "The better to hold up your breeches, sir."

He halted midstep, stunned by the sudden surge of passion within the passion. When he started walking again, he wondered aloud, "How do you do that?"

She quoted slyly, "How easily you rise to the fly."

His grasp on her forearm tightened until it hurt her, but her discomfort didn't last long because he soon drew her into a thicket of rambling underbrush in which he had fashioned or found a thick bed of leaves. Before she knew it, she was lying down on top of the shirt he had spread out for her. Her hair was fanned out behind her. Her pantalets were cast aside, along with his buckskins. And he was next to her.

His hands were on her shoulders, her breasts, her waist, framing her hips, slipping beneath her buttocks, bringing her to him. Her hands caressed his neck and shoulders and back, kneaded the lean muscles along his sides. He rolled her over him, once, and let her turn full circle to lie next to him again. He rolled himself over her, once, and stayed. He had her where he wanted her. He had himself where he had wanted to be for a very long time.

Mapping her body with his. Surveying the luscious territory with his fingers. He had experience with feminine geography. He knew to an inch and a fraction of an inch what might give pleasure. He took a lover's pleasure in learning which inch, which fraction, which way gave this woman, this one woman, his woman, the most pleasure. He lined up her fertile ridge with the sight of his inquisitive telescope, then began moving inland. Taking pleasure and pleasure and then more pleasure. As much pleasure as he had previously had pain.

The feel of him, the fit of him, this was all new to her. Frightening, too, at first, when he stretched himself beside her and took possession of her body with his hands. At once exploring and claiming, assuming his right, asserting his right. Making her flounder against the force of his strength and his desire, selfish and savage. Still, she knew that if she were to cry *No, stop! Please stop!* he could cease his kisses and caresses on the instant. That would be the end of it, and she would never know what the tantalizing end of all her teasing would be. So she struggled against her fears and her old desire to be ever sought after but to remain ever pure from male assault.

As he moved her beneath him, he positioned her legs around him, making her vulnerable to be touched and taken in whatever way he wanted. And what he wanted was to touch her where he would join with her, to stroke her, to prod and press her. He wanted to tease her in earnest the way she had teased him in play, with no thought of bowing to the consequences. He wanted her to slippery-slide past embarrassment and chastity, past modesty and restraint. He wanted to waken something inside her. A woman who had been wondering, all these years, what all the fuss was about. A woman who now wondered why they had waited so long to touch each other when she had been hungry for him for days and days and nights and nights.

But when he staked his claim, she felt as helpless as a swimmer in an ocean tide who was being carried on a wave that had no regard for her person. She was fighting to surface, hoping to ride the crest of that wave, but before she could adjust to the extraordinary intrusion and swirling emotions of this experience, the waves crashed, sparkling and splintering, on an unknown shore. For long minutes she lay deposited there, awash. When she came once again to rational thought, she felt both exhausted and exhilarated and perhaps happier than she was willing to admit.

She was mighty curious, too, more so now than before, about the intriguing dimensions of the various possibilities of his body joining with hers. She took feminine pride in the tangible feel of his satisfaction as he lay with his head buried in her neck, his shoulders cropping the world for her and his hands framing her hips. He was holding her down, holding her steady. As if he did not wish her to move. As if he himself could not move. Her teasing self, having had its first tiny taste of passion, had been transformed.

She let her arms flop out on either side of her. She

relaxed her knees so that they fell apart. She wriggled her hips. He moaned. She rolled her hips. He groaned. She took his earlobe between her teeth and whispered, wickedly, "Is that *all* I'm going to get from you?"

He breathed, "God save me from eager virgins."

"You started it."

He lifted his head, looked down at her. His eyes were glazed with satiation, then shaded into a gleam that quickly became a blue glint. "You're asking me to finish it, perhaps?"

She batted her eyes, innocently, seductively. "I don't know what I'm asking for," she admitted.

He set about showing her, not without some inconvenience to himself. He was required first to untangle his pleasure-tired limbs and muscles from her, then to apply what he knew of the delicate arts with care and consideration. When she was teetering on the delicious precipice, driven by a most lovely, luscious, lusty desire to devour him, he found that the only inconvenience to himself would be in denying himself further pleasure, and he promptly availed himself of the opportunity to claim her a second, thoroughly satisfying time.

Thereafter they dozed, laced and happy, while the sun held high in the sky without moving.

Sarah awoke first, as if from a drugged stupor. She lifted heavy lids and beheld a curve of a broad, bronzed shoulder, turned slightly away from her. She let her lids flutter down again, while she breathed in his warm tang and temperament. All was well in her corner of the world. She was lying on soft earth. She was intimate with a man who had overpowered her but not threatened her. She was cuddled by gentle, curling breezes that were braided with prairie perfume and promises. With the tent of trees above, the wealth of fish in the spring beyond and berries all around, she knew that this was comfort, this was abundance.

Powell stirred, shifted, regained consciousness. He moaned, moved toward her, spread his palm across her breast. He drew his fingers up over a pretty pink bud, tweaked it to a peak. Her languor fled. Her spine harped. Her heart leapt. Her eyes opened.

He was already leaning across her, with intention.

She opened her arms to receive him, placed her hands on his forearms. Her teasing self, softened and strengthened by sensuality, slipped inside out to become a seductress. "On two previous occasions," she whispered into his ear, "you had me working to your commands all day, only to make me travel the night through." She rubbed the arch of her foot against his calf. "If you try that a third time, by making me work for you now and travel tonight, you will discover the errors of your ways."

His response was quick. His hold on her relaxed. He rolled on his back and cried, "I plead mercy."

She propped herself on an elbow and nodded, approving of his instant capitulation. However, the next thing she knew, she had lost whatever advantage she might have thought she had, and she was flat on her back, while he was poised above her.

She laughed, charmingly alarmed since she was unable to push him off her. "You really aren't going to exhaust me now and make me travel miles and miles tonight, are you?"

For a response, he adjusted his grip on her shoulders and positioned his legs just how he wanted them. His eyes demanded.

She said, with resignation, "We're pushing on to Windlass Hill tonight, aren't we? Or is it Ash Hollow where you think we might meet up with my family?"

His hold relaxed again, and he drew away from her. This time, judging from the shadowing of the gleam in his eyes, he wasn't playacting.

"What is it?" she asked, her mock alarm becoming real. "You know something I don't?" When he still didn't answer her, she said point-blank, "They're dead. You've discovered that they're dead."

He shook his head. "No, my sweet and courageous Sarah, I have not discovered anything so final." His smile was nevertheless regretful. "We mounted Windlass Hill last night," he told her gently, "and this is Ash Hollow."

She held his eyes, which didn't flinch or waver from her gaze. "This is the next meeting point on the trail, isn't it?"

He nodded.

"And they're not here, are they?"

He shook his head.

"I'm certain those…those wagons we saw earlier don't belong to my family." She paused. "Do you think I could be mistaken?"

He shook his head again.

"What *do* you think, then?"

"I think our best bet," he answered, "is to find the other three surveyors on my team and enlist their help in our search. Your family could be anywhere within a hundred-mile radius or more."

She had to ask. "Do you think they're still alive?"

"There's a chance," he said. "I don't know how many Sioux were out looking for me, but not all of them could have fallen upon your wagon train, and I'm pretty sure those that did suffered some casualties. What was left of the attack party might not have been sufficient to have wiped out the whole train."

She considered this analysis, then asked another question. "Is that your honest assessment?"

The demeanor of a lover vanished. A man, plain and simple, appeared before her. "Have I yet misled you?"

She knew he was answering that question on more than one level. Here they were lying together, naked under the trees, lately awash in passion and ready for another moment of infinite intimacy. Had he deceived her, knowing they were already at Ash Hollow and willing to take advantage of her in the absence of her parents? Had he deceived her? *Had he?*

She didn't think so. She had wanted this as much as he had, and how could he be responsible for knowledge of the whereabouts or well-being of her family?

"No, you haven't misled me," she answered with a slight, sad smile. "In fact, you've stayed the course despite all the difficulties and brought me to the very place you said you would."

His smile mirrored her own, and for an answer, he took her hands and drew her to her feet as he rose. He picked up his shirt, brushed her back with it, put it around her shoulders, then gathered the rest of their belongings before he pulled his breeches on. She appreciated his delicacy. This was hardly the moment for renewed lovemaking now that her thoughts were so distracted by new worries for the fate of her family.

They left their bed of leaves, walked around the pool. He took care of the knife and dead snake. She retrieved her dress from the spot, now shaded, where it had been drying out. The afternoon sky was bleeding into evening. They had easy tasks to occupy them to dinner and beyond. They spoke companionably, each contained in gentle activity and their own thoughts. He rekindled the fire, then went to tend to Lucky. She roasted the fish. They ate, and when they were finished, he took her hand and they strolled around the hollow.

At the edge of the clearing, they paused to admire the night sky. Their eyes strayed in unison to the ridge opposite.

She asked, "Do you see him?"

He didn't need to be told she was asking about the prairie wolf. He scanned the horizon, searched the tricky shadows, eyed the gray-black contours of the land. He nodded. "He's there."

"Watching over us?"

"Maybe." He shrugged. "We can use the protection."

"Like the nice warm blanket we don't have."

He turned to her. One black brow rose. An irresistible look came into his eyes. He put his hands at her hips, bunched the skin of her dress until he could grasp her bare bottom.

"Speaking of warm," he said, lifting her dress higher and slipping his hand between her thighs, "now's the time to make use of that rock."

With a quick shedding of buckskin and deerskin, they hurried to the rim of the inky pool. There she discovered, sure enough, the delight of the sun's heat trapped in stone against her back; and this marvelous feeling, mingled with the feel of his body against her front, created in her instant appetite for him. But the rock wasn't a place they could stay comfortable for long, so when they had satisfied their desires, they returned to the campfire, where he had arranged their bed of moss and leaves.

He fiddled with the fire to make the flames low and long lasting. She brushed her hair and braided it. He stretched out and patted the space before him in invitation. She lay down next to him. He spread his shirt and jacket over the both of them. Her front was to the fire. His back was to the darkness.

"You see," he said, putting his arm over her and hugging her to him, "it is as I promised you. You've traveled no further than the rock and back."

She closed her eyes, snuggled against him, and slept.

Chapter Sixteen

Sarah awoke rested. They had shifted during the night, for their positions were reversed, and she was holding him, her front to his back. At her stirring, he woke too, and before he let her up, he put her under him. Later, he remained stretched out, dozing in sublime satisfaction. She rose, feeling a twinge of discomfort in the pit of her stomach that hadn't been there the day before. Perhaps she was suffering from belated moral reflections on the inevitable consequences of teasing a strong, good-looking man on whom she was completely dependent.

She put herself to rights, dress and belt, and sat down cross-legged in front of the ashes of the night's fire. When she heard him move, she asked, "Is this the day we try to find your team?"

He pulled on his breeches, rolled over and sat up next to her. "It is." As he reached behind him to grab his shirt, he looked up into the blue blaze of the sky. "I've just been trying to figure what we're going to carry water in. Whatever else we do before we set off, we must make sure there's enough water for ourselves and for Lucky." She was surprised. "We're starting out by day?"

"Late afternoon. With four surveyors at your service, we'll find your family in no time."

She pulled her knees up to her breast and wrapped her arms around them. She put a cheek against a forearm, so that she was facing him. He looked dear to her and, oddly, distant. Now that they were a couple, she had a vague sense that a line more threatening than physical intimacy had been crossed—and perhaps this was the source of her early morning unease.

He returned her regard a moment, then asked, "Want breakfast?"

She shook her head and looked away from him. "Not yet."

He grunted. She heard him scratch his stubbly chin.

Staring into the middle distance, she observed, "At least you have a razor."

"And you the comb and brush."

"We both have decent clothing."

"Two knives and a horse."

"Not to mention a protective prairie wolf."

"Ah, yes," he said, "our security blanket, I think you called it."

"Mmm, a blanket would be nice, wouldn't it? A blanket would see us through the nights at the end of summer, as well as through any of the downpours that are sure to come."

To this he added, "I know I've said this before, but a rifle would improve our lot in an instant. The knives are useful but rely too heavily on hand-to-hand contact. I'd like to come to some terms with the prairie wolf who's been roaming around in my back garden, but I'd rather do it at arm's length."

She smiled at that. "While you're hunting down our

friend in your back garden, I'll go into my mansion and issue orders to any number of my many domestics."

His smile was broad enough to produce dimples. "Is that what you hanker for, then? A mansion filled with servants to step to your command?"

"Of course," she answered readily, "and I want the wardrobe to match. My mansion has closets full of shoes and dresses and petticoats and shawls and gloves and hats and parasols."

"Why stop there?"

"Why, indeed?" she returned, letting her fantasy loose. "But most of all, I want position with a capital *P*." She turned to him and arched a pretty brow. "I have an ambition to be the belle of Baltimore. To perch gracefully atop the crispiest crisp of the upper crust."

"You have my vote for the position."

She instantly assumed her role. "Mr. Powell, social position is *not* something for which one votes or, even, *can* vote. And that, of course, is the beauty of it—the desirability of it."

"I'll concede, Miss Harris, that you have the high-and-mighty airs for it."

Her arched brow turned haughty. "That, sir, is precisely what a no-account, uncivilized man-beast who has not the least idea what constitutes good breeding and manners would say."

He laughed. "You rate my powers of perception so low? Recall that I recently credited you with being from the illustrious Harris family of Baltimore, and although I declined to make you its belle—a strategic concession, you understand, in the presence of the pinch-faced Mrs. Wilkins—she was duly impressed." He paused to grin. "I invite you to admire me for having hit upon the very thing you wish most."

She, too, laughed, and retorted, "I admire nothing at all about you!"

"Well then, the least you can do is thank me for having complimented your pretentious self."

"*Complimented?*" she echoed, torn between amusement and indignation. "You deem it a compliment to call me *pretentious?*"

"Since you judged me less than human, I was merely following your own lead of honest assessment of the other's character," he replied, his expression suspiciously bland. "Given that, then, I'll confine myself to asking you to thank me for not having insulted your intelligence."

Her eyes narrowed. "I'll thank you for nothing," she said roundly, "and as long as we are airing our opinions so frankly, I should like to be able to evaluate *your* secret dream, so don't be shy and tell me what—" She stopped, mouth half-open. "But, no, I think I already know what it is."

"Do you? Then you're ahead of me."

"You want to marry some unattractive thing who does good works at the hospital and comes from an illustrious family—" She halted again, crowed, "Aha!" then continued, "Oh, no, no, I was not *wrong* to have thanked you for nothing when you pretended to compliment my intelligence. All you did was to *underestimate* it—and *not* for the first time. That was not *my* dream you were spinning out for Mrs. Wilkins, but your own, sir. Which means that you weren't pandering to *my* vanity but rather expressing your own desire for a wife with wealth and position."

Sarah paused dramatically, then said with the superior voice and smile that always annoyed him, "You are quite right to look for an unattractive woman among the ranks of the illustrious, for such a woman would be the only one likely to entertain a proposal from you." She added, judiciously, "Assuming, of course, that she was desperate enough."

Instead of answering her gibe, Powell planted one arm behind her and stretched the other one around her so that she was trapped. He began to lean against her. He put his lips to her neck.

Sarah stuck her elbows out behind her for support, but even then she was still having to lie back under the force of his superior weight and strength. Despite the obviousness of his intentions, she asked, alarmed, "What are you doing, sir?"

"Taking advantage of the situation."

"Ouch! You're hurting me with your beard."

"You'll have to live with it."

"I don't want to live with—"

Her words were cut off by his lips on hers. She squirmed all the harder away from his scratchy bristles. When she broke her mouth free long enough to speak, she said, "We've already done this once today," and, "It's broad daylight," but neither of these utterances persuaded him to stop, and soon enough she was stretched out beneath him.

Pinning her with his shoulders, he put his hands at the hem of her dress and began to push it up her thighs and over her hips, so that animal skin was lifted off and twisted around human skin.

It was undignified. It was confusing.

"Why are you doing this?" she asked next.

"When you tease a man-beast," he said, "this is what you can expect."

He had taken her by surprise. The day before at the pool, she had been undressed and—she admitted it!— ready for his advances. Last night on the rock they had made warm, shadowed love by mutual consent, lavishly indulging in their pretty, precarious togetherness. This morning had seemed more like a lazy bodily kiss, a prolongation of the secret pleasures of sleep. But now—

"I don't really think you're a man-beast."

"Too late."

He had bunched the deerskin around her waist. He caught her thighs and wrapped them around him as he shoved buckskin away from his own skin.

She pushed at him. "No."

He didn't budge. "Yes."

"Why?"

"Knowing that you have no underwear," he said, "is like an open invitation."

Her waist-down nakedness left no private part hidden from him. He exerted no arts of the lover. "I mean, why now? Why like this?" she asked, still spurred by surprise and fear in this unequal struggle. "One minute we were discussing our dreams, and the next—"

"No," he said, moving his hand under her dress to grasp her breasts, "one minute you were behaving like a beautiful idiot and the next I took action. Ten days late."

"Ten days late?"

He moved to possess her vulnerability. "I should have done this within the first five minutes of catching you in the glade."

She gasped. "What?" she breathed.

"And now I'm doing it."

He wasn't gentle. He wasn't considerate. Her position was still undignified. She was still confused, but something about the thought of her man-beast doing *this* back *then* jolted her from alarm to excitement, and she was responding to him and the fit of his body in a way she had not suspected she could.

When he was finished, he didn't kiss her, he didn't

caress her. He got up, hitched his breeches and said, "*Now* I'm in the mood to make better acquaintance with that prairie wolf."

She could barely lift her head to ask, "Why should you have done this within five minutes of catching me in the glade? I would have hated you, you know."

He looked down at her. "I know, but I wanted to then, and so I did it now."

When he quit the clearing, she was still lying there, hardly able to move. She had pushed her dress back down her legs for decency's sake, but heaven knew there wasn't one of God's creatures around to care, and it hardly mattered whether she was decent or not anyway, because she had never felt quite so indecent in all her life. Stripped, right down to the skin and then some. Her body at his disposal. No doubt about it, and no questions asked. How odd. How unsettling.

She should have felt worse about it, a whole lot worse, but she didn't. But that might have had something to do with the fact that even if he had wanted to overpower her in the glade, he had restrained himself. But, really, restraint had had nothing to do with it. He had been too weak at the time to have done anything so...so brutish as to rip her clothes off and...and... No, he had been too weak. For pity's sake, he had just run fifty miles over open plain naked, so how could he have had the energy to even *think* of such a thing? And yet he admitted to having thought and *wanted* just that.

Men were strange creatures.

This was a particularly strange creature.

Her man-beast.

To want something and to do it.

If he had thought she was beautiful upon *first* seeing her, then she should feel flattered. However, she didn't want his good opinion of her looks but of her character, and if she didn't have that *now* after all she'd done for him, she would tease him and tease him until he couldn't stand it any longer, and then she'd tease him some more and make sure he'd never enjoy her body ever again.

That bracing thought succeeded in rousing her to a sitting position, and just as she was lumbering to her feet, the shocking report of a rifle reverberated through the hollow.

Before she could compose a coherent thought, her heart wrenched in fear for Powell's life. She ran to the edge of the clearing and was going to run out into the open to look for him, to help him if need be, but then her reason reasserted itself. He was unlikely to have made himself an available target for some person's rifle, and he wouldn't appreciate her making an open target of herself if the person holding the firearm was hostile to them. No, she wasn't an idiot—whatever Powell might think of her on occasion.

Thus, she kept to the trees, darting in and among them, keeping a desperate eye out for whatever had happened. She ran halfway around one side of the hollow until she had an obstructed view of the east side of the ridge opposite. From that vantage point she saw a series of events unfold that at once elated her and broke her heart.

Powell left the clearing and his woman, feeling as good as a man in this world could feel. After ten days of dancing on the edges, he had stepped into the wilderness figuratively with both feet and literally with his most bestial body part, and now he was going to hunt down the prairie wolf and tame that alien creature, too. He wanted to get close enough to the creature to hold his neck at knifepoint and let him know who was master of the wild.

He was glad of his breeches, glad of his moccasins, most glad of his knives. The shirt on his back was none so bad. He knew he was carrying her woman's scent on his person but decided that it was all right for the moment, as long as he was downwind. He would bathe later, when the sun was vertical and dropped its flood of heat and light on the land.

It was plenty hot now, even this early in the morning, which was why he had taken care of Lucky first thing upon leaving Sarah's side. The air was sticky, too, and for comfort he had gathered his uncut curls and pulled them into a thick queue, which he secured with a thong he had fashioned from the plentiful fringe growing from the side seams of his breeches.

He had tracked the wolf down and kept his distance. The clever puppy knew how to make use of the shadows to blend into the landscape. Well, so did he, and he was glad again of buckskin and the burnt brown skin of his chest and shoulders, which made him one with his surroundings. With his eyes fixed on the dusty earth and the pattern of pawprints, he calculated the length of the wolf's stride and the speed of his trot, then reckoned the distance to the corner of the ridge. He was counting out how many more steps it would take before he was face-to-face with his quarry, and then it was one, two, three...

He adjusted the grips on the knives, one in each hand. Four...

He heard the pant, smelled warm fur.

Five...

He pressed his back against the rock.

Six steps.

He inched around the corner and brought the first sliver of himself into view and sunlight.

He was crouched in order to execute his plan of bringing his knives up and under the wolf's neck. When he registered the sight before him on the east ridge, he was so far into his motion of catching the wolf up short that he was unable to stop himself completely. A man, not a wolf, stood directly before him and caused him to deflect the trajectory of his knives, but he could not prevent the appearance of attacking the man before him. He didn't hurt the man, but the man had had to raise his arms to defend himself and counterattack.

In the midst of this Powell exclaimed, astonished, "Sean O'Donnell, I'll be damned!"

In unison the man uttered, "Jesus, Mary and Joseph! Is it Wesley Powell I'm seein'?"

Unfortunately, the commotion between Powell and O'Donnell had upset the balance of the main drama going forward on the east ridge, and in that first flash of a half second, Powell was aware that his entrance had precipitated a tragedy that he was powerless to prevent.

The prairie wolf had been cornered by the three surveyors, who were lined up such that O'Donnell was nearest to Powell. Douglas Grant stood between him and Jeremiah Lewis, who had his rifle cocked and aimed at the wolf. At the time of Powell's entrance, the three surveyors were circled about ten feet from the prairie wolf, who was poised and ready for strategic retreat. However, when O'Donnell responded reflexively to Powell's attenuated attack, the prairie wolf lunged at O'Donnell, and Lewis released the trigger.

"Nooo!" Powell howled as Lewis's forefinger twitched, but it was too late. Before his very eyes, he saw the body of the poor, mangy prairie wolf convulse midair and rip open with a bullet. Its life and blood spattered in a terrible arc across the thirsty dirt of the earth.

"No!" Powell repeated, moving toward the body of the

animal, who was shuddering his agonizing last. He knelt beside it, emotions roiling. He snapped his head up and accused, "How could you, Lewis? He's been following us for days and days and hundreds of miles. *How could you?*"

Lewis was spared the necessity of reply by the arrival of yet another player on the scene. In a voice calm and deep, this man said, "I'm an impartial witness to the way the wild animal went after Mr. O'Donnell. If you've lost your valuable hunting wolf, sir, I'm sorry for it, but Mr. Lewis had no choice."

This comment was evidently directed at Powell. Still kneeling at the dying animal's side, he didn't take his eyes off the pitiful carcass when he bit off the words, "He wasn't my hunting wolf."

To the threesome, the man said, "You seem to know this man, and he you."

Grant and O'Donnell replied in unison.

"He's the one we've been looking for."

"He's the one we've been tellin' ye about."

Lewis was less interested in introductions and more interested in exculpating himself. "He's right, you know. I couldn't allow the critter to get Sean. I couldn't allow that, Wesley."

"Wesley Powell?" the man queried. Keeping his calm, he continued, "I am glad we've found you."

"I would say rather that I have found you," Powell replied none too pleasantly, for he was not yet disposed to cordiality.

"Whatever the case, your fellow surveyors assured me that you of all men would be able to help me locate my daughter. We were separated from her during a Sioux attack ten days ago."

At that Powell's head came up. He was looking straight

into the face of a man pushing sixty. It was a sixty the man wore well.

"I am Morgan Harris," the older man said, extending his hand, "and I must ask for your kind assistance in helping us to find my daughter Sarah."

Powell rose to his feet and slid the knives into the waistband of his breeches. He accepted the man's hand. Morgan Harris was tall and thin, almost gaunt, but had a look of stringy strength about him. He was not wearing a hat. His hair was dark, almost black, streaked with gray at the temples and pulled back at the nape, much like Powell's. His eyes were blue and of a keenness undiminished by age. At the moment they were clouded with concern and held an unmistakable expression of entreaty.

"My wife and I are worried, you understand, Mr. Powell," Morgan Harris explained, "because Sarah is a gently bred young woman. Do you think you can help us?"

Powell glanced down at the dead body of the prairie wolf, then back at Morgan Harris. Restored to the company of his colleagues, he knew himself to be rescued, but this knowledge did nothing to lessen the waves of grief and despair that were washing over him, and his emotional storm surged now with a fatalism he did not yet fully understand. He struggled to compose his response. At last he said, "Your daughter is safe and sound down at the hollow, sir."

As Morgan Harris absorbed the impact of that statement, the look of worry and entreaty in his eyes receded. His expression assumed a remote, rather chilling dignity. "Thank you, son," he said, politely enough. He might have had the impulse to extend his hand to Powell a second time, but checked it before he made the first motion. "You'll understand if I quit you with no further words, for I'm anxious to have my daughter once again under my care.''

Morgan Harris raised a hand and signed in the direction of the south ridge, then he departed.

Powell looked over his shoulder at the hollow and saw a tempting oasis of fresh green shimmering in the morning heat and light. Before his very eyes, the earthly paradise seemed to recede, then vanish.

Chapter Seventeen

Sarah's sorrow over the prairie wolf's demise was suspended by the subsequent interactions of the four distant figures on the ridge. It was clear to her that the three men knew Powell and that Powell knew them, and she suspected that they might be the three long-lost surveyors. When the fifth man came onto the scene, she could hardly believe her eyes, but her heart knew better. It traced the lean outlines of the tall, gaunt man and began to soar before her vision confirmed that the man was well and truly Morgan Harris.

Not caring whether Powell would judge her an idiot or not, she came out from behind the trees and ran into the open, heading straight for the man who was now striding purposely in the direction of the hollow. When he caught sight of her moving toward him, he broke into a run, and not too many paces later she was in a crushing embrace of shuddering, shattering relief.

It was several long, loving minutes before either could find voice or strength or desire to break the embrace, but finally Morgan spoke. His cheek was against her hair, his voice was a hoarse whisper. "I lost you once, Sarah love, when you were a baby. Once was bad enough, and then

it was only for a day. This time—'' his voice broke
''—this time I could hardly bear to think of losing you,
since I feared that it would be for all time.''

When she was five months old, Sarah had been kid-
napped by the widow of her natural father, General Robert
Ross. The tale of that incident had been woven tightly
into family folklore, so Sarah knew the story well. However, only at this moment did she understand in every cell
of her body how that loss must have felt for her mother
and Morgan all those years ago. And only now, as she
stood in the generous circle of her stepfather's arms, did
she understand what it must have cost him emotionally to
have normalized her relationship with Mrs. Ross in England.

''I was all right, Father,'' she said, ''really I was, and
I knew, I just *knew* that you were still looking for me,
just as I've been looking for you.''

Morgan eased himself away from her, framed her
cheeks with his hands. ''I considered riding ahead to
Oregon to fetch Laurence to find you.'' His expression
was still bemused, as if he were looking at a dear mirage.
''Laurence found you last time, you know, and I desperately wanted him to help me find you this time, too. But
I was torn by the mere thought of leaving your mother
and the girls.'' He paused, swallowing an emotion, and
repeated softly, ''Your mother.''

Sarah's heart quailed. She jumped wildly to conclu-
sions, fearing the worst. ''Mother is—'' she breathed, unable to complete the question, half horrified, half hopeful.

Morgan's smile softened the harsh lines of his weath-
ered face. His blue eyes smiled, too. ''She's in the wagon
on the southern side of the ridge.'' He glanced over his
shoulder, then quickly back at her, as if keeping her in
his line of vision would prevent her from vanishing again.

"I signaled to her to bring the wagon round. She should be here shortly."

Her heart throbbed, once, with pain. She asked quickly, "Martha and Helen?"

He nodded. "They're with your mother." He enfolded her again in his arms. "We're together again. All of us."

She clung to him and absorbed this miraculous news. Together again. All of them. The world had taken everything away from her, then given her back what she valued most.

"How did you get away?" she asked. "I mean, from the Sioux attack."

"I followed directly in the wake of the Kellys' wagon, and it acted as a kind of shield for us. I would have offered the same protection for the Kellys, if our positions in the train had been reversed, but such as it was, I saw no reason for both of us to present our fronts to the attackers."

Enlightenment dawned. "So that's why there were only nine sets of wagon tracks leading away from the campsite."

He frowned, remembering that fateful day. "I followed Kelly for a half mile or so. But he veered off at one point, and the few Sioux that were left followed him, not us. I don't think he made it very far."

"Neither did the Clarks," she informed him sadly, "and, of course, there was the Widower Reynolds, who never even had a chance to flee. Not to mention the four wagons that are crashed at the edge of the far trees behind us."

"It was foolish of Jonas Reynolds to have raised his rifle so quickly when the Sioux party came upon us. There were hardly more than twenty of them, and they didn't appear openly hostile to us. But Jonas jumped the gun and opened fire, and they had no choice but to defend themselves. They suffered a half dozen dead in the first few minutes, and between those Sioux who went after various wagons and those who remained behind to carry off their dead, there was no one left to bother with us.''

"So you were lucky."

Morgan nodded. "Just lucky."

"And since then?"

"We went straight to the highest ground we could find and hid out with the Fletchers and the Dales, who, like us, escaped injury. We met up first with some trappers, who will now accompany us to the Oregon Territory, and then with the three remaining surveyors from Washington, D.C.''

At that point, he paused. He narrowed his eyes in a way she had known from childhood that meant she would have to account for herself. So close to him, still wrapped in his arms, she felt his moody disapproval. She lowered her eyes and waited for the horrible, embarrassing questions.

However, instead of asking about the particulars of how she had survived these past ten days, he said simply, "You're alive and in one piece, and that's all I need to know for now. When your mother and sisters get here, you can recount your adventures. But just tell me one thing, Sarah Ross. Were you in the company of the fourth surveyor—this fellow Wesley Powell—the whole time?"

She nodded.

"Was there anyone else with you during your time together?"

"That's more than one question," she replied.

His expression momentarily betrayed surprise. Then he drew her to him again. His heart was pressed to her cheek. His chin rested on the top of her head. "If I wasn't sure at first that you were my daughter, so changed is your appearance, I'd be sure of it now. You're as saucy as ever, Sarah love.''

Holding her the way he was, she could detect the muscles in his arms and chest relaxing. He was happy to have her delivered to him. He was happy that she was safe. She wondered how long-lived his happiness would be when he heard how she had spent the last ten days, and she knew the sounds of wagons clattering up behind them meant that the issue was going to be pressed.

''Here come your mother and sisters now,'' Morgan Harris said on a note mixed with tenderheartedness and tough-mindedness, ''and we'll all be eager to hear your adventures.''

When Morgan Harris disappeared around the side of the ridge, Powell looked down at the dead prairie wolf, then up at his three companions. Happiness and hopelessness still clashed violently in his breast, tore at the interior doors that had lately been thrown open. Their unstable hinges began to creak and swing. Reproach for Lewis's wanton killing of the seemingly insignificant, yet noble, animal still hovered on Powell's lips. He opened his mouth, then closed it again, unable to speak for the battle waging in his breast.

Sean O'Donnell might have guessed at Powell's confusion. He attempted to smooth over the moment. ''We've found ye, then, Wesley, or rather ye've found us, and after an eternity of lookin' and givin' ye up for dead.''

Douglas Grant joined in. ''It's a wonder O'Donnell recognized you at all.'' He was taking in the details of Powell's transformed appearance, with a pointed eye at the two handsome knives in his waistband. ''You look like a Sioux warrior come to life.''

"Mandan," Powell corrected.

O'Donnell's brows shot up. "Not Sioux, then? No wonder we were havin' such a devil of a time trackin' ye down!"

"I was taken first by the Sioux, then by the Mandan."

"About the critter," O'Donnell said, "ye said, 'He's been followin' us for days and days and hundreds of miles.' I gather that Morgan Harris's daughter is part of that 'us'?"

"She is."

"And the others?"

"There are no others. We've been alone, Miss Harris and I."

The pause was pregnant.

Grant broke the silence by saying, "If she looks anything like her mother, she's a rare beauty."

"She's a rare beauty," Powell confirmed.

Lewis demanded, "Well then?"

Powell looked out over the plain that separated the ridge from the hollow. In the center were two spots clinging to each other, a tall lean spot with a smaller one enclosed within it. He yearned, but he did not quite know for what. He clung to his old dreams as if to old shoes, practically useless and more comforting than comfortable. His old dreams responded by cowering in the dark safety of their deep closets.

He dredged from fractured memory those circumstances of his experience with Sarah that would count as facts. "I met her—ran into her, you might say—on the second day after I was taken from our camp. At the Platte crossing about a hundred miles east of here. Her wagon train had just been set upon by the Sioux."

"That's right," O'Donnell confirmed, "and am I guessin' correctly now to think the Sioux attack party was lookin' for the likes of you?''

"You are. In any case, I happened upon a hiding place in the riverbed, where I met Miss Harris, who had left the wagon train to refresh herself at the very minute the Sioux came upon them. One white man was killed outright, and we came across two wagons not far from the original site. Four more wagons stand empty and broken over yonder. I believe there were ten wagons in all.''

Grant confirmed this and added the fact that the remaining three belonged to the Harrises, the Fletchers and the Dales. These three families had survived to remain together, and they had been greatly helped by the Indian trappers in the region, who were from the Salish tribe in the Oregon Territory and, thus, no friend of the Sioux.

Powell nodded. At that moment, the three wagons in question, which had come out from behind the south ridge at Harris's signal, rattled slowly by, giving wide berth to the body of the dead animal. In the lead was a wagon guided by an older woman who bore a striking resemblance to Sarah. Next to her sat two girls, dark contrasts to the mother's fairness. Their big brown eyes were as round as greatcoat buttons to behold the sight of the dead prairie wolf and the white man who was strangely dressed in the Indian fashion. It was plain they considered the whole drama a fascinating affair.

When the little train had passed, Powell resumed his story. "We waited out the first night, walked west throughout the second night, were captured by the Mandan on the third day and taken to their village on the fourth. I engaged in a hunting challenge on the fifth. We escaped and rode through the night, whereupon I fell ill as a result of a prolonged rain shower the following day. Eventually we met up with another wagon train—they're about a day's ride behind us, as you already know, since I heard that you met up with the wagon master, Mr. Rogers—and I was restored to health throughout a day and night. I rested the day after that, and then we rode through the night to the hollow. It was my intention to begin tracking you down today."

His fellow surveyors murmured their surprise and sympathy and expressed as one their belief in Powell's great good luck in finding them this morning.

"Good luck, indeed," Powell said, wondering why this extraordinary coincidence did not make him feel particularly lucky, "and here I am more or less back where I started ten days ago. Minus my chain, level, telescope and maps, of course. It's been full circle. Or almost."

"Never mind the equipment," Grant said encouragingly. "It can be replaced."

"And weren't we right," Lewis remarked, seemingly pleased with the overall turn of events, "to have told Mr. Harris that our own Wesley Powell would be the very one to help him find his daughter."

"Oh, yes, mighty right!" O'Donnell said on a nervous laugh. "And weren't we right to have regaled Mr. Harris and company with stories of our fine fourth."

"Stories?" Powell queried. "About me?"

O'Donnell continued on a humorous note turned apologetic. "Oh, entertain 'em we did around the campfire with tales of yer exploits in Washington. We told 'em how the ladies cried when ye left town."

Powell's brows shot up.

"Cried and cried, but only the married ones! Understand, too, that we also told 'em if ever a man would be stranded in the wilderness, he'd do no better than to be stranded with the likes of Wesley Powell!"

Powell was beginning to understand the change in Morgan Harris's reaction upon discovering Powell's name, and the courteous dislike that Sarah's father had displayed toward him suggested that the older man had not discounted the tales he had been told of Powell's tomcat prowlings all over Washington, D.C.

Not without some irony Powell said, "Then, no doubt, Mr. Harris is delighted that his daughter was stranded all this time in the wilderness with the likes of me."

"Well, ye've returned the beautiful daughter to her father safe and sound, haven't ye?"

Powell did not immediately respond.

"Haven't ye?" O'Donnell pressed.

Powell knew what O'Donnell was asking. Because he had been thinking of Sarah Harris as his woman and not his wife, the present circumstances made his intentions toward her entirely dishonorable, and he could not admit the true state of affairs without doing her further dishonor. The only way to make right what he had done would be to propose to her the conventional sanction of marriage. Although completely new to him, the idea was not entirely disagreeable. He even found it appealing, appetizing....

O'Donnell must have understood that this was the moment for a certain measure of honesty. "Sittin' around a campfire leads a man to disclosures, as we all know," he said, then cleared his throat once or twice, "and although Mr. Harris acknowledged that his daughter is not what you'd call wellborn, he has every expectation of making a fine match for her."

"Do they imagine some fine match for her out in the wilds of the Oregon Territory?" Powell asked, surprised and skeptical.

O'Donnell shook his head. "They don't expect her to settle down there permanently, and they brought her with them because—" Here he scratched his head. "Well! I don't know why they brought her with them, but I do think they mean to return her to Baltimore sometime in the future.''

Powell felt doors slamming shut inside and out. Intriguing possibilities were aborted. New pathways were closed off before they could be pursued. He was aware that there was much about Sarah and her life that he didn't know, but he did know her dreams. These included a mansion and servants and social position—in short, all that he could not give her but someone else could.

He had his dreams, too, his old dreams, which, having refused their earlier chance for freedom, now settled down behind the bars that caged the wounds deep in his heart. There was no place in that familiar prison for loving a rare beauty who craved what he could not give and who could not assure him the peace and security he wanted most.

He looked for a second time down into the plain that stretched from the ridge to the hollow. For a long moment he observed an affecting family reunion in progress. Then he resolutely turned his back on that scene and looked down at the prairie wolf for the last time.

"Never worry, Sean, that you gave Mr. Harris the wrong impression of my abilities to ensure his daughter's survival. I did indeed return Miss Harris to her family safe and sound. Now, let's bury this poor thing here, as my way of paying it my last respects.''

Sarah exhausted the last of her emotion into her mother's breast. When she was finished, she raised her head and smiled into wise and loving brown eyes so like her own.

Lifting one arm from around Sarah's shoulder, Barbara Harris made a shooing gesture over the top of Sarah's head at the small assembled audience. "Now, my daughter," she said to the young woman in her arms, "you must answer my next question truthfully."

The reduced train of three wagons had ventured to the edge of the hollow. The various members of the traveling party had spread out to fish and bathe and nap and play. Sarah had greeted the Fletchers and the Dales with nearly as much happiness as she had greeted her own family. Whatever had been her annoyance with Mrs. Fletcher before, it was gone now, and she had hugged the nosy old harridan warmly and expressed her real joy in seeing her alive.

Then Sarah had seated herself with her mother at the back of the wagon, with their legs hanging out, and with Morgan and her sisters standing outside in a ring around them. Martha and Helen had exclaimed over Sarah's brown skin, had declared that she looked like an Indian princess, and had promised never, *ever* to plague their older sister again. Sarah had laughed and given them liberal permission to plague her whenever they wanted, and then she had launched into an emotional, disjointed account of her exciting adventures until Barbara gave the others the signal to leave.

The two women were alone. Sarah guessed what her mother's next question might be. She was happy that the asking of it had fallen to her mother, rather than to her father.

"It's about Mr. Powell."

Sarah nodded. "What about Mr. Powell?"

"Mr. O'Donnell, Mr. Lewis and Mr. Grant were, perhaps, prone to exaggerating the reputation of their professional friend, but even accounting for exaggeration, I'm afraid there might be a lot of truth to what they said."

"What did they say about Mr. Powell?"

"To be blunt, they said he has a taste for the ladies, all kinds of ladies and lots of them. He was portrayed as a...man of loose morals. Now, this did not concern us very much, because we had no idea that you were with him alone this whole time, and we were looking forward to finding him so that he could help us find you. But now I'm remembering the many stories they told about him— discreetly enough, I suppose I should add, for they never told any of the stories in earshot of the girls or Mrs. Fletcher. I only learned of Mr. Powell's reputation because they did not realize I was there when they were recounting some tales to your father."

This information about Powell did not initially square with Sarah's understanding of his secret dream for a proper, mousy wife. But then she reconsidered him in the light of a lover and suspected that his knowledge of the seductive arts was high. Her gut wrenched, and a wave of heaviness seized her, but she faced the situation head-on. "And the question you wish to ask, Mother?"

Barbara's expression was kind, her tone gentle. "Did he take advantage of you, my love?"

The phrasing of the question threw Sarah off course, and she gave the first honest response that sprang to mind. "Advantage? Of course he didn't take advantage of me!" Then she reframed the question that her mother was really asking. "No, I mean...of course...what I mean to say is..."

"Yes?" her mother prompted.

Sarah blinked. She felt herself flush. Her soft innards cramped again. She clapped a hand across the deerskin covering her abdomen. "It's come."

"What's come, my dear?"

Sarah pushed herself out the back of the wagon so that she could stand up and shake out her dress. She smiled lopsidedly at her mother. "My women's courses." Then she put her arms around her mother's waist and put her head in her lap. "How *glad* I am to be with you, and how *wretched* I would have been alone in the wilderness without you—or any other woman—at this time of the month!"

She lifted her head and looked into her mother's eyes. "I wasn't trying to avoid the topic just now, but it's always so *relieving* when the blood finally starts to flow, you know, even though the whole thing is a nuisance. You see, I was dragging myself around earlier today, and some of yesterday, as well, feeling so heavy and irritable. And now to answer your question—"

Her mother pressed her fingers to Sarah's lips to silence her. She smiled and shook her head. "In just these past few minutes, I've realized that you aren't answerable to me for anything anymore—difficult though it is for a mother to admit! Nevertheless, it's plain to me that since you've managed to survive with Mr. Powell, you're capable of living out the rest of your life without my permission or intervention."

Sarah was thankful for the consideration, because she wasn't sure what the real answer was to the question of whether Powell had taken advantage of her or not. Fortunately, the two women had a very practical matter to attend to, and so they went into the wagon to find the necessary for Sarah, along with a change of clothing.

While Sarah was attending to her bodily needs, Barbara went to Morgan. He was standing in the shade at the edge of the hollow facing south toward the open plain and the ridge. His face was impassive. Only the slight raising of his brows as his wife approached suggested his deep concern for what she might have to say, which was, "You'll be happy to know that there will be no unfortunate, long-term conséquences to Sarah's adventure with Mr. Powell.''

Morgan invited his wife to explain.

''She isn't carrying his child. More, I don't need to know. And neither do you.''

Morgan considered this, then agreed. ''All right, then. Beyond that, we don't need to know what else might or might not have happened between them. I'd hate to think of her having formed an attachment for the man. I didn't like the stories I heard about him, and I certainly don't like the look of him.''

Barbara shifted her gaze to the eastern edge of the ridge, but the figures of the four surveyors were no longer to be seen there. She smiled slightly. ''I didn't get a good look at Mr. Powell as we passed by, but I'd guess he's rather like what you must have looked like at his age.''

Morgan nodded in ironic acknowledgment of that observation. ''Then I have all the more reason to know just how unsuitable a man he is for our Sarah, and if my life is any measure of the matter, he's another ten years away from being capable of properly loving a woman.''

With that Barbara could not argue. ''And what, as parents, are we supposed to do about him?''

''I've already thanked him,'' Morgan replied. ''That's enough. If he has further business with Sarah, he'll come see her before he takes off with his team and tell her what's on his mind.''

''Where is the surveying team headed?''

''West like us, but their base camp is south of our trail, so they have no need to accompany us farther. If this Powell fellow wishes to say goodbye to Sarah, he may do so.''

''But what if he doesn't and Sarah wishes to say goodbye to him?''

"Would you advise her to do that, if he hasn't taken the initiative to come see her on his own?"

Barbara shook her head, wearing a troubled frown on her brow. "Better to let Sarah rest right now. We'll see what the afternoon brings."

The afternoon brought Sarah's readjustment to cottons, hairpins and menstrual cloths. She had put aside her deer-skin dress with a twinge of regret, but otherwise she was clean and happy and felt a fluttery kind of excitement to imagine how her next meeting with Wesley Powell would unfold now that she was reunited with her family. She imagined a hundred different scripts for this encounter, but the one possibility that never occurred to her was the very one that came to pass.

Wesley Powell didn't come down to the hollow, and she never saw him again.

When the Indian trappers who were leading the little train to Oregon came to camp, ready to move on after the midday break, Sarah panicked. She wanted to see Wesley. She wanted to go to him, to say…to say what? Goodbye? Take me with you? Why did you send one of your fellow surveyors to the hollow to fetch Lucky? Why did you let the prairie wolf be killed?

Her mother was urging her into the wagon. Her father told her that he had already thanked Mr. Powell for the immense service he had rendered to the Harris family. There was no time to argue with her parents, no reason to argue with them, no grounds on which to plead her case.

What *was* her case?

No case. She had none. Wesley hadn't come to see her, and that was that. Did he love her? Absurd question! Well then, did he care for her a little? Unanswerable question!

As unanswerable as the question of why the prairie wolf had followed them over miles and miles of open land.

The wagons moved forward. Sarah crawled to the back of hers, looked to the barren ridge and murmured, "Wesley." Then she let grief fill her heart for the mangy prairie wolf who had been killed before he had quit.

Powell had steeled himself to face Morgan Harris. He didn't know what he was going to say to Sarah's father, much less to Sarah herself, but he knew he had to say something, if only goodbye.

He had spent the morning on the south rim of the ridge with his team, sorting out the business that lay ahead of them. While he was debating whether he should borrow a decent pair of trousers for his meeting with Morgan Harris, he decided to shave. That thought prompted him to send Grant to the hollow to fetch his razor and horse. When Grant returned, a fresh complication arose.

A trio of wild and woolly traders had been following the surveyors since the week before, when they had skirmished over a prime stretch of hunting ground and had lost. The traders were out to settle the score, which meant that one minute Powell was scraping whiskers off his chin and the next he was looking down the barrel of a long rifle.

At the other end of the rifle was a man who smiled a toothless smile and said, "If you boys is mebbe thinking of going somewheres, we got news for you."

With a renewed wave of fatalism, Powell thought, *For being in the middle of nowhere, I sure do meet up with a lot of people.*

Chapter Eighteen

After months of open sky and prairie and being exposed like bugs on a table, the wagon train and trappers entered a cathedral of great trees and were swallowed in the majesty of mountains. After five months of sleeping on bedrolls, eating rabbits and cooking on buffalo chips, they were in the home stretch. Spirit weary, they revived to see a board house with windows, to hear the buzz of a sawmill, to smell the beauties of both uncultivated and cultivated land.

It was September. They were in the Willamette River Valley. Mount Hood was in the distance, and Laurence and Cathy Harris's apple farm was in front of them. The Salish trappers went on their way down the river, heading for the ocean. The Dales and the Fletchers accepted the invitation to refresh themselves for several days at the home of the son and daughter-in-law of Morgan and Barbara Harris.

When Sarah saw her stepbrother, Laurence, she cried tears of happiness when he took her in his arms. Few experiences exceeded her joy at meeting his wife, Cathy Davidson of Hillsborough, North Carolina, whom she knew from correspondence but had never met in person.

Upon shaking hands with her two strapping nephews and pretty little niece, she felt sure that she would enjoy getting to know them better, and it was obvious that Helen and Martha had taken to Laurence and Cathy's children as well. Her pleasure was complete to see how happy her mother and father were to be able to live out their days among the next generation of Harrises.

The Harris homestead was thriving. The house had been added on to with each successive child, so that it now rambled amiably. It was sparsely but comfortably furnished. Cathy, the expert apple grower, had conjured an extensive orchard in the fertile valley of the Willamette, and many banks of her best trees were already producing plentifully.

Laurence had good relations with the community living in the Hudson Bay Company settlement, and he had learned enough Chinook Jargon to hunt and fish with the Salish. The Harris household feasted on salmon at lunch and Salmon Boy stories at dinner, stories Laurence loved to tell and his children loved to hear.

Sarah had last seen Laurence eleven years earlier, and she was much struck by the change that existed between Laurence the proud, angry young half-breed and Laurence the proud paterfamilias. She had always stood in awe of her stepbrother's cool and unusual hunter's instincts. Now that his self-possession had matured into self-assurance, she was frankly impressed by the man he had become. Although he would never be called a "big talker," he spoke easily with all the members of his family, was openly demonstrative in his love for his wife and lavishly affectionate with his children.

Cathy was not a beauty in Sarah's eyes, but she plainly was in Laurence's. As Sarah watched and listened to the two of them together, she was happy for them, and she envied them. When Cathy and Laurence went to bed at night, they went to bed together. The sight of their bedroom door being closed behind them, closing out the world, closing them in together, gave Sarah a pang that did not decrease over time but only grew and stretched. Every night brought Sarah another opportunity to lie awake, wishing Wesley Powell next to her, wanting him near her.

No matter which way she turned the final events in that distant corner of paradise, she couldn't avoid the fact that Wesley hadn't come down from the ridge to the hollow to say goodbye to her. He had stayed away. He had resisted.

But had she failed? That was the question.

In the Mandan lodge and out in the pouring rain, she had planned his amorous downfall. He had *wanted* her then, and she had known it. It made her smile to recall that he had warned her against the dangers of magic water, when the only magic had been the desire foaming in his veins. As long as she was admitting hard truths, she would admit that she was no longer sitting on the sidelines of this fearsome, fascinating man-woman dance. Wesley Powell had taken her onto the ballroom floor with him, and she had danced with him, body and soul.

That was the force of it. The essential nugget. That morning of brutal, unembellished togetherness. She couldn't stop thinking about that awful, awesome moment when her man-beast had possessed her, all power and purpose, with no regard for her wishes or desires, only his. No superfluous words. No extra actions. Just him to her. All of him. To all of her.

It had been unthinkable. But it was also undoable. And unforgettable. A pact.

So. It could not be undone. It could not be forgotten.

What was she supposed to do about it?

Play with her nieces and nephews. Sew with her sisters. Cook with Cathy. Clean with her mother. Meet the many unmarried men who, upon learning of Sarah's existence, found reasons to stop by the Harris homestead, found ways to get themselves invited to Sunday supper or an evening around the fire eating apple pies and apple tarts and dried apple candies. Watch the cold winter rains come and go through wet and wavery panes of glass.

She was carrying no baby in her belly, but she had plenty of ideas to hatch.

One fine day, with the winds whipping at her skirts, Sarah went out to the fields to find Laurence mending fences with Morgan. She came up to them, nodded to her father, looked at her brother, her expression inquiring. Laurence placed the rail he was holding, then brushed his hands on his trousers. Morgan found something to do elsewhere.

"You've changed, best of my brothers," she said.

His black eyes twinkled. "No more so than you, dear sister."

"No!"

"Yes!" he replied, matching her mock surprise. "First, I've noticed that you speak to your sisters as if they were human beings instead of annoying pets. Second, I'd have expected you to have the male population of the Willamette Valley at your beck and call—and you do—but I'd not have expected you to refrain from sowing the seeds of murderous dissention among your many admirers."

"I wasn't that bad back in Maryland," she protested.

"You were worse."

She let her gaze roam lovingly over his high-cheeked, chiseled features. She shook her head, smiling, and began again. "You've changed, best of my brothers, and so I'm thinking that what I have to ask you may no longer be as appropriate as it would have been eleven years ago, before you were married and had a family.''

"Let's find out. What is it you have to ask me?"

"A favor."

"I was wondering when you'd get around to it."

She blinked in true surprise. "You were?"

"A young woman who stares out the window as often as you stare out the window, and who displays nothing but polite interest in the richest men in the entire territory, has a special man on her mind."

"I do?"

"Do you deny it?"

She shook her head.

"And you want me to help you find him."

"Right again. You're good at finding things."

"I am. Now where did you last see him?"

"At a pretty hollow between the Platte crossing and Chimney Rock."

"And where do you think he is now?"

"I don't know. Perhaps Washington, D.C."

Laurence's expression didn't change.

"It's the other side of the world, I know."

"Only the other side of the continent. Not so bad."

"You'll help me?"

"Do I have a choice?"

"I'm hoping you don't."

"You may have changed in other ways, but you're as persuasive as ever, Sarah Ross Harris." His eyes and voice teased. "Which makes me wonder how you let your man get away in the first place."

"I won't let it happen a second time," she said with conviction, "and I won't let him settle for the mousy, obedient woman he mistakenly thinks he wants."

* * *

When the weather was warm enough to figure the snow had melted in the mountain passes, Sarah and Laurence, accompanied by a band of Salish trappers, set out on their cross-country trek.

Cathy was understandably concerned that her husband chose to embark on such an extravagant journey. However, she knew that Laurence, as a boy of fifteen, had traveled from Canada to Maryland to find a father he had not been sure was even still alive, and so she figured that Laurence, as a seasoned man of thirty-six, should be able to get across the continent and back. Since Sarah and Laurence would be traveling light, she figured that Laurence could cut the usual travel time in half and accomplish the round trip within six months. She never doubted that he would return to her by the end of the summer.

When Sarah had broken the news to Barbara and Morgan, they had not been happy about the idea of her traveling to Washington, D.C. They had no fears for her safety in Laurence's company, but they feared other, negative outcomes for this unladylike goose chase after a man who had not even had the courtesy to tell her goodbye. Their willful daughter was likely to be either disappointed in the man she would reencounter a year later or openly rejected by him.

She had responded that at worst she would return with her brother to the Willamette River Valley—which wasn't a bad outcome at all.

"But to travel across the entire continent," Barbara protested, "and perhaps back again, without being sure of your goal, is…is—" here she groped for words "—outrageous and absurd. No, it's more than that! It's simply unheard-of!"

"You will recall, my wise mother, that you desired me

to make the original journey to, let us say, improve my personality, and you will admit that it has done just that!'' Because there was no denying the truth of that observation, Barbara said nothing, and Sarah continued, ''Consider, then, the possible benefits of my making the trip twice more. Think how agreeable I will be!'' Having registered her point, she turned to Morgan and said, ''Now, Father, you must tell me the magic word.''

Morgan's face darkened. He folded his arms across his chest. He pressed his lips together.

Sarah cocked him a knowing look. ''You're considering reminding me that I'm not privileged to know that word until I am five and twenty, aren't you.''

Morgan nodded.

''And you're also realizing that I've matured at least two years in the past twelve months and am likely to mature another year in the next few months.''

Morgan nodded again.

''Well then, since my years on earth will soon enough number three and twenty, to which I add another three for maturity, I'm sure you'll agree that I'm *beyond* the age of having access to that which is destined to be mine.''

''I don't agree with you, Daughter,'' Morgan said, his expression still stern. ''However, since you and your brother have joined forces, I'm faced with the unpleasant prospect of knowing you'll be going back east with or without my blessing and with or without proper financial resources.''

Sarah smiled. ''You'll tell me the magic word, then?''

Morgan relented. ''It's Tohin-ontan.''

Sarah's eyes widened. ''I might have guessed it at any time these past eleven years!''

''You might have.''

''Well, at least it's fitting!'' she said, shaking her head

in bemused wonderment. Tohin-ontan was Laurence's Huron name, meaning Bird of Fire. His fine Indian instincts had found her twenty-two years ago in the hands of her kidnappers and delivered her to her parents. It seemed right that his Indian name should have safeguarded her trust fund all these years.

Sarah and Laurence set off with their Salish friends, bound ever east, and experienced the arduous trail in reverse. They crossed the Blue Mountains, traded with the Cayuse, waded over the Three Island Crossing on the Snake River, rafted where they could. Then it was the Portneuf River to the Bear River, and the land bloomed pink and purple, trees leaved and antelope ran. This corner of the world was unusually busy with fur traders and would, later in the summer, find the trains of wagons even more numerous this year than the last. No wagon ruts were in the earth as yet, but Laurence's sharp eyes could discern the faint trail of pioneers past as well as he could sniff out the merest trace of Sioux, and thereby avoid them.

With rivers and springs and water so plentiful, they could almost imagine the dry prairie ahead to be more of a bad dream than a reality. When they passed the final rock bastions and battlements before the plains and encountered the buffalo, the bad dream became the reality. In the company of Laurence, however, Sarah did not fear surviving the rigors ahead any more than she had had to fear the rigors behind. At Chimney Rock in the valley of the North Platte, the Salish trappers split off, and Laurence and Sarah traveled several days alone until they met up with some white traders. All along the way, Laurence was gathering what information he could of the trail of the four government surveyors who had passed this way the year before.

The return to the East had its sobering, civilizing effect. In Missouri Sarah put aside her deerskin dress and adjusted to her cottons. She also had to reaccustom herself to the fancy crepes and crinolines of the white women she now traveled among and to their sidelong glances, curiously sizing up her handsome half-breed companion.

When they finally entered the town of Baltimore, Sarah felt shabby and conspicuous in company with Laurence and oddly proud of it. She hoped she would run into one or all of those stuck-up rich girls she knew so that she could show them just how little she cared for their opinion. However, when she did run into Claire Cleveland and Isabelle Dupont, on Eastern Avenue by the harbor and around the corner from the First Bank of Maryland, she did not feel the least bit feisty. Rather, she was delighted to see them, and genuinely so.

"Why, Claire and Isabelle, by all that's wonderful!" Sarah exclaimed. She took in her former friends' studied elegance. "You're both looking just as beautiful as on the day I last saw you, from the tops of your parasols to the tips of your toes."

"S-S-Sarah? S-S-Sarah Harris?" Claire and Isabelle stammered in unison. Their eyes widened, and they turned red, evidently embarrassed and aghast at what they were seeing.

"Yes, it's really me!" Sarah returned, laughing at their consternation.

Their eyes were still wide. "We thought you left for the Oregon Territory. We thought you lived there now."

"I do, or rather my family does, but I'm not sure where I'm eventually going to settle down." She waved these trivialities away and linked elbows with Laurence. "Perhaps you don't remember my brother because he left Maryland so many years ago, but I'd like to present him to you now.'' She performed a pretty introduction and was gratified, once they recovered their wits, that they didn't give either Laurence or her the cut direct. Instead, she pressed them for the latest Baltimore gossip and learned, by the by, that William James had married none other than Olivia Hamilton.

"Did he marry Olivia, then?" Sarah replied happily. "I'm glad for him and for her. They make an excellent couple. And I'm sure Mrs. James is delighted with her daughter-in-law."

Since Sarah had said this with no trace of irony or wounded feelings, Isabelle was left speechless, and Claire was moved to say slowly, "You've changed, Sarah."

Sarah laughed again. She looked down at herself and stretched out her trail-roughened hands and fingernails. "Although I don't plan to be in Baltimore more than a day or two, you'll be doing your fellow citizens an inestimable favor if you can assure me that Miss Lulu's Dressmaking Shop is still open for business with the smartest styles around. I wish to make myself instantly presentable again to the eyes of my former townsfolk."

Claire and Isabelle exchanged a significant glance at Sarah's mention of the most expensive needlewoman in Baltimore, then assured her that Miss Lulu was, indeed, where she always had been on Franklin Street. Presently, they took their leave.

Sarah was unmoved by the snub that her former friends had not made any overtures to see her again, and said to Laurence with perfect equanimity, "Now, wasn't that pleasant to meet up with old friends? Well now, if I'm going to make myself and you, dear brother, fashionable, we had better line our pockets with Mrs. Ross's gold."

Matching word to deed, they went around the corner and into the hallowed marble interior of the First Bank of

Maryland, whereupon Sarah asked for Mr. Charles Duguid, known to her as Mrs. Ross's American banker. This reliable functionary came out from behind his teller's cage while shrugging hastily into his jacket. His glasses were perched on a long, thin nose, his vest and tie were askew, his fingers professionally ink-stained. His eyes widened to see a rather ragged, though remarkably beautiful, young woman in company with a—with an *Indian*. He hardly knew what to make of this circumstance, however, since the Indian was carrying no weapons and the young woman looked calm, going so far as to extend her hand to him and to greet him by name—

"Oh! It's you, Miss Harris!" Mr. Duguid exclaimed, relieved but still puzzled. "But you're in the Oregon Territory!"

"I'm here in Baltimore," she corrected, "and I have come to withdraw funds from my account for the very first time."

Mr. Duguid frowned and performed a rapid calculation. "You will not have access to that money for two more years."

She winked, rose on tiptoe and whispered the magic word into his ear.

Mr. Duguid was plainly torn. He wanted to do his duty by Mrs. Ross and Mr. Harris, both of whom were convinced, as recently as the year before, that Miss Sarah Ross Harris was no fit person to have access to a sum invested and large enough to produce a respectable yearly income. On the other hand, here she was in front of him, looking confident and oddly mature. Not to mention the quiet presence of that Indian, who was bearing no arms but whose expression was turning ever more threatening with each passing second.

"Well!" Mr. Duguid decided. "I'm legally bound to

give you what you want, in response to the password, but I'm hoping you don't mean either to clear out the account or even to eat into the principal. No, indeed, I would advise you against such an unwise course! Now, what can I do for you?''

Sarah named the figure she had in mind and requested a letter of credit for her use in Washington, D.C. By the end of the day, she had outfitted herself with several modish frocks, transformed Laurence—against his wishes and better judgment—into a paragon of male fashion, and hired a fancy open carriage that would sweep them into the capital city.

The next day the sun was shining, and Sarah and Laurence were looking very smart as they bowled down the Mall on Constitution Avenue. They glimpsed the White House beyond the Ellipse and passed the Treasury Building and the Archives before pulling up in front of an impressive red sandstone building whose brass plaque proudly proclaimed the offices of the War Department.

While Laurence remained behind to hold the reins, Sarah stepped down from the carriage and into the bustling main corridor of the building. Following the instructions Wesley had given her long ago in the Wilkinses' wagon, she approached the first man she saw. She requested, politely enough, that he tell her the address of Miss Alice.

Since she figured the name to be the honorific title of the woman who must be Mrs. Powell, the reaction she received was contrary to what she had expected. The man looked her rudely up and down, uttered the name ''Miss Alice'' suggestively, and fairly leered when he issued an address that he said could easily be found in the neighborhood of Georgetown. Then he asked for her name, saying that he would be sure to call on her at Miss Alice's in the near future, perhaps even that very evening.

Sarah left the building without giving that rude man her name and feeling somewhat besmirched by the encounter. She would have sent Laurence back in to settle the score if she hadn't been so anxious to hear the latest of Wesley's news from his mother. So they retraced their course down the Mall, angled up Pennsylvania Avenue, negotiated the traffic circles, and were soon surrounded by pretty green streets and spacious parks.

On a quiet, residential street Laurence drew rein before a beautiful, perfectly manicured brick house. About it hung an aura of deep respectability. Or, at least, it looked as if it should be a residence of deep respectability, but for some odd reason, Sarah had the uneasy feeling that this was not at all a respectable establishment. Perhaps it was the way an older, portly gentleman with a florid complexion came out of the front door just then, looked furtively to his right, to his left, started slightly at the sight of Sarah and Laurence in the street before him, then scurried away.

Sarah looked at her brother. He looked at her.

"Do you know what you're getting into?" Laurence asked.

Sarah shook her head. "Not really, but I'm beginning to form an idea."

"Are you ready for it?"

She laughed and said, "I didn't cross the continent to give up now."

Laurence nodded approval. "Good girl."

Chapter Nineteen

Laurence handed Sarah down from the carriage and stood on the curb holding the reins. With only one backward glance at him, Sarah walked up the short brick path to Miss Alice's house and trod the five shallow steps to the front door. She took a deep breath and resolutely plied the brass knocker.

The green door swung open on well-oiled hinges, and a matronly woman in a white starched apron and cap greeted Sarah pleasantly. Upon learning Sarah's desire to meet the mistress of the establishment, this comforting-looking woman opened the door wider, permitted Sarah access to the interior, then told Miss Harris to wait in the foyer while she went in search of her employer.

The relief Sarah had felt at the sight of the matronly woman was dispelled as soon as her eyes had adjusted to the dimness inside and she was able to take in the details of her surroundings. Her first glance confirmed that she was in exactly the kind of house she feared she might be entering, and she had a pretty fair idea that Miss Alice's business boomed with clients from the War Department.

The central foyer was gracious and afforded views into the rooms that opened on either side and would, in other

houses, have been called the parlor and the dining room.
The style and luxury of the furniture and decoration in
these rooms, however, covered as they were in deep red
velvet, made the parlor look more like a sultan's harem,
while the dining room with its chaises and sofas had more
the look of a Roman bath, without the bath. Now Sarah
did not know exactly what either a harem or a Roman
bath might look like, but she had heard tell of such decadent places, and the rooms she beheld were as decadent
as any she could conceive.

The grand, sinuous staircase ahead of her curved into
the upper story and the rooms where, she guessed, the
real business of the establishment was transacted. At the
moment, a well-endowed young woman was descending
that staircase in her chemise and pantalets, her hair tumbling wantonly around her shoulders. At the foot of the
stairs, she yawned luxuriously and cast sleepy eyes over
Sarah's person. She seemed to calculate Sarah's attributes
with one glance, shrugged as if indifferent to possible
competition, then disappeared down the hallway that led
to the back of the house.

From the other end of that hallway came another
woman, walking toward Sarah. As she approached, Sarah
saw that she was no less generously endowed than the
undressed young woman and no less beautiful, but she
did not look at all sleepy, and she was outfitted in a different fashion altogether. This woman had ebony hair,
swept up on her head, and sapphire eyes, and she was
wearing, despite the early hour of the day, sapphire drops
at her ears, which were matched by a magnificent circle
of sapphires displayed to advantage on the dazzling white
expanse of her exposed bosom. Her dressing gown was
of black satin with a blue revers several shades lighter
than her eyes and her jewelry. On her feet were black

satin mules that click-clicked daintily across the polished wood floors to be muffled by the thick-piled Oriental rug upon which Sarah was standing.

Sarah saw the ebony-and-sapphire woman sum her up as quickly and neatly as had the undressed young woman. When she was in front of Sarah, she held out her hand, charmingly, as if to a dear old friend or to a man who might be tempted to kiss the offer of alabaster skin. Her pretty lips were smiling and murmuring words of welcome. This, then, was Miss Alice, but she was surely not also Mrs. Powell.

Sarah was at once appalled and enlightened. Her heart sank and cried out for Wesley. Because she had not come for a job that Miss Alice evidently supposed she was hoping to find, Sarah did not take her hand, but she did permit herself to sum up the woman before her as openly as she herself had been estimated. Although Miss Alice did not appear old enough to have a full-grown son, she did look as if she had been around the block more than once; and apart from a similarity in coloring, her hard beauty found no echo in Wesley Powell's striking masculinity.

When Sarah didn't take her hand, Miss Alice's expression changed from one of gracious welcome to cool inquiry. "You wished to see me for some reason, my dear?"

"My name is Sarah Harris, as your woman may have told you, and I have come—perhaps mistakenly!—to speak to you as a mother."

Miss Alice's look of cool inquiry shaded into one of amusement. "But my dear Miss Harris! You have come to speak to me as a mother? How very…*original* of you!" Her musical tones tinkled with sophistication, condescension. "I am sure that I have never been approached in quite such a fashion before, my dear, my *very* dear Miss

Harris. Nor do I truly wish to waste my time with such foolishness now!"

Sarah was being put at a disadvantage by this bewitchingly beautiful woman. She had faced worse in rain, cold, hunger, God-fearing pioneers, a Mandan medicine man, Indian braves, a wild prairie wolf, a twelve-hundred-pound stallion and a testy man-beast. The strength she had acquired from those experiences was not going to serve her in the present circumstance. Instead, she had to reach back to an old self, one that now felt very brittle and had been used to showing up in the presence of Claire, Isabelle and Olivia.

Although Sarah didn't think she could teach Miss Alice anything about feminine wiles, she was determined to give her a run for her money. She smiled sugar sweet and said, "I'm sure we can conclude our business quickly enough."

Miss Alice assumed an equally artificial frown. "You have come to discuss motherhood in connection with… business?" She ran her eyes once again over Sarah's person, let them linger on Sarah's flat stomach. Her expression cleared, became clever. "I must tell you that I do not, repeat *not,* make it my business to harbor girls who are to experience the joys of motherhood. Instead, I can give you an address of a very discreet physician you may find useful."

Sarah dismissed this hideous turn in conversation with a shake of her head. "I'd rather you tell me the address of your son, if you know where he's keeping himself these days."

"You credit me with a son?" the woman queried.

"Yes."

"And you have come to this house for the extraordinary purpose of asking me—a woman you have never met before—for news of this supposed son of mine?''

"This supposed son's name is Wesley Powell. Of the U.S. Geological Survey."

Miss Alice gave herself away by looking over her shoulder to assure herself that they were quite alone. They were.

"It hardly matters to me whether or not you acknowledge him." Sarah figured it was time to call the madam's bluff and turned to go. "I began by admitting that I might have made a mistake in coming to you, and you countered by saying that you didn't want your time wasted. So I won't compound my obvious mistake by wasting any more of your time or mine."

When Sarah's hand was on the door handle, Miss Alice said quickly, "You could always ask his father if he knows where his son is these days."

Sarah didn't lift her hand from the knob. She turned back slowly and repeated coolly, "His father?"

Miss Alice pursed her pretty lips and said, "It's usually the other way around, you know." She paused. "You don't know, do you."

"What's the other way around?"

Miss Alice's lips spread into a smile. "People generally know who Wesley's father is but not his mother."

Sarah cocked her head meaningfully.

"Yes, Miss Harris, I admit to being Wesley's mother, but what I didn't know was that he knew it—or, rather, that he was ever willing to admit it." Her sapphire eyes narrowed. "I don't acknowledge him, he doesn't acknowledge me, and nobody knows of our relationship. Since I'd like to keep it that way, I can now guess the nature of your business. How much do you want?"

Sarah smiled pleasantly. "No money, only information."

"You come very cheap, Miss Harris!"

At this new insult, Sarah's smile didn't falter. "It's your lucky day."

Miss Alice considered that comment, then looked down to study her long white fingers and to admire the thin gold bangle on her wrist. "I can tell you what the whole world seems to know except you. Wesley's father is Major General George Powell."

Sarah blinked. A major general? She began to take heart. Perhaps the situation had a bright spot, after all.

Miss Alice looked up and continued, "As for his precise address, I wouldn't know. I keep my distance from him but tend to hear if he is in town or not. At the moment, he is, I believe. Is that all the information you wanted, then?"

"Almost." Sarah swallowed once, hard, straightened her spine. "Can you tell me whether he has been married in the past year?"

Miss Alice's laugh was melodic. "Married? Wesley? No, my dear, I fear you must be thinking of a different Wesley Powell!" She recovered from her merriment enough to say, more seriously, "Although it's true that Wesley has not been quite so *busy* since he returned to town some months ago, I haven't heard the least breath of a rumor that he is settling down." With a hard edge of unmaternal malice, she added, "What respectable woman would have him, anyway?"

Sarah took this news with a further lifting of her heart. She opened the door and answered, "A respectable woman wouldn't have him, of course, but I will." Before she stepped out, she said, "I thank you for the information, Miss Alice, and will keep my end of the bargain.

You can decide whether or not you wish to attend our wedding when you receive the invitation.''

Sarah finally succeeded in disconcerting the sophisticated Miss Alice. Her features softened in understanding, and she became truly beautiful. She said, ''I've just remembered something I heard recently. Wesley is being sent off soon to another surveying assignment in—'' she wrinkled her smooth brow ''—that new Republic of Texas. So if you're eager to marry him, you have no time to lose.''

Sarah smiled. ''Thank you, Miss Alice. I am eager.''

''Surprise is the essence of attack.''

Laurence had taken up the reins and was urging the horses to a walk down the cobbled street. He did not immediately respond to Sarah's enigmatic pronouncement. Instead he glanced at her and said, not entirely with approval. ''You've changed, little sister, all in the space of a few minutes.''

Sarah had been lost in abstraction, but she was interested enough in that remark to respond, ''You mean, I've changed *back*.''

''Back?''

''Yes, I've changed back to the woman I was before you saw me in the Oregon Territory. The agreeable woman you met at the end of her trip west had been taken down a notch or two. She could finally see beyond the end of her nose to be kind and considerate and caring of others.'' She gave her head a careless toss. ''This one feels just like her old self again!''

Laurence's appraisal became more searching. ''You do remind me of a very different Sarah I used to know.''

Sarah was pleased by his perception. ''What a shrew I must have been in those days, although I don't think I realized it until this very moment. I was always grasping and grasping—but for what? For acceptance, I suppose, but I never quite knew what it was or when to let go. I only knew that I wanted more and more of it—*it!*—from every man and woman I met. And woe to those who didn't recognize my superiority!''

''And that is the person you wish to become again?''

Sarah laughed and said cheerfully, ''For the next hour, at least. I feel as though I've come full circle and am back where I started, but not exactly where I started—if that makes the least bit of sense!'' The thought had a familiar ring. ''You know, I recall Wesley saying something like that at one point. Hmm. I wonder if he thinks he's going in circles, too. Well, if he is, I'll straighten him out.''

''Don't try to straighten him out completely. You couldn't even if you wanted to, and you probably don't even want to.''

She paused to absorb the import of these recommendations, then said, ''I have told you, I think, of my experiences among the Mandan.''

Laurence accepted this abrupt change of topic with his customary calm. ''More than once, dear sister, and I have been pleased upon every hearing to note how well you learned the lesson that the cultures of the original Americans are varied and rich.''

She waved a hand dismissively. ''Oh, pooh, *that!* This isn't the moment for dreary moralizing!'' Her glance smoldered. ''And you needn't criticize me for repeating myself in your sly way, dear Tohin-ontan.'' She paused, then exclaimed, ''How I have *longed* to call you that all these years, and I will tell you now that you never looked like a Laurence to me. Never!''

They had arrived at an intersection. Her sly, long-suffering brother inquired, ''Which way?''

"We return to the War Department," she commanded loftily, "but I digress, and you will not turn me from the subject! Now, I do not wish to discuss your Iroquois name or your Iroquois customs. I do not even wish to discuss Mandan customs, for at the moment I am rather more interested in *spirits!*"

"Did Miss Alice give you something to drink?"

"Very funny." She tapped his arm in reprimand. "Listen. I have told you that I spent a night among the Mandan—in a very comfortable bed, yes—but I never told you what happened when I awoke at one point. The fire was burning low and continuously, and every time I blinked, the flames changed shape and took the form of men from my past. I thought at the time that those hallucinations came from the magic of Mandan spirits."

"And now you think otherwise?"

"Of course, silly! *You're* not the only ones who know about spirits, Tohin-ontan. White people do, too, and besides, *I'm* the one who saw the images! What I'm telling you is that I can feel the spirit of my father on my shoulder—one of my fathers, anyway. General Robert Ross of the British army." Her heart swelled with happiness and pride. "And he is telling me that surprise is the essence of attack!"

"He is?"

"Yes, and to think that the General has been just out of my reach all these years and that all I had to do for him to come to me was to…let go! It was that simple." She shook her head in wonderment. "He's also telling me that my troops should be on high ground and well covered, which is good advice in any case, but what am I to make of the principle that cavalry must not be used before the enemy has suffered considerably from our infantry and artillery? It does not seem at all useful at the moment, I can tell you!''

"I'm glad you're in contact with your spirit father—"

"Thank you," she interrupted graciously.

"But for the benefit of those of us in this life, I pray you will tell me the worst." Laurence's expression was stern, but his voice was laughing. "Are you planning to kill someone?"

"No, I am not planning to kill anybody," she reassured him, then suggested brightly, "Oh, but you can, if you want! I met a very rude man on our first visit to the War Department, and I would like you to take care of him for me on this next visit." She reflected judiciously. "However, I think killing him might be extreme, so perhaps you will only want to punch him in the nose."

"If I agree to punch him in the nose, will you tell me what you *are* planning to do?"

A militant light danced in her eyes. "I am planning to pay a visit to Major General George Powell, whose offices, I don't doubt, are in the very building we lately visited."

"I see. Since you are evidently preparing for war, you may wish to consider your spirit father's advice concerning the cavalry, artillery and infantry."

After a puzzled moment, understanding dawned, and Sarah smiled approval at her brother. "You're right, of course. I need a battle plan." She nodded, once, decisively. "You will drive, and I shall contrive!"

Sarah spent the rest of the short drive to the Mall contemplating her plan of attack. In happy communion with her spirit father, she rejected and revised any number of possible strategies, reviewed her strengths and weaknesses, along with the risks and pitfalls of her campaign.

She didn't have to wonder what her spirit father thought. She didn't have to second-guess him. She simply *knew*.

At one moment, she broke through her heavy thoughts to say aloud, "He never showed himself to me before because I was blinded by selfishness. He came now that I am finally pursuing a worthy objective."

Laurence needed no further explanations of those statements, and his reply was pertinent. "Your spirit father is wise."

Some moments later, Sarah said, "One's dignity is a fine thing *only* when one does not take it too seriously."

Laurence turned this statement over once, twice, and replied, "I am inclined to feel sorry for Major General Powell, but I suppose you think he will get whatever he deserves."

Her manner displayed satisfaction. "One usually does, myself included. Well, here we are!"

Laurence had drawn up in front of the red sandstone building. This time, instead of staying behind in the carriage, he found a boy and tossed him a coin. He told the boy to hold the reins and advised him to walk the horses up and down the Mall if they should get restive. He walked toward the building and the entrance marked with the brass plaque bearing the words War Department. He asked conversationally, "By the way, is my dignity at stake?"

His sister cast him a laughing glance over her shoulder. "That's for you to determine."

"Well then, is my freedom perhaps at issue?"

"Your freedom?"

"Last time I heard, the Bureau of Indian Affairs was part of the War Department, and that's a fact that tells its own tale. What to do with *us* is the Great White Father's most pressing foreign policy problem."

Sarah ran her eye over Tohin-ontan's white-man elegance. "We can always claim that you're an Asian prince—or maybe just my brother."

"All right, then," he said, following her into the building, "tell me what to do. That is, tell me who to punch."

"Tell me first how I look."

Sarah struck a pose. It was one she had used to carry her through the first critical moments upon stepping into a drawing room or a ballroom. Its effect had been to draw the men and to show the ladies just how far they fell short. A year ago she had thought this pose held grace and dignity, but she now realized that it had been hollow. She filled that empty space with power gathered for a purpose.

Laurence's response was to the point. "Formidable."

The foyer was just as busy as it had been the hour before, but the rude man was nowhere in sight, which meant that Laurence was not obliged to spoil Sarah's plans by creating an instant riot. The strategy she had chosen—ignoble, underhanded and quite simply brilliant—called for scattering seeds of rebellion that would lead up to a riot. Eventually. In five, ten minutes, maybe. So she sashayed up to the first man she saw, and instead of asking for the address of Miss Alice, she asked him with a smile of melting submission if he could tell her how to get to the offices of "General Georgie. You know, Major General Powell."

The young man stammered that the major general's offices could be found one flight up, center of the building, Mall side, and he offered to escort her there until Laurence made his presence known. The young man stammered some more, inarticulately.

Sarah patted his chin, giggled and said, "You're cute!" she rose on tiptoe and whispered something in his ear that made him frown, then raise his brows, then blush.

She proceeded down the hallway to the wide marble staircase. In her wake, she left several blushing, consternated men, and many more who were not blushing but only consternated by what Sarah had whispered into their ears. The buzz she left behind in the hallway was growing in intensity.

When she took the first step up, she asked her brother, "Do you think I am overdoing the simpering bit?"

Laurence's reply was unequivocal. "Yes."

Sarah nodded. "Well, it's working."

"That it is."

At the top of the stairs she turned right as she had been instructed and walked a short way down the hallway, dropping more incendiary remarks into available ears. At a certain door, she requested that Laurence stay outside in the hallway, and he obeyed. She gave her head a tiny toss, opened the door without knocking, and entered the room in such a way that all eyes focused instantly on her.

The space was large and masculine and paneled in a rich walnut. It was filled with dark furniture and staffed with a half dozen young men in smart blue uniforms and shiny brass buttons. It was also bathed in sunshine from its three large windows, which opened onto green lawn and blue sky. Off to the right, out of the corner of her eye, Sarah saw a door that was ajar, and which evidently gave onto another room. She guessed she would find her quarry in that second room.

The young army officers stopped as one at her entrance. Some broke off midsentence or froze with hands in filing cabinets, while still others held sheaves of paper midshuffle. They acted as if they had never seen a woman— much less a beautiful young woman—in these offices before, which, in fact, they had not.

Her bright smile encompassed all of them and promised

everything. Then she raised their expectations by waiting an exquisite second longer, at which point she nodded toward the half-open door on her right and said, a little breathlessly, "I'm here to see *him*."

One young man in blue had enough presence of mind to clear his throat and ask, "Is Major General Powell expecting you?"

"Not at all!" she was pleased to tell him.

He did not think of asking her to leave. Instead, he said, "May I tell him who is calling?"

She moved toward the door, smiling benevolently. "Oh, no," she cooed, "I'd much rather surprise him." She reached the door handle before anyone could stop her, threw one last, lingering smile over her shoulder, and inquired, "Have you heard the news about Miss Alice's?"

Six eager faces were blank.

"You will!" she assured them, before she entered the lion's den.

The second room was even larger and more masculine than the antechamber. The walls were covered with maps of the world, and one entire wall was devoted to different regions of the United States. Pins were sticking from several of those maps, and Major General Powell was seated below one of them at a massive mahogany desk. An assistant was at his side, showing him a file. He had just dipped a quill into the ink pot at his side, and the pen was poised to sign one of the papers before him.

At her entrance he looked up. There was no mistaking whose father he could be. There was no mistaking the expression of extreme displeasure on his face.

Sarah prayed for strength from her spirit father. She loaded her guns, took aim and said at her most charming, "Just the man I was hoping to see!"

Chapter Twenty

Major General George Washington Powell was an unhappy man when disturbed, and he was being disturbed now. But he was also surprised, as Sarah had intended, and therefore at something of a loss. Instead of taking control from the very beginning and refusing to have anything to do with her, he snapped, "How did you get in here?"

She was happy to answer him. "Several of the men downstairs were so kind to tell me how to get to your offices, and then the men in the other room—they're so handsome in their uniforms!—helpfully directed me here."

She was aware that those handsome, helpful men had gathered close to the other side of the door, which she had deliberately not closed.

"What do you want?"

Her well-practiced smile would have melted a lesser man. "The address of your son in Washington, D.C."

The major general's expression did not change. "My son lives in Annapolis."

"No, I mean your *other* son, Wesley." She spoke in

carrying tones. "The one who works for the Geological Survey."

At that the major general put down his pen. To his assistant he said bluntly, "Get out, and close the door behind you." Then he stood up and walked around the desk.

Sarah took several steps into the room to meet him head-on. The assistant scurried around her and made a hasty exit, shutting the door behind him, but not before something of a ruckus was created on the other side. She didn't doubt that many ears were pressed to the heavy wood that had been forcefully shut.

Major General Powell was tall, and his frame was filled out with age. His hair was black and silvered at the temples, and his eyes were the snapping blue of Wesley's. He was more classically handsome than his son, but far less attractive to Sarah, and his expression was informed by decades of having had his slightest command obeyed on the instant. When he stopped before her, he spread his feet, locked his legs and clasped his hands behind his back. He fixed her with a gaze that had caused many a man under his command to quake.

Sarah was unmoved. She had once survived an encounter with a naked man-beast. She was determined now to outface his father. Her smile remained beatific.

The major general was scowling. "I have no son in the Geological Survey."

"Oh, I know you don't *acknowledge* him," she said sweetly, "but the resemblance *is* striking, and all I really want to know is where I can find him."

"Why should you come to me?"

"His mother suggested it."

This announcement momentarily robbed him of speech. She pressed her advantage by adding, "Oh, and she told me that Wesley was soon to be sent out of town on another one of those dreadful surveying assignments, and I was hoping that you—'' here she had the audacity to reach out and curve her finger along the gold fringe of one of his epaulets ''—would give him a reprieve.'' She raised a limpid gaze to him and said, as if unsure of herself, ''If that's the correct term.''

''Why should I give him a reprieve?''

''Because the Geological Survey is in the Bureau of Indian Affairs, and the Bureau of Indian Affairs is a division of the War Department.'' She went so far as to bat her eyes. ''Now, you're the head of the War Department, aren't you?'' She looked as femininely stupid as she could. ''Or as good as such?''

The major general was gathering his wits. ''Do I know you?''

''No, sir,'' she said, ''but you might have once met my father.''

This seemed to interest him, as a stable place would interest a man standing on ground that was shifting beneath his feet. His expression lightened. ''Your father?''

''He served during the Second War of Independence,'' she said. ''He was stationed in Maryland during the summer of 1814.''

His expression darkened again. ''I was part of land defense in New Orleans.''

Sarah did not reveal the disappointment she actually felt. ''Oh, too bad!'' she said breezily. ''Then you could never have met my father, but no matter! I did not come to discuss him but rather your son's whereabouts.'' Her half stupid, half alluring smile lingered. ''Can you tell me where Wesley lives?''

The major general did not seem capable of fulfilling that request.

Sarah cocked her ear. She heard a gathering din penetrate the walls of the major general's inner sanctum and was rather pleased with herself. "Perhaps you can tell me where Wesley works?"

The major general had recovered enough to respond to her gentle assault with cannon fire. In his most authoritarian accents he boomed, "No, I cannot! And I have never in my life, missy, been confronted with such impertinence!"

Given that the sounds she heard coming from beyond the walls of the major general's office were increasing in intensity, she felt it safe to say straight-faced, "Well then, this is new to you, isn't it? How happy I am to have been able to enlarge your experience. Now, concerning Wesley's whereabouts—"

"I am sure that I do not know!"

"In that case, you can simply assure me that when I do track him down—for I will, you know—you will make sure that he won't be sent off again on some assignment or another that will take him away from the capital!"

"Just who do you think you are?"

"Miss Sarah Ross Harris."

The major general had had enough. "Then I would like to know, Miss Sarah Ross Harris, what you hope to gain by confronting me in such a manner!"

"Oh, you see, I'm trying to maneuver you into acknowledging your natural son."

He blinked in disbelief, then fired away. "It is more to the point to ask you why you think that I—Major General George Washington Powell—should have anything further to do with you, much less accede to your outrageous demands, which flout all decency!"

Sarah didn't flinch and was happy to answer him. "Because I'm the only one who will be able to help you out of the difficulty that is about to visit you—''

She paused to listen to the roar that could be clearly heard coming from the antechamber. Under her breath, she counted down, ''Five, four, three, two...'' She smiled charmingly.

''Now.''

At that moment the door between the antechamber and the major general's office burst open and, just as if a dam had broken, a flood of young men in blue tumbled into the room on a swelling tide of angry exclamations.

''What is this we hear about Miss Alice's house being closed to custom from the War Department?''

''How could you have sold us down the river to the *senators!*''

''You could have secured the War Department budget without having promised those soft-bellied politicians on the Hill all the best women in Georgetown!''

''You're responsible for barring us from Miss Alice's? *Miss Alice's?*''

The major general had never been so befuddled in his life. Not even during the worst of the fighting in the Second War of Independence, when the American forces were in disarray and the damned British were about to bring the fledgling United States back under their rule, did his world seem to spin so completely out of his control. He had no idea why this hussy was in his office making absurd demands. Nor could he determine why the majority of the United States Army officers under his command had stormed into his office and were shelling him with incomprehensible accusations. Whatever else he did not understand about his present, exposed position, he was becoming dimly aware that he was going to have to deal with the young woman in front of him, and he was realizing that he might just have to deal with her on her own terms.

The major general looked down at her. He was sure he had never seen her before. "Sarah *Ross* Harris?" he muttered with a vague feeling of doom. "You are going to help me?"

Her smile was particularly dazzling. For his ears only, she whispered, "Only if you first concede defeat, then do what I ask."

Wesley Powell had come to the War Department with important papers in hand. He had convinced the head of the Bureau of Indian Affairs that his upcoming assignment to the Republic of Texas should be extended to include a trip to the Oregon Territory, and he was rehearsing the arguments he would now be making to the officer in charge of approving bureau allocations. He felt confident that he would secure the team and equipment he was requesting, but it didn't matter in the end whether he succeeded or not, for he was going to the Oregon Territory with or without the approval or funding from the United States government.

During the past twelve months since he had last seen Sarah, he had thought of her nearly every day, and when he hadn't been thinking directly of her, he had been planning how he was going to get out to the Oregon Territory. The first month after having been expelled from Eden had been the worst, when all he could think about was what Sarah must have thought of him for not having come to see her.

The grizzled old traders who, at gunpoint, had stopped him and his fellow surveyors from doing anything more productive than raising their hands had not been the most trying of his ordeals. There had been a long series of obstacles and encounters, none of them pulling him west, all of them driving him inexorably east. If it wasn't the traders, then it was the trappers. If it wasn't the trappers, then it was the unfriendly Indians. If it wasn't the unfriendly Indians, then it was the friendly Indians, the ones who demanded they stay to partake of their hospitality. Then Sean fell sick and needed tending. Then Douglas got shot and needed tending. Then Jeremiah begged Wesley not to leave with the team in such disarray.

East, east, then Washington, D.C., and it was October and no time at all to undertake the trip to the Oregon Territory when the western mountain passes were already covered with snows that wouldn't melt before the next spring. So he did what he could, which was what he was supposed to do anyway, and that was to go south and survey the swamps in Florida with a new team.

He would have been happy to have stewed the winter in the heat had it not been for the new adventures that beset him. What had been planned as a short four-month foray had turned into a seven-month ordeal, and the time had unfolded like a bad dream in which he was running, running, trying to get home, but never quite able to reach it.

But now, at last, he had returned to the capital and had accomplished what he needed to accomplish before he could set out again. He was some months behind schedule, but that didn't matter anymore. Nothing was going to stop him now. Not his work. Not the weather. Not his health. Not any living creature, human or otherwise. He would begin tomorrow. By day's end. *Right now.*

Yes, he'd file his papers, get his team together and ride out of town. He'd leave the team in Texas and forge on. It would be fine and dandy to have escort and equipment for the rest of his trip, but it was not necessary. He could do it on his own—

His energized thoughts were given an abrupt turn when he entered the foyer of the building that housed the War Department. A hubbub was bubbling. Exclamations of outrage crackled in the air. References to "the major general" and "Iron Butt Powell" could be heard, along with more obscure mutterings concerning "Miss Alice's." Bodies were bustling, gathering, mobilizing in one direction, moving toward the central staircase.

Powell was intrigued enough to join the group, since it wasn't often—or ever—that he had heard his mother's and father's names spoken in the same breath. So he joined the flow of the crowd, whereupon he was told the startling particulars of the situation. Although he had difficulty believing the story, he was happy to continue along with the crowd, for it seemed that he was to be entertained at old Iron Butt's expense. This suited him just fine, given how much grief had always come his way either directly or indirectly as a result of his relationship to this man.

He moved up the stairs, down the hallway and into an office whose threshold he had never before dared to cross. He registered the presence of a tall dark man standing outside the door, seemingly uninterested in the exciting goings-on, his arms folded across his chest. He didn't give the man a second thought, for it was his luck to have been situated on the outer edge of the crowd that squeezed into the major general's antechamber, such that he had a direct line of vision through the open door of the inner sanctum. He had full view of the little drama that was going forward there, center stage.

He could not believe his eyes. No, it couldn't, it really couldn't be—no, no, of course not. He was imagining things. Nevertheless, there was something so real, so familiar about the way that woman was standing there, fearlessly, foolishly facing down her opponent, that his disbelief began to crack and give way. He blinked, once, twice, and realized, yes, he was really and truly looking at *the beautiful idiot.*

There she was, standing up to Major General George Washington Powell, smiling, posturing, heedless of the danger she had run by bearding the lion in his den. Nothing in her demeanor suggested that she thought anything out of the ordinary to be speaking to this fearsome man in front of a large male audience, and one look at the major general's abashed, befuddled face informed Powell that, indeed, nothing was out of the ordinary for her. She might as well have been winning the war of nerves with the prairie wolf or speaking to the Mandan medicine man and securing them an honored welcome or outfacing Mrs. Wilkins while she nursed him back to health.

He decided that he might as well relax and enjoy the show, since she was going to take care of whatever she had come to take care of. That led him to wonder just what, exactly, she had come to take care of. While the happy thought was sinking in that she had just saved him an arduous journey across the continent, the less happy one occurred to him that she was not in this particular office, speaking to this particular man by accident. When he actually started listening to what she was saying, he couldn't decide whether to be scandalized all over again by her beautifully idiotic behavior or to be thoroughly amused and maybe even a little proud of the way she was twisting his father around her little finger.

The major general had boomed an order for "Quiet!" and the excited babble of complaints and protests had died down. He had turned his quelling eye on the beautiful idiot and had demanded, "Now, just what is it, missy, that you're asking me to do?"

The major general's success in bringing his troops under his thumb did not extend to Sarah. His harsh, commanding tones and magnificent bluster produced no effect whatsoever on her. She answered placidly, "But I've already told you what I came for, namely a piece of information, a request and an acknowledgment." She glanced over her shoulder at the eager crowd, bestowed on them a winning smile, then returned her attention to her prey. "I'm sure you don't need me to repeat the exact information, request or acknowledgment now, do you?"

"And why should I give you what you want?"

"We've been over that before, too," she said patiently, as if to a wayward child. "You will give me what I want, because, as I have told you, I am going to help you out of your present difficulty." She wagged an admonishing finger at him, keeping to her role of the disciplining parent. "But only on the condition I have already given you."

Although he was looking harassed, the major general didn't immediately capitulate to her demand, whatever it might have been, for he didn't say or do anything other than try to disconcert her with one of his fierce looks.

Instead of backing down, Sarah shook her head sorrowfully and addressed her attentive audience in mournful tones. "A naughty rumor is circulating about the deal your General Georgie made with those fat old men in the Senate to bar all the handsome young officers in the War Department from visiting Miss Alice's." She turned a pitying smile on the major general. "I would love to be able to tell these fine men here that they can go to Miss Alice's this evening just as they have always done, but I'm not sure I can, unless…"

At mention of Miss Alice's, a ruckus broke out again among the men. They loudly protested the major general's dirty politics and jeered his sputtering exclamations of "It's not true! Not a word of it! This hussy is *lying!*" This last disclaimer only made the major general's case worse, and he was shouted down for adding insult to this lovely woman to the injury he had already dealt his men.

Powell watched in astonished admiration while his far from sweet, rather tart Sarah Ross played her part to the hilt. Powell was almost beginning to feel sorry for his overbearing father. He reflected on the possible scenarios that had brought Sarah to this point and came to the conclusion that the author of the "naughty rumor" must be Sarah herself, and that it was most likely as untrue as it was naughty.

It was an outrageous bluff. Risky, too. Powell figured it was likely to work only if it could be pulled off quickly, before the major general had time to regroup his mental forces.

With his world crumbling rapidly around him, General Georgie wasn't in a position to find that time. In another minute, he might have realized that Miss Harris was bluffing. However, in that same minute, he might just have an insurrection on his hands. It seemed the only way he was going to get quit of this confusing mess was to give this Sarah Ross Hussy what she wanted—which was his to give, and easily, too.

Ross? *Ross?* What was it about that name?

General Georgie couldn't quite place it as he strode to his desk, scrawled across a piece of paper and strode back to Sarah, fairly thrusting his capitulation into her hands. He said a few more words to her, which could not be heard above the noisy commentary of the crowd.

She read what he had written, nodded once, then turned

to the crowd, which instantly quieted. "I'm so pleased to be able to say that the rumor about Miss Alice's has been a silly misunderstanding! How glad I am to know that General Georgie—" she put an overly apologetic hand to her mouth, then corrected herself "—Major General Powell has made no improper deals with those senators!"

"I never said I did!" the beleaguered major general protested.

"Oh, but now the naughty rumor is put to rest, and you get all the credit for having squelched it before it got out of control. And I don't mind telling you that those senators eat too much and smoke nasty cigars. Well! You did a fine thing today, Major General Georgie, yes, you did!" She waved her hand expansively in a gesture halfway between blessing the masses and breaking them up. "You may all go freely to Miss Alice's this evening, just as you did the evening before!"

"They could have anyway," the major general insisted, not quite willing to acknowledge that he'd been beaten.

"Yes, and isn't that pleasant?" she agreed readily. When the crowd began to disperse, she assumed a more businesslike demeanor. To the major general she said, somewhat obscurely, "I'll send you the address we both want, and we'll meet there tonight. At eight o'clock." Then she reverted to character by pinching his cheek and squealing, "You're cute!"

Sarah figured she had better get out while the getting was good. Her absurd gambit had worked thus far but was sure to collapse in the next few moments. She had in her hands what she had come for, and that was Wesley's release from his latest surveying assignment, along with the name of the bureau officer who would have Wesley's address on file. As soon as she had his address, she would send it to the major general so that he could meet the two of them at Wesley's at eight and wish them happy—

Well, expecting the major general to wish them happy might be pushing it, and she would settle for him simply showing up and looking his son in the eye. What he chose to do after that about his son's existence was his affair. In any case, she had achieved her primary goal when he had handed her the note and said to her the magic words, "I concede defeat."

As she turned to leave the inner office, the major general stopped her with the words, "Sarah *Ross* Harris?"

"That's right."

He looked puzzled, suspicious. "Your father was in Maryland in the summer of '14?"

"Right again."

"There was a General Ross in Maryland in '14. A British general. Was *he* your father?"

"Why, yes, indeed he was."

The major general's mouth fell open. His expression suggested that he was beginning to realize that he had just conceded defeat to the daughter of a famous British general.

She wanted the impact of his realization to dawn on him fully after she had gone, so she said merrily, "See you tonight at eight!" and quickly merged into the departing sea of blue.

Once out of the major general's reach, she cast her eyes heavenward and said under her breath, "I hope you will rest peacefully now, spirit father." She had a feeling he would.

She had much to do before eight o'clock, which included having Laurence drive her to the location where she would get Wesley's address, then tracking Wesley down. Her brother could find anyone and anything across thousands of miles and great stretches of time, so she didn't imagine that he would be unable to find Wesley within the confines of Washington, D.C., in the course of one afternoon. However, when she exited the outer office to the central hallway, she wasn't quite prepared for the fact that Laurence had found Wesley so soon. Nevertheless, there her brother was, just where she had left him, speaking to her love.

Her first thought was *I never realized how much Wesley reminds me of Laurence.* Then Wesley looked up and over at her, and her second thought was *It looks as if he thinks I've done something incredibly idiotic!*

She didn't have time for a third thought, for Wesley grabbed her arm and was taking her away.

"But...but...but...Laurence," she protested.

He cut her off. "Your brother will be just fine for a few more minutes on his own. Although I am concerned about the insanity that seems to run in your family—how your brother could consent to accompany you across the continent and allow you to indulge in this outrageous freak in Iron Butt's office, I'll never understand!—he did get you here safe and sound and seems to realize that nothing can stop you when you take a...a...a perfectly idiotic idea into your head!"

Wesley had swept her to a relatively secluded corner of the hallway. Their privacy was paradoxically assured by the large numbers of people still milling about, rehashing recent events. Only the occasional under officer stopped to thank Sarah for all she had done for them.

She crowed, "I knew it, I just *knew* it! And I'm not sorry you were witness to one of my better performances." Her manner was lofty. "You have no idea the favor I have just done you—as well as for myself—and you *would* condemn it as idiotic before you had the least notion what I was up to.''

He had resigned himself to being amused. And relieved. And satisfied. To feeling every shade of pleasurable emotion. ''Well,'' he demanded, ''what *were* you up to in Iron Butt's office?''

''I'm the illegitimate daughter of a British general. He died in Maryland at the end of the Second War of Independence. Yes, isn't that funny? Well, of course, not the fact that he *died*, but you can see that there was something extremely necessary about me settling the score with your father for my father's sake, and then, not irrelevantly, I got your father to release you from your assignment in the Republic of Texas. Oh, and by the way, he'll be meeting us at your house tonight at eight.''

''What?''

''You heard me. I believe he'll have calmed down from the great trick I played on him. I'm almost amazed that it worked so well! In all events, it's high time he acknowledged you, and I think your mother is not at all a bad person, truly, despite her profession.''

''You saw her, then?''

''You sent me to her, as you'll recall, if ever I was to come to the capital. At present she's considering whether or not to attend our wedding.''

''Our wedding?''

''I didn't come all this way and go through what I went through in there just now for *nothing*, you know!''

He was feeling a strong desire to take her into his arms and kiss her. ''But what about your dream of the mansion and the servants and the social position with a capital *P?* I can't give you those things, you know.''

She laughed. ''As for the mansion and servants, I'll have you know that I have come into a reasonable allowance from General Ross's side of the family. Not enough to buy a mansion and servants, but enough to live on in some style. However, after my performance in your father's office, I'm sure I can forget about achieving position with a capital *P* anywhere along the East Coast.'' She was experiencing some of the same emotions he was feeling. She lowered her lashes, then peeked up at him. ''And what about your dream to marry some desperate, unattractive, highly respectable woman?''

''She wouldn't have to be either unattractive or desperate.''

''She would have to be very much of both! And respectable, which I certainly am not. But it hardly matters, since she can't have you.''

Wesley was coming to a proper acceptance of his fate. ''I gather that my release from the assignment in Texas is to allow us to have our honeymoon, but I should tell you that I don't plan to give up my profession of surveying.''

''And neither should you. Since we're bound to be social outcasts in this town, I'll be coming with you on all your assignments.'' With a mischievous gleam in her eye she said, ''Besides, you can't bear to be parted from me, remember?''

He laughed. ''I remember the bald-faced lie you told Mrs. Wilkins while you had me at your mercy in her wagon.''

Sarah ran a critical eye over him, noticing the details of his person for the first time. ''Yes, and you were wearing far less clothing than you are now. I'm not saying that your uniform isn't smart. In fact, you look very dashing in it.'' She frowned as she pondered an important point. ''However, I suppose that, given the circumstances of our first meeting, I will always prefer you wearing nothing.''

A knot of emotion choked up Wesley's throat. Desire flamed under his fine blue uniform. He placed his hands on her shoulders, looked down at her and whispered, "Sarah."

She looked up at him, all her love for him in her eyes. "Wesley, I know I'm not the woman of your dreams."

"Nor am I the man of your dreams, Sarah." He smiled. "No mansion. No servants. No Position." Before he kissed her, he said, "We'll just have to settle for being happy."

* * * * *

Author Note

In the summer of 1836, the year during which most of *Sweet Sarah Ross* is set, the trail to the Oregon Territory had hardly been blazed, and it wasn't even yet known as the Oregon Trail. This famous route west became better traveled in the 1840s, boomed with the forty-niners and was well beaten by the close of the Civil War in the mid-1860s.

The Mandan, Plains Indians of Siouan stock, were alive and well in 1836. In 1837 a smallpox epidemic reduced their numbers to between one hundred and one hundred and fifty. At the end of the twentieth century, the total Mandan population reported on the Fort Berthold Reservation in North Dakota was about three hundred and fifty.

The Bureau of Indian Affairs ceased to be a division of the War Department in 1849. Instead of pursuing an openly hostile policy against the Indians, the bureau turned its attention to assigning large tracts of land in the West for the exclusive use of specified Indian tribes. By the 1870s, however, westward expansion and the building of the transcontinental railroads had resulted in a series of bloody Indian wars and had raised questions about just how peaceable were the government's Indian policies.

And the Winner Is...
You!

...when you pick up these great titles
from our new promotion at your
favorite retail outlet this June!

Diana Palmer
The Case of the Mesmerizing Boss

Betty Neels
The Convenient Wife

Annette Broadrick
Irresistible

Emma Darcy
A Wedding to Remember

Rachel Lee
Lost Warriors

Marie Ferrarella
Father Goose

Look us up on-line at: http://www.romance.net   ATWI397-R

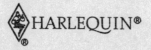

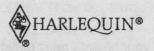

You are cordially invited to a

HOMETOWN REUNION

September 1996—August 1997

Bad boys, cowboys, babies. Feuding families,
arson, mistaken identity, a mom on the run...
Where can you find romance and adventure?
Tyler, Wisconsin, that's where!

So join us in this not-so-sleepy little town and
experience the love, the laughter and the
tears of those who call it home.

WELCOME TO A
HOMETOWN REUNION

Tyler's vet, Roger Phelps, has had a crush on
Gracie Lawson for fourteen years. Now she's
back in town and he still wants her madly. But
Gracie couldn't possibly carry on romantically with
the boy who used to pack her groceries. Even if
the man he turned out to be is gorgeous, gentle,
funny and passionate.... What would people say?
Don't miss *Puppy Love* by Ginger Chambers,
tenth in a series you won't want to end....

June 1997
at your favorite retail outlet.

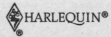

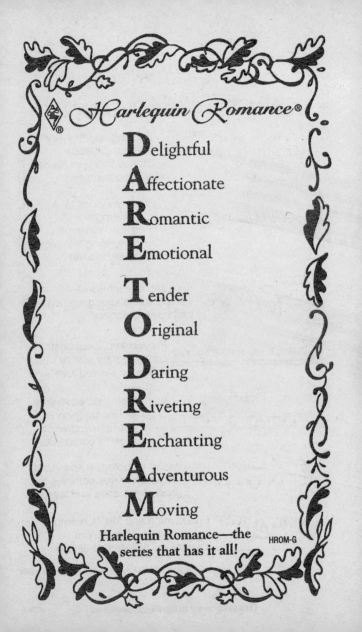

Harlequin Romance ®

Delightful

Affectionate

Romantic

Emotional

Tender

Original

Daring

Riveting

Enchanting

Adventurous

Moving

Harlequin Romance—the
series that has it all!

HROM-G

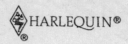

Not The Same Old Story!

 Exciting, emotionally intense romance stories that take readers around the world.

 Vibrant stories of captivating women and irresistible men experiencing the magic of falling in love!

 Bold and adventurous— Temptation is strong women, bad boys, great sex!

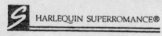 Provocative, passionate, contemporary stories that celebrate life and love.

 Romantic adventure where anything is possible and where dreams come true.

 Heart-stopping, suspenseful adventures that combine the best of romance and mystery.

LOVE & LAUGHTER™ Entertaining and fun, humorous and romantic—stories that capture the lighter side of love.